MARIA FRANKLAND

Hit and Run

He was dead before she really knew him

AUTONOMY
PRESS

For John Stephenson (1955-2019)

A dad who was as supportive, present and wonderful
as the dad in this story

Join my 'Keep in Touch' list!

If you'd like to be kept in the loop about new books and special offers, join my 'keep in touch list' by visiting www.autonomypress.co.uk.

You will receive a free novella as a thank you for joining!

Prologue

All couples have issues, don't they? Everyone has their ups and downs. That's life. I'll get through this. But how?

A bike ride usually calms me down. As I ride out of Otley towards Ilkley, I don't feel the hill that normally challenges me. Today I'm at the top before I notice that my breathing is laboured.

On any other day, I would enjoy the freewheel down the other side, the summer air whooshing in my ears, impressive scenery as far as the eye can see.

I'm always grateful that I live around here. But today I don't feel grateful for anything. The demons that have been chasing me have finally caught up.

I pedal faster, as though trying to escape them, glancing over my shoulder to see how far away the approaching vehicle is. I've got time to get around the narrow bend onto a straight and wider run. Give it room to get past me. I know this stretch well and enjoy getting my speed up. My tracker normally clocks me at forty miles an hour here. As I take the corner, I glance around again to the roar of the engine, now right behind me, the sound feeling as though it's vibrating through my chest. The driver is not slowing and is not going around me.

I don't know whether the sickening crunch is caused at the point of impact or as my body lands. Agonising pain shoots through me, and the world turns black.

Chapter 1

Mum rams her make-up bag into the side of her suitcase. "It's not like I ever ask much of you Fiona." She glares at me. "I never have."

"You're asking me to lie for you. Again. It's not fair Mum."

She swings around to face me. "I'll tell you what's not fair, Mrs Know-It-All." Her face bears the expression that scares me as much as it did when I was seven years old. "What's not fair is being trapped in a marriage with a boring man, whose idea of living is work, dinner, TV and bed, day after day after day." Her angry voice echoes around our sparsely furnished guest room, steam still curling through the door of the en-suite after Mum's recent shower. "You think you've got it all sussed, don't you? You're happy settling for your crap and mediocre life. I can do so much better."

"Dad's a good man. He loves you." Not wanting Rob to hear me arguing with Mum, I battle to keep my voice low, hoping she'll follow suit. I hate it when she slags Dad off. It's him who could do so much better.

"I'm only with him because of what he might do if I leave. You know that." She pulls a comb through her damp hair. "It's emotional bloody blackmail. And I don't know how much longer I can go on like this." She slams herself onto the bed, her bracelets rattling with the force. "If you tell him the truth, on your head be it, do you hear me?"

1

"What do you mean?" I walk to the window and twist the blind to let the early June sunshine in. I can't bear to look at her cold eyes and tight mouth. Really, I know exactly what she means, and it runs much deeper than the danger Dad might pose to himself.

"It would be a shame for you and me to sever our ties again. Jack certainly enjoys his Granny Maggie being here." Her voice softens. It always does for anything to do with Jack.

"You've only been here for one night."

"We're making up for lost time though, aren't we? At least that's what you'd better be saying to your father."

Deep down, I wish we *were* making up for lost time. That she could be the mother she never has been. "You don't need to convince yourself of that – you've already got Dad fooled. One night is hardly making up for anything really, is it?"

"Don't get all high and mighty with me, lady." Mum's eyes narrow. "You're never too old for a slap across the face."

"You can't hit me anymore Mother. Have you not noticed I'm a grown woman now." I've got to stand up to her, though I'm quaking as I do.

"So stop giving me grief. As far as your father knows, I'm here for two weeks. I might even spend another night here on my return journey from Devon." She squirts some perfume onto her neck. I remember when she would squirt it on me when I was a girl. When she was in a 'good mood' with me. When she was in a 'bad mood,' I got ignored. She continues. "At least I can get another live video with Jack to put on Facebook."

"I can't keep lying to Dad. I feel lousy about it." I lower onto the side of the bed, beside Mum, staring at the pattern on her blouse. She's got some nice clothes. Better than what I have. She's a good-looking woman. It's a shame she's not the same on the inside.

"It's a white lie Fiona. What he doesn't know can't hurt him? You're

2

saving him in the long run. And yours and Jack's relationship with me." She zips up her suitcase. "Because you realise, that if you betray my trust, I will cut you off again. Forever this time. From your father as well. You know from experience that he will always stand by me." She pauses and looks momentarily thoughtful. "If he was to succeed next time with the suicide thing, I would more than likely get nothing. No life insurance, no mortgage pay-off, not even his pension. Nothing. If he's going to find anything out, it will be when I'm ready to tell him, and when he's ready to know."

"As if you're referring to what happened as *the suicide thing.* Nor can I believe you're so reliant on any money Dad could generate. Do you know Mum, you could always get a job and live your own life? Make your own money. I'd look after Dad. You've at least a dozen years of working life left." I sound like a snob, but I don't care. I'm sick of her threatening me.

"Like you do, you mean? It's alright for you, isn't it?" She points her hairbrush towards my face. For a moment I think she's going to hit me with it, but instead she stands, towering over me. "With your grandmother's money that should have been mine, and with your big house and your executive husband. You don't deserve any of it."

I will not let her intimidate me. I also stand. "At least I have worked and earned my own money." I load a confidence into my voice, which I'm not feeling. "Not just what Grandma gave me."

She grabs me by the scruff of my t-shirt, twisting the neckline around her fist. I can smell the sourness of her breath. "What, you mean at poxy jobs in offices and shops, where you haven't lasted five minutes?"

"Get your hands off me."

She lets me go, pushing me backwards. Something within me shifts as I realise she really can't hurt me anymore. She just thinks she can. I continue staring into her eyeballs. I can't quite believe she has just grabbed me.

"What have you ever done with your life Fiona?" She's almost snarling at me now.

"Rob likes me being at home. At least I can look after the house and Jack."

She leans forward and looks at me as though I am diseased. "If Rob knew what you were really like, he would drop you like a ton of bricks."

"What do you mean, what *I'm really like?*" Anger rises in me. She's always done this. Made me feel like there's something inwardly awful about me. Ever since I was little. The only thing she's ever approved of about me is that I brought Jack into the world. Even then, she was grimacing about becoming a grandparent. About appearing old to others. Jack's always had to call her Granny Maggie, rather than Grandma. Personally, I think *Granny* sounds older than *Grandma* anyway. And she didn't broadcast her new role, like most new grandmothers would. Dad was over the moon. Until the depression got hold of him. He's done amazingly well coming back from where he was. I can't let her destroy him again.

At every turn, Mum throws my inheritance in my face. She hated Grandma, her mother-in-law. Even Dad stopped visiting her because Mum gave him such a hard time, calling him a mummy's boy and accusing him of being tied to Grandma's apron strings. I was always close to her though. Through my childhood, it was Grandma who came to school plays and sports days. I remember her staying up half the night to sew my costume for a fancy dress day. Throughout my teens, it was Grandma I ran to when I had a problem or wanted some adult company. She was the one who would tell me it was 'his loss' when I got dumped, and would be proud of me if I got good grades.

"Mum. Where's my book bag? I need to learn my spellings before school." Jack's voice hollers from the landing. "What's up?" He looks at me with concern as I swing the door open.

4

Even at seven, he can always read when there is something amiss with me. I thank my lucky stars every day that Jack and I have such a strong bond. Now that I'm a mother myself, I can't understand my mother's lifelong rejection and contempt for me. Occasionally she can be OK, it all depends on what sort of mood she's in. Whenever she is having an affair, she's usually nicer than this.

"You should have learned them last night Jack." I try to inject a sternness into my voice. "It's a good job you're up early, isn't it? It's under your PE bag in the hallway." I point towards the stairs. "Look at them whilst you finish your breakfast." It's my fault really that he hasn't learned them yet. I let him spend time with his gran last night, given that her visit is so fleeting, and he doesn't see much of her.

"Will do Mum. Morning Granny Maggie." He hurtles downstairs without waiting for a response.

"Look Fiona." Mum slides her feet into her shoes. God knows how she drives wearing heels like that. "I don't want to leave things on a bad note. I'll try to get back here on my way home."

"When?"

"In a couple of weeks."

I close the bedroom door. "But what am I supposed to say to Dad when he rings here?"

"The usual. Tell him I'm in the bath, or that I've gone for a walk. You'll think of something. You always do."

"Thanks for putting me in this position Mum. As long as you know I'm doing this for him, not you, if he wasn't still on those anti-depressants..." When I think about it, I'm definitely braver than I used to be when I'm dealing with her. "I can't believe you're carrying on behind his back again."

"It really isn't any of your business." She applies lipstick onto stretched lips, sliding each lip back and forth over one another. I used to love watching her apply make-up. In fact, the only job I have known her to have was as an Avon lady.

"I don't want it to be. But you're making it my business!"

"Look I don't want to talk about this any further. If your dad gets in touch, text me straightaway. I'll get away from Shane and call him back."

"I don't know why you don't just answer your phone yourself when he rings you. Keep me out of things."

She sighs. "We've been through all this Fiona. Don't you ever listen to me? I don't want to speak to your father in front of Shane – for the same reason I don't like him speaking to his wife in front of me. Shane and I keep our phones on silent when we've got our precious time together. Besides, we're too busy doing other things, if you know what I mean." She smiles to herself.

Ugh. "On that note, I'll leave you to get sorted. I'll put the kettle on."

"Not a word to Rob, eh? He was quizzing me last night about my plans. My love life is none of his business either." She pulls a brush through her hair. At fifty-six, she easily looks ten years younger than she is. Not like Dad, who, at the opposite end of the spectrum, looks ten years older than his fifty-eight years. It's the decades of being Mum's puppet on a string. But he's old school and believes marriage is for life. He might moan about Mum, but it would break his heart if he found out she was having an affair. Again.

"Trust me. Rob wouldn't want it to be his business."

The last time Mum left Dad, Jack had been three. She went off to Corfu with some married man she'd been carrying on with for months. Luckily, I found Dad in time to get him to hospital. He had to have his stomach pumped and months of therapy. He was extremely sorry afterwards, saying it had been a moment of madness and desperation. But he's been on anti-depressants ever since. He daren't come off them.

"Shame you found him," Mum had said when I rang to tell her what had happened. "I don't know why you're even telling me. I've got a new life now. If you want to take your father's mental problems on, that's up to you."

I had put the phone down on her and it was over eighteen months before I spoke to her again after her callous attitude. I couldn't bring myself to. I helped Dad put himself back together, but then Mum's boyfriend left her in Corfu to return to his wife, daughter and sons in the UK. Mum returned to Dad, her tail between her legs. Of course, he naively believed her apologies and promises that she wanted to make a go of things with him. Neither of them had started divorce proceedings, so they just picked up where they had left off. But I was worried when I discovered Dad had increased his life insurance, and let Mum talk him into re-mortgaging the house so they could have more holidays. Rob ordered me to keep out of it.

I've kept my distance from them since, not really going over to visit, and only ringing Dad when I knew Mum wouldn't be around. But a year ago, she started approaching me again and making a big fuss of Jack. Then within a couple of months, it emerged what she really wanted from me. An alibi. For her latest affair with another married man. Maybe the re-mortgage money was running low, and she wanted excitement.

Chapter 2

At the sound of Rob's voice, I pause outside the kitchen door. "Ring me back the minute you get this message. I've been trying to get hold of you for days." There's an angry edge to his voice, one I don't hear often. He's normally easy going.

He jumps as I walk in, slopping the protein shake he's making. He looks as though he's got the woes of the universe on his shoulders. His phone is still lit up on the counter beside him.

"Who were you on the phone to?"

"Just something to do with work."

"No prizes for guessing what you're up to today." I look at his lycra-clad body and notice his cycle helmet on the breakfast bar. "Are you not at work?"

"Not until this afternoon. I booked a half day." He flicks the switch on the kettle. "A bike ride will blow away a few cobwebs."

"Are you OK? I noticed you were up half the night." He's in the same league as Dad at the moment, looking ten years older than his thirty-eight years. "It's not like you to suddenly book a half day either."

"Yeah. I'm fine. I'll have a brew with you before I set off. Let the traffic die down, especially on that back road."

"I take it I'm dropping Jack off at school then?" I rummage through the letter rack for his school trip letter.

"I assumed your mother would want to go with you to drop him off.

It's been months since she's seen him." The sarcasm in his voice is not lost on me.

The thundering of footsteps through the hallway stops our conversation. Jack bursts into the kitchen. "Granny Maggie's going to take me to school," he announces.

"Where is she?"

"On the phone in the lounge." He takes a loud slurp from his cup. "She said I had to leave her alone for a minute, then we will set off. She's closed the door."

No prizes for guessing who she's on the phone to. I drop some bread into the toaster.

"Back in a minute. I need to find my watch." Rob strides past me. He's got the morning off and he's going out on his bloody bike. We could have done something together. Of course, he probably thinks my mother is still going to be here. He might think he's doing us a good turn by giving us some time together.

"Can Granny Maggie pick me up from school as well?" Jack's expression is a cross between pleading and excited.

"We'll see."

"You'll have to show me where your school is." Mum breezes into the kitchen and swipes a slice of toast from my plate.

"I'll come with you," I say. "Maybe we could go for a coffee afterwards." I'm feeling a renewed sense of strength. She can't keep doing what she's doing to Dad, and I don't want to keep covering for her. The worry makes me feel ill but I'm going to tell her straight before she sets off. It's better discussed on neutral ground. She can't kick off as much in a coffee shop.

"Sorry, no time." She looks uncomfortable as she checks her watch. "I'm going to take Jack to school and then get on the road."

"But you only got here last night. Surely you can make time for a coffee?"

9

"You know I've got plans." She checks her reflection in my mirror on the kitchen windowsill. I always do my eyebrows in here as it's a good light.

"Mum, we need to talk."

"It'll have to wait. I've got a long drive in front of me." She winds a chiffon scarf around her neck. I have the intrusive thought of strangling her with it. "Where's Rob?"

"Upstairs."

Jack looks at the clock. "Granny Maggie, it's after quarter to nine." He knows all his o'clocks, halves and quarters. "I'll be late for school if we don't go now."

"Come on then." Mum plucks her jacket from the back of a chair and picks her case up. "I'll see you when I see you," she nods towards me. I know she won't hug me. She never has. She has no problem with grabbing me by the scruff of the neck or threatening to slap me though.

"A couple of weeks then?" I've tried to talk to her. I can't do any more. It would be easier if Dad didn't insist on ringing landlines first, and mobile numbers as a last resort. Maybe this visit to Devon will be the one where she and Shane will split up. Her affairs are usually short-lived.

"I'll do my best Fiona. Come on then, Jack. Have you got your things together?" She ruffles his mousy-brown hair as he stands. It's the same colour as Rob's. Jack's like a miniature Rob, with the same blue eyes, olive skin tone and lankiness.

I remember when we had to empty Rob's dad's house a couple of years ago. Because it was a council house, they only gave Rob a month. I couldn't leave him to do it on his own, and his dad's death had hit him hard. Looking at old photos of Rob was like looking at Jack. They're as close as Rob was to his dad. At least, they have been until recently.

Rob has become suddenly preoccupied. I'm waiting for him to spill whatever is bothering him. He's like that. He'll only brood on things for so long, then his solitude or conscience will get the better of him.

Perhaps, soon, he will let me know why he's been meeting up with his ex from when he was younger, Bryony. I thought I was seeing things when I saw them leaving a café a fortnight ago. They didn't look, well, together, but a man meeting his attractive ex-fiancée, without mentioning it to his wife will never bode well.

"Where's my coat?"

"You don't need one Jack. It's cracking the flags out there. What's his school called, Fiona?" Mum turns to me. "In case he forgets the way or something."

"The Whartons," Jack replies. "It's up the hill. I know the way."

"Remember what we talked about before," says Mum, turning back from the kitchen door. "It's my life. My business. I hope that's the end of the matter."

Chapter 3

Rob takes the milk from the fridge. "How long's she staying?"

"She's on her way down to Devon today." I raise my eyes from the counter I'm wiping, knowing he'll have something to say.

"One night! You're joking. She's still seeing that bloody man, I take it?" He slams the milk onto the counter.

"Rob. Calm down. Yes, she is. I'm not getting involved, and neither are you."

"But you're bloody covering for her again?"

"I've no choice, have I? You know what it could do to Dad if he found out." I take two cups from the dishwasher and slide them towards Rob. "Anyway, I'm sure it'll blow itself out like it did last time. The man's married. He'll come to his senses."

"Your mother can have it away with half of Yorkshire if that's how she wants to carry on. But without dragging us into it. God, I've got enough going on right now?"

"Like what?"

"It doesn't matter. Really. What bothers me is her making you lie for her. She makes my skin crawl. Making out like she's mother and granny of the year."

Things are often up and down between Rob and my mother, but the abruptness of his words makes me bristle. "I couldn't cope with her

12

here for two weeks, anyway. I wouldn't want her here. She makes me feel like a child again."

"You need to get over that Fiona." Rob swings around to face me. "Get a grip. You're a grown woman with a son of your own now. Sort some counselling or something. Whatever it takes to stop letting that self-centred woman control you."

His voice is on the rise. I hate rows. I've got to calm this down. He's every right to be annoyed, but I'm taken aback at how angry he seems to be.

"It's just a shame she's not doing what she's telling your dad. What is it? Spending quality time with her daughter and grandson? Making up for lost time?"

"I've told you I wouldn't want her here for any length of time, anyway. But it's got nothing to do with you Rob." I try to move past him, but he steps towards me, blocking my path.

"Nothing to do with me! It's bad enough what she's doing to your dad," he begins. "But if you think I'm going to stand back and watch as she emotionally blackmails you, I'm not. She's had far too much control for too long."

I keep my tone low and even, hoping Rob will follow suit. I hate rows. "I know you mean well. But they're my parents. I'll deal with it."

"Whether or not you like it, I'm involved too. Jack's my son. I'm telling you now Fiona. If Maggie doesn't stop issuing threats and ultimatums, and doesn't leave you out of it, I'll tell your dad what's going on myself, when I answer the phone to him."

"You wouldn't. You saw what happened before." We face each other as opponents, rather than as husband and wife.

"Fair enough. I'll drive over then. Tell him to his face. Stay with him afterwards. I mean it Fiona. We're not lying to protect her."

"I'm not asking you to do anything."

"You're asking me to lie if I answer the phone. Whilst she gallivants around at the other end of the country."

"Well, let the answerphone pick up then." Dad's always had the belief that it's cheaper to ring the landline. Then I realise that if I were to simply unplug it, he'd have to ring my mobile, reducing the chances of Rob intercepting his call.

"Fiona. For God's sake." He places his hand on my arm, but it's a grip rather than a placating touch. "Why has that woman got such a hold on you. Let her go. She does absolutely nothing for you. And never has. You need to give her a wide berth."

He's right, I know, but it still hurts, hearing it said out loud. "But Jack loves her. So she can't be that bad."

"Jack's seven years old." He glances towards the picture of him on the fridge. "And easily won over with a new toy. Your mother knows exactly what she's doing. She's one of the most manipulative women I've ever met."

"I know."

"Then do the right thing Fiona." Rob steps back from me now. "Tell her to go home. Sort her marriage out."

"I can't tell her anything. She's not coming back after dropping Jack off."

"She's going straight to Devon? Selfish cow."

"She's really unhappy Rob. And I don't think she realises the effect she has on other people."

"I don't give a shit how unhappy she is. She has no right expecting you to lie for her. I'll tell her for you."

"No," I blurt. "I know you're right, but it needs to come from me. I stood up to her before - when we were upstairs, and I've got to keep doing it."

He shakes his head as he turns away. "Like I said, you need to see someone about this. You're not a little girl anymore. And if you're not careful, you'll be hitting the bottle again."

14

I notice the pitying expression on his face, and the rarely felt kick-ass woman deep inside me fires. "No, I will not. You've room to talk anyway Rob. About lies and deceit."

"What's that supposed to mean?"

"My mother isn't the only person keeping secrets. I know there's something going on, Rob."

"I don't know what you're talking about."

"Well, maybe a bike ride will be a good time for you to think about it. You said you're off out to blow away the cobwebs. We'll talk later." Part of me wants to have it out with him now, but I've had enough this morning. I just want some peace.

Rob reaches for his cycle helmet. "You need to talk to your mum first. Ring her. Or I'll be speaking to your dad."

I sigh as the side gate clangs after him. He's right about my mother though. What the hell did I ever do to deserve her? I feel drained every time we part company, no matter how briefly I've been around her. If I had siblings to compare notes with, it wouldn't be so bad. Dad's blindsided by her because he's terrified of being on his own. He probably wouldn't know what to do without her ordering him around all the time. It's like he's become institutionalised.

I decide to give him a ring. Get in there first. There's less chance of him ringing later and Rob answering then. I'll speak to Rob again when he gets back. Hopefully, he'll be in a better mood and I can persuade him to keep out of it. I want to speak to him about the Bryony situation too. I was planning to yesterday, after he was late back for the Sunday lunch I'd spent ages cooking, but Mum arrived.

"Hi Dad, it's me." I walk through the kitchen and out of the conservatory door towards the garden swing. It's too nice to be inside.

"Who's me?" He does it every time. He thinks it's funny to pretend not to recognise my voice. I can't be bothered going through the usual rigmarole of it today.

"Me, Dad." I lower myself onto the swing.

"What's up with you Fiona? You sound stressed. Your mother isn't on your case already, is she?" I know what he's getting at. At every given opportunity since Jack was born, whenever Mum gets the opportunity, she'll criticise my parenting skills; she can never resist. She criticises everything, from how I feed and dress Jack, to his routine and activities.

Then if it's not that, it's the inheritance. It's not my fault that Grandma left me half a million. Dad decided at the time to respect his mother's wishes and let me have it. Mum despised him for it. Grandma left him fifty grand as well, which meant there probably wouldn't have been any grounds to contest the will. When I'd offered Dad a proportion of what I'd been left, he refused. "She adored you love," he had said. "And it was you who took care of her when she was ill, not *us*. She wanted you to have it. It's rightfully yours."

"I'm OK Dad. Mum's taking Jack to school." I'm not lying, am I? "Jack was delighted when she arrived last night."

"That's nice dear. It makes me feel better. I'm rattling around the house, here on my own, but I'll be used to it in a day or two. It's a shame I couldn't have come over with your mother."

"Oh, Dad." I rock myself gently back and forth on the swing. I wish he could come and stay. At least he genuinely wants to spend time with us. He's still got work commitments though and is still a few years away from retirement. Plus, Mum will have thought of a reason why he couldn't have come over. "Are you not working today?"

"Yes. Soon. I didn't sleep so well last night. I never do when your mum's not here."

"But you have your own rooms, don't you; it shouldn't be too much different?"

"I'm not a fan of being on my own in the house."

16

I feel the weight of responsibility and I hope to goodness Mum's affair doesn't last much longer. That Dad never discovers it. He's still fragile and sounds even more so today. He's like this whenever Mum goes away, but he bounces back.

"Sorry love." My silence must give away my awkwardness. "I shouldn't lay this on you. I'll be fine. It's great that you and Jack can spend some time with your mother. One of these days, I promise I'll make it over to stay with her. I'm sure you can make room in that big house of yours."

"Course I can Dad." I wonder, for a moment, if Dad is getting at something with the big house reference. But I doubt it. Mum has made me paranoid. I stand from the swing and busy myself dead-heading the flowerbeds as I wander around the perimeter of the garden. "Isn't it gorgeous today?" I look into the sky, hoping that shifting his focus to the sunshine will cheer Dad up. I want to ask if he's still on the antidepressants, if he's got anyone he can talk to, but I know he'll never open up to me. After all, I've had my own ghosts to fight. And still have.

When Dad took his overdose, he was deeply ashamed and would never discuss it with me – I'm relieved that I persuaded him to continue with the counselling. The hospital which had pumped his stomach referred him. I know he's got stuff stemming from his own childhood – something to do with his dad, something he'd not forgiven his mother for. I never got to the bottom of that though. I'll mention it to him again, one of these days. I'm dying to know what this family secret is. Even Mum doesn't seem to know.

"It sure is. I might even have a beer in the garden when I get home later. Invite Dave around."

"That's more like it." I laugh. "Beer on a Monday." I don't drink anymore, thank God. I'm free of it. This is something that I don't discuss with Dad. Secrets and lies keep the cogs of our family spinning.

17

"Though Dave will probably be busy." His voice is downbeat again. "What are your plans today? Are you doing something nice with your mum?"

"I'm not sure yet. I'll see what she says when she gets back." *In two weeks,* I feel like adding, but I never would. I pray I can talk Rob around from his current stance on the situation. Dad would take it really badly.

After saying goodbye to Dad, I wander around the garden, dead-heading the plants in the hanging baskets now, before padding barefoot back into the house. I catch sight of my reflection in the hallway mirror. I've lost weight since I stopped drinking and my face is less puffy.

I'm trying to make more effort with my appearance again, wearing a bit of make-up, that sort of thing – not that Rob notices anymore. All he seems to care about is his life away from the house. His work, the golf course, getting out on his bike with his cycling friends – getting away from me no doubt. And now he thinks I'm even more pathetic because I can't stand up to my mother.

I don't know if there's anything I should know about Bryony. When I saw them together, it all looked platonic, but that was only one sighting of them. There's no denying either that he's gone cool on me lately. My gut is saying it should worry me.

I move things around in the kitchen and dining room, sliding pots into the dishwasher and wiping the sides down. The house is pretty clean; I bottomed it as soon as I discovered my mother was coming, whilst preparing the Sunday dinner at the same time. I don't know why I had bothered; Rob had been nearly two hours late back for it. I see his phone flash on the side. It's unusual for him to have left his phone behind, very unusual.

Incoming Call – Bryony. I'm sorely tempted to answer it, but something stops me. Maybe ignorance is bliss. I can't get into his phone, but I can see the notifications on his lock screen. He has missed three calls from her. What's going on? Prior to meeting his first wife Denise, he was engaged to Bryony. They were together for several years. But that was such a long time ago.

Speak of the devil. There's a message from Denise, sent just after seven this morning. *Thanks for letting Simone down yet again,* it begins. *You should try watching a ten-year-old waiting for her da-* then it cuts off. The phone needs unlocking to read the rest.

Rob has always said marrying Denise was the biggest mistake he ever made. They got together not long after his first engagement was broken off. Bryony had wanted travel and freedom – Rob wanted money and career.

Rob felt he had to marry Denise after she became pregnant with Simone. He later discovered the pregnancy was deliberate but didn't learn this until after their wedding. His marriage to her consequently only lasted two years. At least he's beating that record with me. There's been no love lost between me and Rob's ex. And I can just about tolerate Simone, Rob's whining ten-year-old, as long as it's in small doses. She's not too keen on me either, but we seem to have developed an unspoken agreement to keep out of one another's way.

What I want to know is why Bryony is so desperate to contact Rob. I feel like looking her number up and ringing her back. I should have answered the phone when I had the chance, but really, I don't want to know the truth. Maybe I'm more like Dad than I care to admit.

There's the start of an email from an employment agency on Rob's screen. He can't be looking for another job. The subject line states, *Executive Director of Finance.* It must be spam or something. There are three missed calls from an unknown number. It's not even ten o'clock. His phone is having a busy morning. Unlike him, out on his bike, in his own little bubble. He pretends to be all caring, getting involved in this situation with my mother, but I know that he's simply trying to deflect the attention from himself. From his recent behaviour and distance, I know there is something going on with him. I grab my handbag and car keys. I need to get out of this house.

* * *

I had a moment when I doubted my plans.
I even pulled up at the side of the road.
There was a final chance to change my mind.
But deep down, I knew what had to be done.

Chapter 4

I settle on my sun lounger with a cup of tea and a book. I love my peaceful afternoons and usually get through a novel every two or three days. It's my escape into a more exciting life. I've got an hour before I need to collect Jack. He's going to be so disappointed when I arrive, instead of Granny Maggie. I imagine her now, she'll be nearing Devon, without a care in the world, not giving a toss about the stress she's putting me under, and as for Dad, she won't give him a second thought.

She's never really forgiven him for not taking me to court and contesting my grandmother's will, calling him *spineless* and every other name under the sun. He was genuinely happy with his fifty grand and insistent that I had what his mother had wanted me to have. This was all wrapped up inside the guilt he felt at their estrangement.

I'll never forget what Mum said to me after I received my settlement - *your diligence paid off in the end, didn't it Fiona?* Like I'd only looked after my grandmother for what I might get out of it. To be honest, Grandma lived a frugal life, and I had no idea she had that sort of money.

Grandma and Mum despised each other with a vengeance. They'd apparently never got along, and there was always an atmosphere at family occasions. If Grandma had known about Mum's affair and Dad's subsequent overdose, she'd have been spinning in her grave.

21

My dear mother paid Dad's *spinelessness* back by embarking on her first affair – at least it was her first, as far as I knew. She didn't leave him until the third affair. And by then, the hole of depression was too deep for me to drag him out of.

I put my book to one side. I can't concentrate. I want to stop my monkey-mind from jumping around its familiar territory, but the harder I try, the more my thoughts scramble over one another.

I spent my childhood vowing that I would never turn out like Mum, as a mother, a wife, or as a person full stop. She was so inconsistent. If we were around others, she would act like mother of the year, but when we were alone, she would not speak to me at best, or be cruel at worst. And when I say cruel...

She once told me she could feel my presence if I was in the house. I had asked her what she meant, and she replied that my being around gave her a bad feeling. Dad once explained that Mum had suffered with postnatal depression after my birth and claimed to have no recollection of me being born. This, he said, had damaged any potential bond she could have had with me.

Yet for all her indifference towards me, she was also controlling. I had buck teeth as a child, yet she wouldn't allow me to wear a brace. The other thing that still bugs me, is how she always made me wear my hair like a boy. I was never allowed to grow it long; she said it was too messy.

She threw me out of the house at sixteen, whilst Dad was at work. She had caught me drinking vodka from her cabinet. She had slapped my face and screamed at me, saying I was a total disgrace. I took refuge at Grandma's to start with, but was at an age when I was resentful and hormonal. Before long, Grandma gave me some money for a deposit on a flat. I was obviously too much for her.

One of the first things I did after Mum kicked me out was to get a brace for my teeth. I could finally wear things other than charity shop cast-offs and grow my hair long. She was a strange and cold woman, my mother. And still is. We've had a difficult relationship ever since we made up when I was older, and normally keep one another at arms' length. However, something inside me still yearns for her to apologise for treating me as she has and become a proper mother to me.

I spent my late teens and much of my twenties trying to fill this mother-shaped void. Alcohol became my biggest friend and greatest enemy. Rob has stopped reminding me of the fact that he saved me from myself. We met when I was twenty-seven.

This last year is the longest I've gone without a drink. When I first kicked the booze, I envied all the lucky, normal drinkers who could control their intake and their behaviour. Which is why I used to keep going back to it, thinking that perhaps after a time of abstinence, I could control it too. I saw it as relaxation after a stressful day. I turned to it when I was miserable or bored. I poured it in copious amounts. I would control it for so long, then I would be right back where I started. I never found the answers I needed in the bottom of my wine glass. Nor could I numb any of my pain. It would come back, larger than life the next morning, each time worse than the time before. I'm never going back to it now. Jack deserves better. I do too.

I stare into the cloudless sky. Once upon a time, I would plan a sunshine tipple on my return from picking Jack up. That's if I got to school time without one. That's the thing with the booze – it's used on sunny days, rainy days, and anything in between days, to celebrate and to commiserate.

A loud knocking at the front door, then the doorbell cuts into my thoughts. By the time I've hoisted myself from the sun lounger, I hear a voice and what sounds like a radio coming down the drive.

23

"Hello," calls a female voice. "Is anyone there?"

"Can I help you?" I call back, my stomach lurching as I notice a policewoman at the gate. Then through the climbing flowers, I see a policeman towering behind her. Police in one's driveway on a Monday afternoon are hardly likely to yield any good news.

"Detective Inspector Diane Green," she announces, showing a card through the clematis, "and this is my colleague PC John Robinson." He also holds his ID badge up. "Are you Mrs Fiona Matherson?"

"Yes. What is it?" Thoughts of Dad having done something stupid again flood my brain. He sounded down this morning, but he'd perked up by the time we'd finished speaking, I'm sure he had. Or maybe Mum's had an accident. Monkey mind again.

"Can we come in?" she continues. Her face is unsmiling, troubled. She looks around the same age as me. God knows what she's going to tell me.

"Yes, sure. But I've got to collect my son from school shortly. It won't take long, will it?"

Without answering, they come through the gate and follow me to the patio where I gesture for them to sit. I face them at the table, the parasol casting shadows onto our faces.

"I'm afraid there's been an accident," the woman says.

* * *

There was no guarantee of death, even at speed.
There was the possibility of survival,
yet this would be unlikely without some lifelong impairment.
And this was nothing less than what was deserved.

Chapter 5

I stare at her. An accident. It can't be my dad having done something again. They wouldn't describe it as an accident if he had. He didn't sound that bad on the phone this morning, anyway. It must be my mother. Despite our differences, the hairs on the back of my neck stand up. *What the hell will I tell Jack? How will Dad cope?*

"Involving a car and a cyclist," the policeman says.

"My mum." My voice sounds loud amongst the birdsong. "She had a long drive. Is she alright?"

"It happened on the Denton Road between Otley and Ilkley."

"But she left hours ago. She was on her way to Devon. Why are you only coming around now?"

"It's taken a while for us to conduct the investigations at the crash scene. And to get an ID back from the cycle shop."

"Cycle shop?" There's a saying about 'blood running cold.' I think I'm experiencing it.

"There was a sticker on the bike to inform us that the cycle involved had originated from Chevin Cycles in Otley."

I feel sick. It's not Mum they're here about. "You mean…?"

"We've checked the serial numbers and a bike purchased by Mr Robert Matherson in July 2018 has been involved in an accident this morning."

I try to make mental calculations about when and where Rob bought his bike, like it even matters. I can't think straight. I rub at my temples.

"What time did your husband leave the house this morning?"

They could ask me my name right now, and I don't think I could answer them straight. Then I remember he left after Jack and Mum. "Just after nine o' clock, I think. He was going for a bike ride."

"Do you know where he was heading?"

I shake my head. Rob never tells me much about himself anymore. He rarely even mentions work. I was going to book us a table for our anniversary in a couple of weeks in the hope we could reconnect as a couple, instead of continuing as merely Jack's parents and housemates. I'd even planned what dress I was going to buy. "He was going for a bike ride before work. Is he OK?"

They look at each other. "I'm afraid not." The woman looks into my eyes, her eyes watery and her voice gentle. "A male cyclist, who we believe is your husband, has unfortunately been involved in a fatal road traffic accident at about ten-thirty this morning."

I stare back at her. "You must be mistaken. He'd have got further in an hour and a half than Denton Road. Like I said, he left here just after nine."

"We've double checked everything before coming here. The bike itself, the debit card he had on him..."

"Hang on - did you say fatal?" It's as though I'm watching this unfold from elsewhere. It's a strange feeling, like I'm not in my body.

"I'm so sorry Mrs Matherson. Subject to an identification, which we'll need you to do as soon as you feel able, it appears that the victim of the road traffic accident was your husband."

I choke on a sob. I don't know if I can face having to identify him. I stare into the sky. How can news about death occur on such a beautiful day? I tremble in the heat, feeling cold, wondering if there's any brandy left in the house.

DI Green must read my mind. "Can I get you anything?" she asks. "Or let someone know?"

"Are you really sure it's him? I mean, he's such a safe cyclist. And by half past ten he'd have been well beyond Skipton."

"We're as sure as we can be," the PC says gently. "Is there anyone who can be with you? You shouldn't be on your own."

"Can you ring my mother?" I slide the phone across the table. I don't want to take Mum's rejection first-hand, if that's what comes. "She's away, but I'm sure she'll come." Surely at a time like this, she'll put Jack and me before her married lover. Besides, Dad thinks she's here, and he's going to have to know what's happened soon. He'll be straight over, so she needs to get back.

DI Green holds the phone towards me so I can unlock it with my thumbprint. "I take it she's listed in your phone as Mum?"

I nod. I'm totally numb. Rob's not really dead. Until I see him with my own eyes, I won't believe it's true. I listen as DI Green is connected to my mother. Apart from the birds and a rustle through the trees, the garden is so quiet that I can hear what my mother is saying.

"Fiona – what is it? Has your dad been ringing already?"

"Sorry this isn't Fiona. My name is Detective Inspector Diane Green from Weetwood Police Station." She tucks a stray hair that's fallen from her ponytail behind her ear.

"Oh, I see. Is Fiona alright?"

It's the first time my mother has shown any concern towards me. Even in my benumbed state, something inside me warms.

"Yes, she's fine. But she's too shaken to ring you herself and has asked me to do it for her. I believe you're away right now?"

"That's right. I'm in Devon for a fortnight."

"Is there any way you can make your way to your daughter's? She really needs you here. I'm afraid we've had to give her some terrible news."

"What news?"

"Am I alright to tell her over the phone?" DI Green looks at me, her eyes still watery. It must be hard for the police, having to impart this sort of thing. I guess it's what they're trained for though.

I hold my hand out for the phone. It will be better coming from me, not a stranger. Not that it's sunk in yet.

"Mum," I say, my voice wobbling, and the phone shaking within my grip.

"What is it Fiona? Is it Jack? Is everything alright?"

"It's Rob," I begin, knowing as soon as I say the words, it makes them real. An image of him floods my mind. My six-foot-two handsome husband. Yes, things have gone awry, but we were deliriously happy once. Maybe we could've been again. Now I'll never know.

"He's. He's…" I can't say it.

DI Green takes the phone back from me. "Am I OK to tell her?" I nod.

She takes a deep breath. "It's DI Green again. I'm really sorry to be the one to tell you this – have you got anyone with you?"

Mum's made of steel, I think to myself – she doesn't need someone with her.

DI Green continues. "Your son-in-law was involved in a fatal road traffic accident this morning." She looks at me again. "If there's any way you can get here to be with your daughter, then…"

"I can't," I hear my mother say, curtly. "I've got plans over the next few days."

I take the phone back and raise it to my ear. "Please Mum. I need you here." And I really do. It suddenly dawns on me I don't want to be alone and there are not many friends I can call on. My former friends were merely drunken acquaintances. I've become somewhat of a loner over the last year.

"You know the score Fiona. I'll be arriving in Devon shortly. You must have a friend who can come and babysit you. Or get the brandy out."

Momentarily, all thoughts of Rob are swept aside. Bitch. She knows of the problems I've had with drink and she recommends brandy. "It's OK," I say with a mock sweetness to my voice. "You enjoy your holiday. I'm sure Dad will drop everything to come and help me."

"You wouldn't…"

I don't hang around to hear what she's got to say. I cut her off.

"Is she not able to come?" DI Green reaches across the table and squeezes my arm. "Is there someone else I can call for you?"

"I'll ring my Dad shortly."

"Can I get you a cup of tea?"

I nod. "The kitchen's through there." That's it. Yorkshire's answer to it all. A cup of bloody tea.

* * *

I have rarely driven a vehicle at such speed.
My feet shook against the pedals as I neared my target
Right before impact, our eyes locked.
What could I see?
Confusion?
Fear?
It was all over so quickly.

Chapter 6

I am too lost in my swirling thoughts to bother about PC Robinson's presence, or the silence between us. He shuffles awkwardly on the garden bench. Normally I witter away to mask the quiet when I'm in the company of someone I don't know well. He looks young, only mid-twenties, probably unaccustomed to breaking news of this type.

"Fiona, are you there?"

My head jerks towards the gate where my neighbour, Christina is wrestling with the handle.

"Come in. I'm over here." I've never felt more relieved to see a familiar face. I get up and stumble towards her, finally allowing my pent-up self to fall apart in her arms. She's one of the few friends I've got. And I've never needed a hug like I do right now.

"The police - I've just seen them looking around both of your cars - what on earth's happened?" She strokes my hair, which makes me cry harder. It's something my mum should be here doing. But she doesn't want to know.

"Rob's been in an accident. They're saying he's dead."

"Dead. No. He can't be. I only saw him this morning."

"It happened at half ten."

"Oh my God!"

DI Green comes to the door of the conservatory and looks at

Christine who lets me go. "I'll get another cup. Start taking some details please, John."

PC Robinson's head jerks up. I notice he's got a look of Rob. A younger Rob. Same sort of build and it's the hair too. "Will do." He pulls a dog-eared notebook from his pocket and looks grateful to have something to do. "OK. I'm sorry to have to do this now, but I'm sure you can appreciate it's a necessary part of the process." His gaze shifts from me to Christina. "You say you saw him this morning? What time was this?"

"I'm not sure." Christina sits at the side of me. "Around nine-ish. Maybe half past. He was on his bike and waved at me."

"Leaving here?"

"Yes."

"And he was on his own?"

"I think so. I didn't take that much notice to be honest. I was just wheeling the bin back in."

DI Green returns and places a cup in front of Christina. The irony of what we are doing suddenly hits me.

"My husband is lying dead in some mortuary and we're sitting here, drinking afternoon tea," I snap. "All we need is a plate of biscuits. What are we playing at?" Then I remember Jack. "Shit. I forgot about my son. He'll be waiting for me at school."

"Can anyone collect him for you?" DI Green asks. "Whilst we ask you a few questions?" She glances at Christina as she speaks.

"I'd prefer Christina to stay here." It's true. I don't know what good she can do, but I need someone with me. I'm shaking. I grab hold of my left wrist with my right hand to still it. If I'm left on my own, I'm likely to down that brandy. I shouldn't have it in the house. I'm out of options in terms of Jack. Mum won't come back. I can't let Dad know about what's happened, and Rob, the only other person who could collect Jack, well, he's... Fresh tears slide down my face.

"Isn't there an after-school club at The Whartons?" Christina puts an arm around me. "There was when my two were younger."

"Could you ring them for me?" I sniff. "I don't think I could get my words out."

"Do you want me to tell them what's happened?"

"No. Not until I know for definite. Tell them there's been a family emergency. It might not even be Rob yet."

The two police officers look at each other with a look that says *poor cow*. There's a moment of silence as Christina waits for the call to connect.

"Are you OK for us to continue with our questions?" DI Green slides a mug towards me. "I've put lots of sugar in yours. It's good for shock."

I wrap my fingers around it, allowing the warmth to comfort my trembling hands. As I take a sip, I nearly spit it out. She must have put five sugars in it!

"I'm ringing regarding Jack, erm Matherson." Christina stands and walks towards the edge of the garden.

"Can you remember what your husband was wearing this morning?" DI Green asks.

My mind drifts back. "His cycling stuff."

I can't remember the colour he was wearing. I took little notice. He's got stacks of golfing and cycling gear, though I've always told him he looks sexier in the cycling gear. At least, I used to. We've barely given each other a compliment in the last couple of months. Which would tie in with him being in contact with Bryony.

"Did he say where he was heading?"

"My son thought maybe Skipton. But to my knowledge, he sets off and goes wherever he ends up."

"So quite a fit man then? And normally safe and capable on a bike?"

"Yes, always. Listen - before we go any further with this, I want to make sure it's him."

"Like we said, we're..."

"If he's dead, I want to see him. I won't believe it until I do."

"Very well." DI Green sips from her mug and nudges her colleague. "We'll wait until your friend has finished on the phone. Make sure your son is taken care of first. How old is he?"

"Seven. I don't know how the hell I'm going to tell him." I drop my head into my hands.

Christina walks back towards us. "One of Jack's friend's parents was in the office when the school secretary answered." She places her hand over the mouthpiece of the mobile phone. "Anyway, the mum has offered to take him to their house. Give him some tea. Is that OK with you?"

"Whose mum?"

"Someone called Sam."

I nod. "I know her address. I've dropped Sam off before when he's been here. Tell her thanks." I can't believe I'm even capable of making decisions and holding a conversation. Not with all this going on.

She walks away again, completes the call, then comes to stand next to me.

"I'm off to make sure it's him. Rob, I mean."

"Do you want me to come with you?" She squints in the bright sunshine. However, her expression says she wants to do anything but come with me.

"No. This is something I should do on my own."

She squeezes my arm. "Drop me a text when you get back. I'll come over. You shouldn't be on your own tonight. I'll bring over something to eat."

"Thanks."

"We'll drive you there." DI Green offers.

"I'll drive myself. I'll be OK."

"You probably shouldn't. You've had a huge shock." Christina says, letting her hand rest on my shoulder. "Let them drive you."

I don't tell them this, but I want to look at the crash scene for myself first. Try to make sense of everything. So far, I'm holding up well. The old me would probably be drunk by now. I seem to have gone into some sort of autopilot, and I don't know whether or not that is a good thing. Deep down, however, I know that drinking is the last thing I'll be doing.

"She's right, you know," says DI Green. "You've had a terrible shock."

"I'd rather drive," I reply. "Besides, I need to collect my son on the way back. Where shall I meet you?" We could be arranging a meeting at a café, the way I'm talking. Not the identification of my husband's dead body.

"He's at the hospital mortuary." She's all matter-of-fact. The wateriness has disappeared from her eyes, now that I've got myself together. I suppose this is all in a day's work for her. "We're waiting to hear from the Coroner but it's almost certain that a forensic post-mortem will be necessary. Once your husband has been formally identified and the post-mortem has taken place, he can be moved to a chapel of rest."

"That's if it's him." Christina's words are full of hope.

It's unreal that we're talking coroners and post-mortems. Why couldn't he just be injured? Why does he have to be dead? "I'll get changed and I'll set off," I say to the police, then turn to Christina. "I'll text when I know."

"Are you sure you can do this, alone?"

"I'll be fine." My voice exudes a strength I'm not feeling.

"We'll meet you at the hospital reception," DI Green says. "Then we've got a few more questions to ask you, if that's alright?"

* * *

CHAPTER 6

The bang wasn't as loud as expected.
There was something,
but more like a bump in the road.
I got a bigger jolt from the stone I hit as I left him there.
A plan executed like clockwork.
Nearly.

Chapter 7

I slide into my Jeep. Thoughts of the day Rob bought it return to haunt me. Well, I say he bought it. It was out of our savings, which mostly comprised of what remained of my inheritance. The new car was to celebrate getting my driving licence back after a three year driving ban. I had been three times over the limit.

I blink back tears as I reverse from the drive and make my way out of our cul-de-sac. All the neighbours, apart from Christina, probably think I'm off to collect Jack from school. I'm surprisingly calm as I leave the residential area and pull onto the country road. The air conditioning is blasting onto my face, freezing the tears I didn't realise I was crying.

The radio station is tuned into Classic FM, probably from when Rob picked Jack up on Saturday. When life was normal. I imagine that this is how my life is about to become demarcated. Before and after. Rob and post Rob. Normality and well – I don't know yet.

I imagine my husband cycling this route. Toned calves and biceps glistening in the sunlight, head down, legs pumping. I overtake a cyclist, taken aback at his similarity from the back to Rob. After I've passed, I feel compelled to check in my mirror that it's not him. I've heard before that when someone dies, you see them everywhere.

I surprise myself at my ease of driving, especially on this road, after what's happened. I should be more anxious. But I'm numb. Void. Like

I'm not even here. But it's an easier way to feel than what it could be. Rob always felt safe when out cycling. Said he could handle anything. I was never the same on the odd time I went out on my bike with him. I felt out of control going down a hill, and as though I was going to die from lack of oxygen going up one. So cycling became something he did without me. Same with golf. I'd rather watch paint dry. It was like that with most things, eventually. We hardly did anything together. We barely even ate together.

The air freshener swings from side to side as I bring the car to a halt at the end of a line of cars. I've arrived here in record time and can't even recall my journey. There's a sign ahead saying *road closed* and a snaking queue of vehicles turning around in the narrow road. As they turn in the opposite direction towards me, and the queue becomes shorter, I edge closer to the sign. Before long, I'm right in front of it. I get out of the car, poised to walk to the spot where whatever has happened, has happened. I need to see it.

"You can't come through here love." An officer springs from his patrol car that's blocking the road after the sign. It's so sunny that I didn't notice the revolving blue lights. But I see them now, reflecting on his face as he reaches me. "There's a crime scene back there."

"A crime scene?" I stare at him. "What's actually happened?"

"A fatal road traffic accident earlier today. This road will be closed for a while longer, I'm afraid. The crash investigation team are still doing what they need to."

"Wasn't it just an accident?" I ask. I feel sick. I realise I've not eaten anything since the toast, just after Mum and Jack left this morning. If I'm sick, it will just be bile. I swallow hard.

"That's what they're trying to establish." Sweat rolls down the side of his head. "But for now, you'll have to find another way through."

"I need to see what's happened."

He gives me a strange look. "You can't. I'm not letting anyone through. I'm not allowed."

"But I'm his wife."

"Whose wife?"

"The man who has died. Rob. The cyclist. I need to see what has happened."

"I'm really sorry. You shouldn't be here. I can't let you through."

He steps back from me, so I break into a run. He shouts after me. I turn, expecting him to give chase but he doesn't. He's tilting the radio on his shoulder towards his face. I'll probably be intercepted when I get there, but at least I'll get a glimpse of the scene. I get to the sharp bend and stop, now able to see a hive of activity further up the road, through the gaps in the bushes. If I go any further, I will definitely be caught and frogmarched back to the cordon.

People in white suits swarm around, measuring things, taking photographs, writing things down. There's no sign of Rob's bike.

The dry stone wall doesn't look all that damaged from what I can see, from the distance I'm at, and I can't see any skid marks in the road from where I am. Of course, I will come back and take a closer look. Maybe lay some flowers. Apart from a low hum of voices, all is quiet. I close my eyes, allowing the sunshine onto my face and the sound of birdsong to wash over me. It could be just another day.

* * *

The scene keeps replaying.
I'll never forget the sight of him flying through the air.
I imagine the crumpled body as bone and flesh connected with earth.

Chapter 8

By the time I leave the hospital, it's what I used to call wine o'clock. I'm tempted to have a drink, and no one would blame me if I did. It's not as if I have to answer to Rob anymore, is it? I hate myself for thinking this. However, I know drink won't do me any favours, so I'm going to try other things to get through this. I just haven't worked out what yet.

The mortuary staff have stamped my parking ticket, so I don't have to pay. DI Green got someone to make me another sweet tea whilst they asked more questions. They didn't ask anything out of the ordinary, just routine stuff. But the patrol officer was right. It *is* being investigated as a crime. There were apparently no skid marks in the road, just a wheel dent where the car ran into a large stone. They're saying that whoever hit Rob did not even try to stop afterwards.

It's the second time I have seen a dead body. The first was Grandma, ten years ago. I was the only one who went to see her. It helped me accept it. I don't know what I feel after seeing Rob. I only glanced at him. A sheet was pulled up to his neck. I looked at his face and said, "yes, that's him." He apparently died quickly. They haven't worked out the exact cause of death yet, but think it was damage to his brain stem. The forensic post-mortem will confirm that, and whether he had taken anything that might have caused an accident. After seeing me, they were speaking to the farmer that was there when he died.

I couldn't even cry when I saw Rob's body. In fact, I've only cried this afternoon. That might have been more to do with Mum's indifference. And then Christina being nice to me. I guess, in time, the lot will come tumbling out. But I've Jack to break the news to first. I've got to stay strong for him.

I tug my phone from the glove box and search through my messages for Sam's mum's number. She texted me a couple of months ago about yet another birthday party. Jack's got a ten times better social life than I have. He seems to go to a different party every week. I haven't saved her number – she's not exactly what I'd call a friend, but at least she gives me the time of day, not like the other cliques of mothers at the school gates. They used to stare and whisper when I'd walked up to collect Jack, a little worse for wear. Since I've sobered up, they still eye me with the same suspicion. Pious hypocrites if you ask me. I bet they all have their own wine o'clock routine.

The call connects immediately. "Is that Sam's mum?" I don't even know her name.

"Speaking. Hi Fiona."

"How did you know it was me?"

"I've got your number saved."

"I'm sorry. I'm all over the place right now. You must remind me of your name. I can't keep calling you *Sam's mum*." Here I go again, having a normal conversation. Even though I've just identified my husband's body. People will think I'm heartless.

"It's Lynne. Don't worry. Is everything OK?"

"Not really." I steel myself to say the words out loud. I guess I'm going to have to get used to telling people. "It's Jack's dad – my husband. He's…" Out of the corner of my eye, I notice DI Green and PC Robinson, as they drive out of the police parking bay, towards the exit barrier. They're laughing. How can they laugh after what they've just dealt with?

"He's what?"

"He's been in an accident. On his bike this morning."

"The one on Denton Road? Oh, my goodness! I've just heard something on the local news. Please tell me it wasn't your husband!"

"I've just identified his body."

The line is quiet. What can she possibly say? Heat springs to the back of my eyes as I imagine her face – etched with shock and sympathy. Maybe the other mums at the school gates will acknowledge me now. Or perhaps they'll treat me even more like a leper. As if the death of one's husband is something that can be transmitted.

"Hello? Are you still there?"

"Fiona. I don't know what to say. Do you want us to keep hold of Jack tonight? He can borrow some of Sam's pyjamas. I'll wash his clothes ready for school tomorrow. You must be distraught."

"I should collect him. He needs to hear what's happened from *me*."

I watch as people park and leave their cars, or return to the hospital car park, some deep in conversation, some glued to their phones. All around me, life continues. I wonder if I'll ever feel normal again.

"I can make sure Jack finds nothing out. They haven't named your husband yet, have they?"

"No, but it's only a matter of time. Like I said, I've just formally identified him, so they'll release his name soon. Plus, they'll be wanting eye witnesses to come forward."

"You should look after yourself Fiona. Let me help you with Jack. It's the least I can do."

I'm beat. I haven't got the energy to insist on collecting him. At least I can wait until tomorrow before having to impart what's happened. He's seven years old – it's not as though he's going to watch the news, or read a paper and find out for himself.

"OK, thank you. I'll leave him with you. If you're really sure?"

"Of course I am. I'm glad to do something useful. Let me know if you'd like me to collect him tomorrow as well. Sam loves having Jack here."

"No, it's fine." I'm aware of the possessive edge to my voice. "I must tell him what's happened to his daddy tomorrow. At least you looking after Jack gives me chance to try and make sense of what's happened myself first."

"Are you going to be alright Fiona? Have you got someone there with you?"

"My neighbour's coming over." I'm lying. I've already decided that I need to be on my own this evening. We all have our own way of dealing with things, and this is mine.

"If there's anything I can do, all you have to do is ask. I mean that."

"Thanks. I appreciate that."

The standard line when someone has died. *If there's anything I can do...* It's a sentence that I'm probably going to get used to hearing.

I take the long way home, pointing the Jeep toward Denton Road, which has reopened. There's hardly any sign of anything having occurred. It's as though Rob's life didn't count for anything. Here one minute, gone the next.

I pull up and step out into the balmy evening air, which smells of muck spreading and summer meadows. There are a few stones on the ground from the dry stone wall. Apart from that – nothing. I glance over the wall where I saw a police officer earlier, taking measurements. There's a dent in the grass, man-sized. I realise, with a shudder, that this is where Rob ended up. There should be rows of flowers here, marking his life. Yet hardly anyone knows just yet, that he's gone. I climb over the wall, stumbling towards the flattened grass. A closer look reveals dried blood. I fall to my knees beside where he died. I'm comforted because it was quick. That's probably why PC Robinson told me. To comfort me.

CHAPTER 8

* * *

Not a soul passed as I set off again.
I thought I saw the top of someone's head in the next field.
But I'll have got away too quickly for them to have anything on me.
A gamble which seems to have paid off.

Chapter 9

Arriving back home is inevitable. Though the company of anyone else is the last thing I want, the prospect of an empty house is still uninviting. I absently notice the hanging baskets are showing the fruits of my recent labour. They need watering but, in the scheme of things, that seems unimportant.

I usually love being in our beautiful home – my sanctuary and favourite place in the world. It's hard to believe that this time yesterday, Mum, Rob and Jack filled it. Rob wasn't impressed that Mum was here. I had sensed this by his tone whilst they were in the garden. I was busy in the kitchen, so couldn't make out what they were saying. Jack had been over the moon at her arrival and the toy cars she had brought him. Despite the undercurrents, yesterday, it was a family home. Now, I don't know what it is. An empty shell.

There's a tap on the window of the Jeep. I let the window down.

"Was it him?" Christine bends towards me, shaking her mane of chestnut hair behind one shoulder. I've always been envious of her hair. Mine's past my shoulders now, but thin and brittle, not glossy and thick, like hers. I notice she's holding a foil-wrapped plate.

I nod, momentarily closing my eyes against her expression.

"I'm so sorry." She reaches in and touches my shoulder with her perfectly manicured hand, balancing the plate in the other. I'd meant to get my nails done as a sobering up treat but had never got around to it. Somewhere deep inside, I've never felt as though I deserve treats such as manicures. I rarely spend money on myself. Just Jack and the house.

"How are you doing? Sorry, silly question, I know."

I shrug my shoulders. "I don't think it's really hit me yet."

"I can't imagine what you're going through. Where's Jack?"

"He's staying at his friend's tonight – that one whose mum picked him up. I'm going to be rattling around in there." I nod towards the house. "It's probably for the best though. I don't think I'd have the energy to cope with Jack tonight."

"Shall I come in with you? I can stay overnight." She means well, though her expression doesn't carry the same conviction as her words. "You shouldn't be on your own," she adds, as though convincing herself.

"No." I'm surprised at how quickly I reply. "I honestly need to be on my own tonight. Just to get my head around it all."

"I understand." She rises back to her full height. "If you change your mind, just drop me a text. And make sure you get something to eat and get some sleep."

"Yes Mum," I say, wishing I could say that to the person who should really be here for me. Some kids in the street are out on their scooters. Jack would normally be with them. Life continues.

"I've made you a salad." She steps back as I open the door and rise from the car. "It should be fairly light for you to eat." She holds the plate towards me.

"Thanks." I take it from her. "I'll do my best with it."

"You know where I am if you change your mind about having some company."

I let myself in, the slap of silence hitting me as I step into the hallway and kick my sandals off. The tiled floor is cool and comforting against

45

my bare feet. This is normally a noisy house, even just with three of us. Rob listens to the TV at a hundred decibels, and Jack's normally tearing around like a wild thing. None of us ever remember to turn the kitchen radio off and the cat, Milly, trails after whichever of us is closest to the utility room. It's where her feeding bowls are, and she meows night and day for food, whether or not she is hungry. Rob has always said that she's more like a dog than a cat.

She's waiting for me now. "At least I'm not totally on my own tonight." I pick her up and nuzzle my face into the warmth of her fur. Not an affectionate animal in the slightest, she wriggles to be free, and meows. She'll come to us but doesn't like to be approached.

"Come on then." I open a tin of tuna, which is a real treat for her. I watch her elegantly eating for a few minutes. All is normal in her world. I head back out of the utility room into the kitchen, where Rob's phone is flashing on the side again. *Bryony.* I grab it this time before I can change my mind. "Hello?"

She hangs up immediately. I'm so frustrated that I can't ring her back. I don't know the password for his phone. I look again at the lock screen. Two more missed calls from her since this morning. I wonder why she hasn't tried to text him. I can see the beginning of another text from his ex-wife. *If you want to see Simone again, you'd better...* Ten hours ago. It looks as though it was sent hot on the heels of her first one.

I jump as the doorbell sounds. I can see the formidable shapes of police hats through the stained glass in the door as I walk towards it. As if I haven't seen enough of police for one day. I fling the door open and nearly say, *so are you going to share the joke you were laughing at, after I'd identified my husband in the mortuary?* But, seeing their serious faces, I refrain.

"Sorry to bother you again." DI Green takes a step across the threshold into the porch. "Can we come in?"

I hold the door wider, inviting their entry. She walks past me, followed by PC Robinson, who sweeps a cursory glance over the hallway. He even walks like Rob. We stand facing each other in the sun dappled hallway.

"We're here to collect a couple of things," she says.

"Things. Like what?"

"Now we know we're looking at a hit and run, rather than an accident. We need to have a good look at your husband's recent communications. You said earlier that he'd left his phone here this morning?"

"Yes." I think of the missed calls from Bryony. Maybe they'll go after her. Then there're the messages from his ex-wife. At least they'll get access to read the messages in their entirety. Not like me.

"We need to take his phone, and his computer. I'm assuming he's got one?"

"He's got a laptop. It's in the dining room." I'm talking about him in present tense, as though he's still here. But he's not coming home. It's the most eerie feeling. I'm used to him working away from home now and then, therefore it'll take a few days before this becomes reality.

PC Robinson holds his hands out to take the computer and phone from me. "We'll have them back to you as soon as we can."

"They're Rob's, so they're of no use to me. I won't miss them. Keep them for as long as you need to. Although I could do with knowing why Bryony's been trying to get hold of him."

"Bryony?"

"His ex from when he was younger. It's bugging me."

"Which brings me onto another question. We should have asked you this afternoon," DI Green begins, "do you know of anyone who might have done this to him? Did Robert have any enemies?"

"Not really. No one who would want to mow him down." The coloured glass of the window in the front door casts colours over us all. I think of his ex-wife. She's the only person who seems to bear a grudge against him, as far as I know, but it's hardly out of the ordinary for ex-spouses not to be on the best of terms. Rob has a grievance against my mother, though she's totally unaware of it. But I want to know why Bryony has been ringing. And I'll find out.

"Are you sure?" DI Green is staring at me. "No matter how insignificant you think it is, every bit of information might help catch whoever has done this. We don't have a lot to go on. We'll certainly look into this Bryony."

I tell her about the missed calls and messages from Denise as well.

She makes a note, promising to investigate it all once they come back on shift in the morning. "By then, Robert's name will be out in the media, so we might have one or two witnesses come forward. Don't you worry. We'll catch whoever is responsible for this."

"Have you considered that it could be a case of failed brakes on the car, or something? Not a hit and run?"

She shakes her head. "If your brakes failed, and you sent a cyclist catapulting over a wall, would you just drive away and carry on with your day?"

"Perhaps they were going so fast that they didn't realise?"

She half laughs. "Believe me, when you hit fifteen stone of person, and a push bike, you know about it. I expect their car is damaged too."

I step towards the front door to let them out. My head is buzzing. There is no way I'll get any sleep tonight.

"We're going off shift soon." She turns back to me. "But we're passing these items on before we finish." She nods towards the items PC Robinson is holding. "To the digital forensics team. And they officers taking over on night shift will be studying nearby CCTV."

"It sounds as though you're doing all you can."

"Oh yes. Tomorrow, we should know who killed your husband."

CHAPTER 9

* * *

Throughout the night,
whenever I've closed my eyes,
I've seen his body fly through the air.
Parted from the bike at the point of impact,
like one of those Evel Knievel motorbikes from the eighties.

.

Chapter 10

I wander around the house, picking things up and putting them in different places. Rob has always said that tidying this house comprises moving each pile of crap to a different place. It's true. It's always a clean house, but we have accumulated a lot of stuff between us.

I need to keep busy. I can't shake Bryony out of my head. Why has she been repeatedly ringing my husband today? I wonder if she knows he is dead yet.

Eventually, the anguish drives me to grab my mobile and open Facebook. I'm not a big Facebook user. I follow *Otley Chat,* and an earlier post shows at the top of my newsfeed, asking why Denton Road is closed. I scroll down the thread, noticing several people have grumbled about the inconvenience and how it's made them late. Selfish sods.

Someone has then posted - h*ave a heart you lot. A man has died there this morning.* Then there's an outpouring of do-gooder wishes and speculation who it might be and what has happened. I feel sick. Here's our situation, out in the public domain, for people to pass the time of day with. They'll then forget about it and it will become tomorrow's chip paper as Grandma would say.

I don't know Bryony's surname. I type Bryony into the search bar and a whole list of them come up. I've seen her in passing a couple of times, so can quickly rule out the women listed. I click through to Rob's profile page. His cover photo is one of the golf course, and his profile picture is one of Jack. Rob wasn't a big Facebook user either. In fact, the last post from him was two months ago and was something crass about how Leeds United have done.

I scroll down his friends list and there she is, larger than life – Bryony Rose. Why does she have to have such a nice name? She's one of these wholesome yoga and meditation types. I've always felt resentful of her. She smiles up from her profile picture and is so pretty that I hate her.

When Rob and I first got together, he carried on meeting Bryony for coffee for months. They even had yoga sessions together. I had to put my foot down. Who wants to get into a relationship with someone meeting their ex? I'd offered to step back whilst he decided who it was that he wanted to spend his time with. I clarified that he couldn't have both.

I had more kick-ass about me in those days. Rob promised he would stop seeing her, but now, it appears it was all rekindled. For a moment, anger absorbs my reality and I have to remind myself that he's dead. Gone. I'll never see him. Ever. Again.

I couldn't understand why they'd split in the first place if they couldn't bear to stay apart, but it was apparently all to do with finances. Rob told me Bryony was a liability and squandered everything they had. He'd described her as 'a non-conformist.'

When it came to money, Rob was as tight as a duck's arse, so I imagine he wouldn't have coped well with that. Since I've known him, he's been governed by money. As a paid-up member of the rat race, he made enough to cover bills and his lifestyle, but could never progress from that. He wanted financial freedom, but few ever achieve such a thing, working for an employer. So whilst he'd tell anyone who'd listen about his ambition and drive, the fifteen-year commitment he had shown Bracken Furniture told a different story.

In opposition to Bryony, who could never rub two pennies together, I'd received nearly everything from my grandmother's estate. Mum once told me that this is all Rob ever saw in me. Perhaps she was right. Maybe that is why Rob decided between Bryony and me so easily when I gave him an ultimatum.

As if Bryony and Rob are even Facebook friends. It's so blatant and out there, seeing it in black and white. Until recently, I've had no reason to check. I scroll down her page, hoping I don't see any evidence of get-togethers between them, relaxing slightly when I see a photograph of her with a young girl. Then with a man. However, the caption reveals him to be her brother, and the girl appears to be her niece. I click onto her *about* information. Because she offers yoga and meditation sessions, her number is publicly available. I copy and paste it into my contacts, listing her as Ex. Then I press call. Just when I think it's going to voicemail, a syrupy-sweet voice says hello. I hate her voice too.

"Is that Bryony?"

"Speaking."

"I want to know why you've been trying to ring my husband today." There's a click as the line goes dead. I try again. Six rings later, voice mail kicks in. *This is Bryony Rose. Sorry I can't take your call. Please leave a message after the beep.*

"This is Fiona Matherson. You know, Rob's wife. He's had several missed calls from you today, and I need to know why you've been contacting him. Please call me back. It's urgent."

I try once more, but this time it connects straight to voicemail. She'll have turned her phone off. I send her a text. *You'll probably hear soon about Rob. I really need to talk to you. Fiona Matherson.* Hopefully, that will intrigue her enough to ring me back.

Next, I try Mum. Straight to voicemail as well. "Mum, I could do with talking to you when you get this. When the police rang you earlier, we didn't know for definite if the body was Rob's. I've been and identified him. I need to tell Jack tomorrow. If there's any way you can get back up here. I'd really appreciate it." My voice wobbles. "I haven't let Dad know yet, but I'm going to have to soon. Please ring me back Mum. I'm in a bit of a state."

Tears drip from my chin. She'll probably be able to hear the desperation in my voice. I can't believe she hasn't tried ringing me back since the earlier phone call. But I should try to give her the benefit of the doubt. She could be on her way back for all I know. That might be why she's not answering her phone. Perhaps she's doing eighty up the M1.

I yank the cupboard door open in the kitchen. The bottle of brandy is sitting there, taunting me. Over the last year, there's been barely any alcohol in the house, but Rob likes a nip when he has a bad throat, or a big presentation to give. I stare at the brown liquid, desperate to pour the lot down my neck, but slam the door shut and run upstairs to the bathroom.

Warm water on my skin makes me feel slightly better, and the scent of the lavender bubble bath reminds me of my grandmother. It's been an endless and stinking hot day. I've sweated more nervous energy than I did when I was coming off the drink. I don't know how I'm going to get through this. Just like when I finally kicked alcohol, I'll take it one hour at a time. If I try to look too far ahead, I'll get overwhelmed. I just feel so alone. There's no one I can talk to. Maybe I should have taken Christina up on her offer to stay with me. But I can be so stubborn.

I locked the door after the police left, so don't need to go back downstairs. I can't face the silence and the emptiness, anyway. Instead, I fill a glass with water, tie my dressing gown around me, and head

53

across the landing to the bedroom. Our bedroom.

The bed is unmade from this morning. I didn't pull the blinds, so I crawl beneath the duvet. It makes a crinkling sound as I tug it over me. I slide in, so I don't disturb Milly who is curled up on the edge of the bed. Her soft body is comforting. Tomorrow I will pour that brandy down the sink. I will also ring my AA sponsor. I have to stay off the drink. But tonight, I'll try to pretend that Jack is peacefully sleeping in the next room and Rob is merely working away.

I'm woken by the doorbell. At first, I think I'm dreaming the sound. It rings over and over, which annoys me. Who is it? I stare at the pattern on the ceiling. Leave me alone! For half the night, my thoughts have been escorting me to the darkest places. At around 5am, I'd decided I would stay in bed this morning. I'm exhausted. And I feel ill. I've barely eaten for twenty-four hours. Christina's salad is still sitting in the fridge.

I keep turning over Rob's final hours, days, weeks. We'd grown apart. Our marriage had become perfunctory. His face no longer lit up when he looked at me. And he was always attached to his phone.

I think of Bryony again with a heavy heart. If she had nothing to hide, she would have spoken to me last night. Rob has gone, and perhaps it will not do me any good to have it confirmed whether anything *was* going on between them. Coming to terms with it all is going to be hard enough. I guess the police will uncover anything that I need to know once they go through Rob's calls and messages.

"Fiona? Are you there?" Christina calls through the letterbox. I'm grateful to her, but I can do without neighbours just now, no matter how well-meaning they are, braying on the door and shouting through the letter box at the crack of dawn. I sit up and take a large swig of water. Its chill feels strange in my empty stomach. I reach for my phone to text her and am shocked to see it's after ten. Not exactly the crack of dawn.

Sorry. Bad night so have only just woken up. I'll text or ring later. X

The icon for my Facebook app says that I have nine plus notifications. I'm lucky to receive one or two normally. I click through and realise that people are posting onto Rob's wall, many tagging me in with their condolences and *sending a big hug*. Like that's really going to help.

One post says they hope that I'm getting well looked after. Yeah, right. There's the expected shock, disbelief, and sorrow, and a ton of photos of him out on the golf course or posing with his bike. I can't bear to look at them. Many of them were taken when things were still good between us, but obviously didn't include me. We ran separate lives. Especially over the last few months. They must have released his name in the media. I click onto BBC Local News and there it is.

Police are appealing for witnesses after a fatal accident occurred between a cyclist and a vehicle at approximately ten thirty am yesterday, Monday the eighth of June. It took place on the Denton Road, about three miles from Ilkley.

The victim has been named as a thirty-eight-year-old local man, and father of two, Robert Matherson, who, it appears, was struck from behind as he cycled. There is no information on the vehicle involved, other than that it will have potentially sustained damage on its front left-hand side. In assessing the impact, it is evident that it was travelling at a significant speed.

Investigations are being carried out on the damaged cycle to look for fragments of paint from the car. Local CCTV is being checked and nearby houses and farms are asked to come forward if they can contribute any private CCTV footage for inspection.

DI Green from West Yorkshire Police is leading the investigation and gave the following statement: "Someone knows what happened yesterday. The life of an innocent man has been snatched away. A husband and a father. Whoever is responsible must answer for what they have done. If you were the driver of the vehicle, please come forward. It will be far better for you if you come to us.

If you think you saw something, no matter how seemingly insignificant, in or around the area of Denton Road, before or after ten thirty yesterday morning, please get in touch immediately. Whoever is responsible made no effort to slow down and to have hit Mr Matherson with the impact they have, quite possibly, sped up as they approached him. It is imperative that we speak to this person as soon as possible."

A phone notification slides over the top of the news report. It's Sam's mum again. *Jack is at school now. Seemed OK when I left him. Do you need me to collect him this afternoon as well?*

No, I type back straight away. *But thank you. I really appreciate your help and support. I'll pick him up later. He needs to hear what has happened from me.*

* * *

I'm glad the wall shielded me from watching him land.
That would really haunt me.
I can't bear the sight of blood.
Or bones.
Or twisted limbs.
A damaged tyre was bad enough.

Chapter 11

Seeing a phone number I don't recognise, I answer it straight away, in case it's the mortuary or some other official calling.

"It's Denise," announces a clipped voice without saying hello. Rob's ex-wife has always been hostile towards me. Probably because he didn't wait a year after their split, before getting together with me.

"I've just seen the news." She pauses as though waiting for me to say something. Her voice ramps up a notch. "How dare you not tell me what's happened to Rob? Do you not think I had the right to know yesterday?"

I can imagine her angry face, shrivelled and red. She loves drama and will hate being the last to know.

"I haven't even told my son yet." I walk into the lounge, realising I didn't come into this room yesterday. All is as it was, from when things were normal. "I only found out myself late yesterday afternoon. And forgive me for being so blunt Denise, but calling my husband's ex-wife wasn't the first thing that entered my mind."

"He and I have a daughter together. She had a right to know."

Don't I know it? "Yes, I'm aware you and he have a daughter. Well, you know now what's happened, don't you?"

"I shouldn't have had to find out through the news. What if Simone had seen it before me? How could you have been so bloody heartless?"

"Do you not think I'm going through enough right now?" I slump into the armchair, staring out of the window. It's another beautiful day. Christina is watering her hanging baskets and her adjoining neighbour is on her knees, weeding the flower beds. It's as though the sunshine is taunting me.

"Alright. I'll let it go." Denise's voice loses its edge. "Luckily, Simone knows nothing yet, at least, I hope not. I'm just about to drive around to her school to make sure it's me she hears the news about her dad from."

I don't know why she thinks I would care about this. I say nothing, so she continues.

"Have you been told any more about what happened yet? They're saying someone has done it deliberately, aren't they?"

"You know as much as I do Denise. I should hear more today. They're carrying out tests and investigations." I've not even been awake for two hours and I'm worn out already. I'll make a coffee when I get this stupid woman off the phone.

"I want to know the minute you hear anything. Do you understand?"

Who the hell does she think she is? "With respect Denise. I've got a lot on my plate. I'll give you the number of the person dealing with the case so you can liaise directly." I fish around in my bag for DI Green's business card.

"What about the will?"

"*The will?*" I feel like I'm hearing things. The callous cow.

"Yes. I want to know what provision he's made for my daughter. He's probably better off dead than alive anyway."

I'm speechless. She's talking about inheritance for her bloody daughter while Rob's barely cold on the slab.

And she continues. "He'll certainly be a better father to Simone now that he's dead. At least he can't let her down anymore. He'll be forced to provide for her."

"I'll get back to you on that Denise." If I'd still been drinking, I'd have shot her down for her selfishness, but at this moment, I'm calmness personified. Nowadays, I seem to take things more in my stride. Denise and I have never exactly seen eye to eye, but then what ex-wives and new wives do? Luckily, I've never had to have a great deal to do with her.

But for her to say, *are you OK?* or *How are you?* is surely a basic kindness when someone's husband has just died. I give her DI Green's number and she rings off. I save her number into my phone, knowing I won't be answering again if I know it is her.

I have no idea about Rob's will. And I don't want to think about it yet. However, I'm going to have to deal with some practicalities. Beginning with formally letting Rob's work know. They could have heard something through the media, but I should speak to them. He might be owed some money, which is a consideration. I don't know what;s going to happen on that front. All I know is that my own funds are seriously depleted after my recent investment. Which is another matter I need to get onto soon.

"Good morning, Bracken Furniture, Yorkshire, Katie speaking."

"Can I speak to Mr Bracken please?"

"Who's calling?" she asks in her sing-song voice.

"It's Robert Matherson's wife, Fiona." I won't be able to say this for much longer. Not now he's gone.

Her voice changes. "I'm so sorry for your loss, Mrs Matherson. I know there's been problems here but, even so…" Her voice trails off.

"What do you mean, *problems?*" God, how much more can I cope with today?

"I'm not sure. I'm sorry. I'll pass you through to Mr Bracken. One moment, please."

I stand and pace the length of the lounge, catching sight of myself in the large mirror above the fireplace. My hair looks like I haven't brushed it for days and the roots badly need doing. I've got a hair appointment booked later today but I can hardly go getting my hair done. It's not exactly the behaviour of a grieving widow. I don't think I could sit still for that long, anyway.

"Phil Bracken speaking." His voice is even more curt than Denise's was. What's wrong with everyone? Am I so goddam awful that no one can be half decent towards me? Maybe Mum is right.

"Erm, Mr Bracken. This is Fiona, Robert Matherson's wife. We've met a few times."

"Yes, I recall." His voice is stone cold. With free bars on offer, I've occasionally indulged in too much seasonal cheer when I've accompanied Rob to his works' Christmas parties. But this isn't the time to recall that.

"Have you heard what's happened to Rob?" I'm taken aback at having to be the first one to mention it. If the receptionist knows, so must he.

"Yes." He still sounds guarded. "What a shock it must have been for you."

"I know you were expecting him in yesterday afternoon so thought I should get in touch."

"Yesterday afternoon?"

"Yes. Obviously, his accident was in the morning, but I know he'd planned to be in the office in the afternoon."

There's a pause. "Actually, we weren't expecting him."

"Oh. Well, *this* morning then." Bryony enters my head again. Perhaps he'd intended to meet her, and that's why he told me he was going to work. My heart is thumping.

"Mrs Matherson," Phil Bracken begins. "Robert hasn't worked here for the last month."

"What? No. There must be some mistake." I think of him, showering, dressing, shaving, grabbing his wallet and coffee, and setting off at twenty past eight. Every morning without fail. "For the last month?

Why? He hasn't said anything to me."

"I can't go into it with you," he replies. "There's an investigation in progress."

"What do you mean – *an investigation*? Into what?"

"I'm sorry Mrs Matherson. I'm not prepared to discuss this with you."

"But I'm his wife. And Rob's dead. I don't see why you can't tell me why he hasn't been in work for a month." If he hasn't been going to work, where has he been going. It must involve Bryony. I remember the brandy in the cupboard.

"I'm going to have to go. Katie is trying to put another call through."

"Mr Bracken. My husband was Director of Finance within your company. He worked damn hard for you for many years. If you won't tell me what's happened, then I'll have to let the police know about your investigation. You'll have to tell *them* what's been going on if you won't tell me."

The line goes dead.

All the calm I professed to feel whilst speaking to Denise has evaporated. My breath is coming fast. *Investigation?*

Just as I'm looking for DI Green's card in my handbag again, the doorbell goes. Not wanting to speak to anyone, I feel like ignoring it. Then I notice Dad peering through the bay window. Shit.

I slide the latch to the door, and he strides in. "My poor girl. I've just heard. An hour ago. I got straight in the car." He steps towards me and envelops me in a hug, his beard tickling my forehead. His smell, a cross between Imperial Leather soap and musk comforts me. Suddenly I'm ten again and he's trying to make it all better. "Why the hell didn't you let me know?"

I sob into his shoulder. "I was going to. But I've been trying to get my head around things myself." I step back and look at him, assessing his possible fragility. Any minute now, he's going to ask me where Mum is. I can't think straight enough to come up with a plausible reason for her not being here.

It's as though he reads my mind. "Where's your mother? Her car's not here."

"She had to go, Dad."

"Go? Go where?"

"I'll put the kettle on." I turn from him and head for the kitchen.

He follows me, the heels of his shoes clip-clopping across the tiles. "I want to know where your mother is, Fiona. How on earth could she leave you at a time like this?"

"She set off before it all happened." I flick the kettle on and take two cups from the cupboard. "She needed to see a friend in Devon."

"A friend? Devon?"

Apart from parroting me, he seems to take this in his stride, better than I could have expected. "I don't know who the friend is," I tell him. "And right now, I don't care."

"It's OK. You're right. I shouldn't be quizzing you about your mother." He puts his arm around my shoulder. "I'm sorry. I'm right here for you and I'm going nowhere. Is Jack upstairs?"

"No. He's at school. I haven't told him what's happened to Rob yet."

My phone, which I've placed next to the cups, bursts into life. "Speak of the devil. It's his school. Just a second Dad. I need to take this. Hello?"

"Is that Mrs Matherson?"

"Yes." Part of me is screaming *what now*, but another part of me has calmed down now that Dad is here.

"Mrs Matherson. It's Kay, I'm one of the lunchtime supervisors. I'm afraid I need to ask you to come and collect Jack."

"Why?" I'd rather he stayed at school, but I don't tell her that. I hope he's not ill. I don't feel as though I can cope with anything else. Not even Jack. Plus, he's better off being in blissful ignorance for as long as he can be. When I tell him, the poor lad's world is going to change forever.

"It's the situation with his father," she says, her voice oozing with sympathy. "Clearly he knew nothing about his death, and one of the year six boys has said something to him."

"Oh God. It only broke on the news this morning." I feel terrible now for thinking I could send him to school and get away with him not finding out. It's only got to lunchtime. "I'm really sorry." What was I thinking?

"No, I'm really sorry. It's absolutely dreadful for you both. If you can come for him, I'll look after him in the library until you get here."

"Thank you. Tell him I've got his grandad with me. That should settle him down a little until we get there."

Dad slides a mug along the work surface to me. "Is he OK? Silly question. Of course he's not. The poor little man."

I feel better having Dad here. Unless he goes to pieces about Mum. "We haven't got time to drink this Dad. We're going to have to get to the school. I let Jack stay at his friend's last night." I take a slurp of the tea, then pour the rest down the sink. "I had to identify Rob at the mortuary. I wanted to keep Jack away from it all."

Dad runs his hand over his thinning hairline. "For God's sake Fiona. Why didn't you ring me? Why do you always insist on coping with things on your own?"

"I know." Tears slide down my face. "I could have happily reached for the brandy last night. I had to go to bed to stop myself."

"I thought you were over all that."

"So did I, but it's not every day your husband dies."

"Have you got some in the house?"

I nod and point towards the cupboard in the far corner. Dad strides towards it and in one swoop seizes it and pours it down the sink. I watch as it mingles with the tea. It smells terrible. I don't know how it could have tempted me.

He rinses it away. "Come on." He reaches an arm out. "I'll drive. Let's get that grandson of mine."

* * *

It's out. His name.
There's the usual outpouring of sympathy.
Flowers laid at the scene.
Condolences on social media.
It will pass.

Chapter 12

Dad and I stride across the playground. Over twenty-four hours have passed since Rob died. Somehow, I'm putting one foot in front of the other, unsure how I'm keeping going. DI Green says after the impact, Rob shouldn't have felt much, he'll have been out of it immediately. He was dead before the ambulance arrived. I'm glad he didn't die alone. The farmer who'd been rounding up his sheep at the other end of the field had been with him as he passed away. He saw nothing other than Rob flying through the air and the top of a car roof driving away. In the bright sunlight, he'd said, he couldn't even make out what colour or shape the car was.

Children hurtle around us as we approach the main entrance. I wonder how long it will be until Jack is running around again, shrieking like the others.

As we get to the door, Dad, as though reading my thoughts, puts his hand on my arm and says, "Jack'll bounce back. Kids are amazingly resilient – you'll see."

The receptionist lets us in and walks us up to the library in silence. She doesn't refer to what's happened, which surprises me. I suppose many people don't know what to say in such circumstances. Kay, the lunchtime supervisor, is reading a book with Jack. My heart breaks as I observe his red-rimmed eyes and trembling lip. As soon as he sees me, his tears well up. As do mine.

"Come here, sweetheart."

He gets up and runs towards me. I pick him up and lower onto the tiny chair with him on my lap. This is one occasion where I can't make it better.

"I'm sorry I didn't tell you sooner." I sob into his hair. It smells of shampoo that isn't ours. He's wearing socks that aren't his either. Guilt creeps over me like a rash.

Some older children are trying to look in. Kay strides to the window and closes the blinds. Then she comes to sit with us.

"Daniel in year six heard the news on the radio on his way into school this morning," she explains. "To be honest, it was the first I'd heard of it. You know what kids are like. It quickly spread around the playground."

I want her to stop wittering so I can talk to Jack.

"You must be Jack's grandad." She smiles at Dad. "Jack was pleased when I told him you were coming. He said he was expecting his Granny Maggie though."

"Can you give us a minute?" I look at her through my tears. "I'd like a word with Jack."

"Yes – sure. I'll be outside." She rises from the chair. It's so small that it's a long way up for her. "Give me a shout if you need anything."

"Jack." I tilt his face towards mine. "What have you been told?"

His face crumples again. "That Daddy got knocked off his bike by a fast car. And that he was bleeding, and that he's been killed, and I'll never be able to see him, ever again."

I pull him closer. "The ambulance people tried everything to make him better Jack. But Daddy was too badly hurt."

Dad crouches next to us, his eyes full of tears too. He places his hand on Jack's back.

"But where's Daddy now? Can't I just see him?"

"He's in heaven sweetheart. And he'll always be able to watch you from there."

"Where's heaven?"

"We've talked about this before. Can you remember when Monty died. Your rabbit?"

He nods, though I doubt he can remember. He was only three.

"Well, Monty went up to heaven." I point upwards, hoping my words bear a conviction that I'm not feeling. "It's where good people and animals go. Up there, in the clouds." I've drifted in and out of religion in my time, but remain unconvinced. If there really was a God, then why have I experienced such utter crap in life? Or perhaps it's because I'm inherently bad like Mum keeps suggesting.

Dad squeezes my shoulder. "You're doing great love."

"How can Daddy watch me, from in the clouds?"

I take a deep breath. "I'm not sure, but he loves you, so he'll find a way."

"If he loved me, he wouldn't have died. He would have been more careful on his bike. Like he told me to be." For a seven-year-old, he says some profound things. Dad and I look at each other again. This has got to be one of the worst moments of my life.

Dad stands and drags a chair towards us. "Sometimes, Jack, accidents happen. I know it feels awful right now, but I promise it won't always be this bad."

"Where's Granny?"

A cloud crosses Dad's face. "I don't know love. We'll find her later. But before that, we're going to get you home. Then we can do anything you want. Any game. Any food. Any TV programme."

"I just want Daddy to come home."

I can't say anything to make it better. I slide Jack from my knee to Dad's as my phone rings. *No number.* "I'd better get this."

"Fiona, it's Detective Inspector Diane Green speaking. How are you doing today?"

"Hello." I glance at Jack, not wanting to say too much in front of him. "As you might expect, really." I can see Kay watching through the glass in the door. I wish she'd leave us alone.

"Have you time to come down to the station today? We'd like to share our findings so far with you, and to ask you a few questions."

"But I answered your questions yesterday."

"I know, but we need everything on record. Especially now that we're looking at a non-accidental situation."

That's one way of putting it. "Just a second." Holding my hand over the mouthpiece, I turn to Dad. "I have to answer some more questions at the station. Can you drop me off, and take Jack home for me?" I know I should probably go home with them, and at least settle Jack down first, but I want to get this out of the way. Besides, I'm anxious to know what additional information they've got. I probably need to keep busy, anyway. If I stop, I might just go to pieces.

"Yes, that's fine love."

Kay puts her head around the door. "I don't mean to rush you, but we've a class in here shortly. Can I possibly move you into the meeting room?"

"We're going in a minute." I say as I lift my mobile back to my ear. "My dad can drop me off in about a quarter of an hour. Will that be OK?"

"See you then." DI Green hangs up without saying goodbye.

* * *

There's speculation that the circumstances might be suspicious.
But they've got nothing concrete.
Nothing.

Chapter 13

It's like a sauna in the police station.

"If you'd like to come through." DI Green pokes her head around the door. "Can I get you a drink?"

It's literally seconds after I've announced my arrival to the man on the desk. A woman in the waiting room scowls at me as I walk towards the door. She's probably wondering how I've got in before her.

"A cup of tea, if that's OK?" I'm taken aback. I bet most people don't get this treatment here.

"If I can ask you to wait in the interview room, I won't be long."

"Are you interviewing me?"

"I'll explain everything in a minute."

I take a seat in the bottle green room. It's even hotter in here than in the reception area. I glance around, noting the lack of a window and the fact that everything is attached to the walls and floors. It's the first time I've been in one of these places since my early twenties when I got locked up for fighting.

The nausea I've been feeling since I woke up intensifies as I become aware of the globs of chewing gum, stuck to the underside of the table. I hope this will not take long.

"Thanks for coming in Fiona." DI Green slides a mug in front of me, then takes a seat. The table is etched with graffiti. She looks towards the door. "Thanks John."

"Hello again." PC John Robinson enters the room and plugs a fan in. "I don't know if this will make any difference. It'll probably just blow all the warm air around." The door of the tiny room closes behind him.

"Right Fiona." DI Green nods towards a machine to her right. "I'm going to hit play on the recording equipment, so everything we discuss is on record."

"OK." This is slightly worrying. I wonder for a moment if I'm under suspicion for what's happened to Rob and think about asking whether I need a solicitor with me. But I don't ask. Perhaps they might misconstrue that.

A long beep sounds and DI Green clears her throat. "My name is Detective Inspector Diane Green of West Yorkshire Police, and my colleague," she nods towards PC Robinson.

"Police Constable John Robinson."

"Will take notes for the transcript in this interview, which is taking place with..." she looks at me.

"Fiona Matherson."

"Thank you Fiona. If you could just state your full address and date of birth, please?

"7 Orchard Mews, Otley, Leeds. My date of birth is 4th April 1985."

"Thank you. As you know Fiona, we've asked you to come in to answer a few more questions in relation to the death of your husband, Robert Matherson. It occurred yesterday at approximately ten thirty am, on the Denton Road between Otley and Ilkley."

"Yes."

"This interview is being recorded and you are here to help us with our enquiries. You are not under arrest at this stage and are free to leave at any time."

"OK." *At this stage.* What does that mean? I wince as a trickle of sweat rolls from my armpit and down the side of my body. I can't remember if I put any deodorant on this morning. I certainly didn't brush my hair.

"Some of what I might ask will have been covered to some extent yesterday, but there will also be some new questions around the inquiry so far."

Just get on with it, I want to say. This tiny box of a room is one of the most oppressive situations I've ever found myself in. I try to slow my breathing. The prospect of a panic attack is threatening to overwhelm me. I need to get back to Jack. I know he's with Dad, but with what he's going through; I need to be there more than I need to be here.

"Right. We'll get started. First, just as you did yesterday, can you walk us through your morning before Robert, your husband, left the house?"

I wipe my palms on my jeans and try again to steady my breathing. *Bryony* wouldn't find herself in this physical or mental state with her yoga and her bloody meditation. "Like I've already told you, we got up as normal, had breakfast and a coffee, whilst our son was getting ready for school. Rob left at just after nine o'clock to go on a bike ride. He enjoyed getting either out on his bike or onto the golf course. There was nothing out of the ordinary, apart from he'd booked the morning off work."

"So he was a fit and active man then?"

"Yes." It sounds strange using the word *was.* Rob being talked about in the past tense. I don't think I'll ever get used to it.

"Was everything alright between the two of you, before he left the house?"

"Between Rob and me? Yes, I guess so. My mother had stayed the previous night, which always causes an atmosphere but other than that..."

"Why does your mother staying cause an atmosphere?"

God. As if they've jumped on that. "I don't know. Just mother-in-law stuff, you know. It's always been fractious."

"Right." DI Green taps her pen on the side of her forehead as though deep in thought. She's acting differently towards me than yesterday. More brisk. Not as sympathetic. "We might come back to that. Are you absolutely sure Robert left the house just after nine? Not any later?"

It's strange hearing Rob being called Robert. I'd heard his father call him it, but his mother had died from cancer before we got together. If there is a heaven, I wonder if they're all together again. Perhaps my grandma is with them too. It's the same whimsical thinking Jack might have. "Yes. Definitely. He left just after my mum set off. She was taking my son to school."

"And how old is your son again?"

"Seven. This has all hit him very hard."

I see a note of sympathy in her face now. "I bet it has. You, on the other hand, seem to be coping really well."

"Do I?" What does she mean by that? "I'm just taking it one step at a time. I could do without being here though, to be honest." I take a sip of the lukewarm tea. It's disgusting. I'm pig sick of tea. "Could we speed things up? I need to get back to my son. He's been sent home from school and my Dad is looking after him until I get back."

"Fair enough. We'll be as quick as we can." She looks down at her notes. "The accident occurred some seven miles away from your home in Otley. How long do you imagine it would have taken your husband to cover that distance?"

"Not long. Twenty minutes maybe?"

"Have you any idea, where he might have got to between leaving home at nine, and getting to Denton Road at ten thirty? Clearly, around an hour and ten minutes is unaccounted for. Did he mention about going anywhere else first?"

"No. All I knew is that he was going for a bike ride." Bryony, yet again, pops into my head. If she had nothing to hide, she'd have spoken to me or replied to the message I sent. I'm going to have to say something to DI Green, but to verbalise the words out loud admits something that I don't want to acknowledge. That they *were* carrying on with each other.

"You look unsure." DI Green tilts her head to one side like a dog waiting for a treat.

"It's just that…" I might as well say it. "He had a few missed calls from his ex yesterday. I've tried ringing and messaging her, but she's ignoring me."

"Do you mean Bryony?" PC Robinson speaks now.

DI Green gives him a look I can't read. Maybe he shouldn't have asked that.

"Yes. Have you been in touch with her?"

"We have," DI Green replies. "We saw the missed calls in his phone log. But she claims not to have seen him yesterday morning. Obviously, our enquiries are ongoing – we're still waiting on CCTV results as well."

She looks uncomfortable. Whatever she knows about them having an affair, if they were, she probably can't tell me. I know where Bryony lives, so I must pay her a personal visit. I'll *make* her tell me the truth. I have to know.

"I've also had his ex-wife on the phone." DI Green places her pen gently on the notepad in front of her. "Several times in fact. What were relations like there?"

"Not good. Rob had apparently let his daughter down at the weekend when he should have picked her up."

"Do you know any details about this? Why he'd let her down?"

"I didn't know of the arrangement." I can feel the heat rising in my face. "I seem to have been the last to know anything lately. And I found out earlier that he hasn't been at work for the last month."

"Really? Where's his work?"

"Bracken Furniture. He was the Director of Finance."

"And why hasn't he been at work?" She's frowning.

"I've absolutely no idea. He's been leaving each morning as though he's going to work, so why he's been lying to me, I don't know. The MD, Phillip Bracken, won't tell me a thing. Maybe he'll tell you."

PC Johnson is writing this down. "We'll get in touch with him. That could be useful."

"There's apparently some sort of investigation in process. It appears Rob was in trouble."

"Thank you." DI Green offers me a hint of a smile. She's possibly pleased at being given something to follow up. "Back to his, Robert's ex-wife, Denise isn't it? What do you think are the chances that he might have gone to see her yesterday morning?"

"Well, normally, he would avoid her as much as possible. Apart from when he's picking his daughter up of course. I don't know. I doubt he would have been there. Simone would have been at school, so I don't see any reason for him going round."

"I know we've already asked you this, but you have had more time to think about it since we spoke - are you aware of any enemies that Robert might have had? Someone that might be out to get him?"

"Nobody that would want to knock him flying off his bike. Nobody that would have wanted to kill him. You mentioned Bryony before – have you found anything out about her from his phone or computer?"

"I can't really go into it at this stage, but I can say that we've found one or two interesting things on his computer."

"Such as?"

"We'll let you know as and when we've followed things up. One person of interest is listed in your husband's phone as JT? Any ideas?"

"JT? No. I can't think of who that would be."

"A financial connection perhaps? There's a suggestion of money being owed."

"By whom?"

"We're looking into it. If you come up with any ideas on who JT could be, let us know straightaway."

"I will." JT. Maybe there was another woman as well as Bryony. I stare down at my hands.

"There's also a couple of recent texts sent by you, that we'd like to ask you about."

"By me? Which ones?" Rob and I rarely texted each other, apart from to say *get some bread on the way home,* or *I've been held up.* Not like we did in the early days. I used to live for his messages. My stomach would flip as one came through.

"We're particularly interested in the money-related messages." DI Green runs a finger down her page. "There's three over the last month."

"Go on."

"Ten days ago. *What about this money then?????*" She looks at me.

"Oh, that. It was to do with a shares opportunity he was investing in. I put some money in to increase his investment."

"What shares opportunity was that?"

"I don't know too much about it. Much of this stuff goes straight over my head." I'm not lying. It really does. I know one investment was to do with property - a new shopping complex in Harrogate."

"What about the other one?" She does that thing of tilting her head to one side whilst waiting for an answer. It's quite irritating.

"It was to do with some Chinese company or other, something about this cryptocurrency that everyone is jumping on. I wish I'd taken more notice of what he was saying now."

"So that would explain the other two texts then. Have *you paid it in yet? This could change our life.* One month ago."

"I think so."

"What *was* your own personal investment?"

"I can't remember exactly. About thirty thousand."

"That's quite a sum to sink into something you know nothing about."

"Rob reckoned I'd get that back ten times over. And since I'd nearly spent the inheritance I received from my grandmother when she died in 2011, I thought it was worth a go to get some money back."

"Thirty thousand is more than just a go." PC Robinson raises an eyebrow.

"Rob knew his stuff as far as the stock market was concerned. He had some sort of adviser or broker as well." I take another sip of tea and shudder at how awful it tastes. "He handled everything to do with the money. He knew what he was doing."

"It sounds like there was a lot of trust between you both."

I'm not sure if DI Green's words are a question or a statement, so I don't reply. I definitely trusted Rob with money. Though with other matters, I definitely did not.

"What do you know about this adviser, or broker?"

"Nothing really. To be honest, I would glaze over when he talked about it all. I tried to be interested but didn't really understand it."

"He must have mentioned the name of his broker at some point. Surely you have some idea of where we could find him?" PC Robinson's pen is poised over his notebook. "Or can you find out?"

"Or her," DI Green says.

"No. But there must be something in his messages. You've got access to those."

"You might not have been interested in his financial dealings and connections. But you were interested in the ultimate outcome?"

"Of course."

"The subsequent text about the top of the range Audi and the Maldives holiday. Was this related to the expected windfall then?"

"Yes. But what I don't understand is what all this has got to do with him getting killed yesterday?"

"We're just putting the pieces together at the moment." She twists the wedding ring around on her finger. "We got minimal forensic evidence from the scene."

"What about CCTV?" Although I know there won't be any around there. The road where Rob died is in the back of beyond.

"My team are doing some house-to-house. We're hoping for dashcam and maybe some neighbouring farm footage."

I wring my clammy hands together. If I don't get out of here soon, I may well pass out. "Is that everything now? I need to be getting back to my son."

"Right you are." DI Green closes her notebook. "We'll come back to you if we have any more questions. We also must have a word with your mother. Can you leave us her number?"

"My mother? Why do you want to speak to her?"

"Because along with yourself, and your son, she is one of the last people to have seen your husband before he died. It's procedure. We need to rule her out of our investigation. And your neighbour who was taking her bin out."

Fair enough. I take the page she slides towards me and write Mum's number down. I scroll through my phone to find Christina's number.

"Just one last thing Fiona."

"Yes." I'm taken aback at the sharp edge her voice has suddenly taken.

"Where were you at ten thirty yesterday morning?"

* * *

So far. So good.
It was always going to be a gamble. All of it.
Either the police are keeping their cards close to their chests,
or they've nothing to investigate.

Chapter 14

J ack wipes his eyes on the sleeve of his football pyjamas. "This has been the worst day ever. I just want Daddy to come home."

"I know, sweetheart." I cup his chin in my hand and kiss his forehead.

"It's my birthday next week. I don't even care about it anymore."

"Daddy would still want you to try to enjoy it." I think again of our wedding anniversary in a fortnight. Perhaps getting dressed up and going out together might have breathed some life into our marriage. Or perhaps not.

"I thought you said Daddy would be always watching over me." Jack leans back against his pillows.

I smooth my hand over his hair. "He will. Always."

"So why can't I see him?"

"You can't see people after they die, but they can still see you." Here I go again. Talking twaddle which I can't back up.

His lip trembles. "You won't die too, will you Mummy?"

"I hope not." I smile through my own tears. I hate seeing him like this. "Look Jack, I know it all feels terrible right now, but in time, if we look after each other, we'll start to feel better."

"How long will it take to feel like we used to again?" He looks wrung out, staring at me in the gloom of his bedroom. The late summer evening light is fighting its way around the edge of the blackout blind.

78

I pray that sleep will rescue him soon.

"You must try to get some rest Jack. You'll feel poorly at school tomorrow if you don't."

He grips my arm. "Please don't leave me Mummy."

I don't feel as bad now for letting him stay at Sam's last night. Jack's such a sensitive soul, and this is going to take some coming back from. "I'll only be downstairs with Grandad. If you need anything, all you have to do is give me a shout."

He sniffs and reaches for his bear, which normally he only bothers with when he's exhausted, or ill. "Can Grandad come and tuck me in?"

"Yes. I'll send him up now." Relieved that Jack's feeling able to let me go, I kiss him on the forehead again, and rise from my perch on his bed. I could do with a few minutes to myself. I'm knackered.

"He's asleep." Dad creeps into the lounge twenty minutes later. He ruffles the top of my head before dropping into the adjacent armchair. "The cat is stretched out on his bed as well."

"How on earth did you manage that? He wouldn't let me leave him at one point."

"He dropped off whilst I was reading him a story. I think the cat helped too. Bless him – poor little chap." Dad shakes his head and his eyes seem to moisten. "How anyone could kill the father of an innocent boy is beyond me. If I could get my hands on them."

"It's only speculation that it was deliberate." I stare at the TV. "Actually, it's just been on the local news again. They're not giving anything away yet – just appealing for witnesses and for people with dash cams or CCTV to come forward."

"Aren't they doing house-to-house for that?" He rubs at his temples, looking as weary as I feel.

"Yes. It sounds as though they're doing as much as they can."

Dad plucks his phone from his top pocket in response to its ringing.

I always laugh at his phone. Well, I did when things were normal. I can't imagine laughing at anything for the foreseeable future. It's one step up from the phones of the nineties, with their pull-up aerials. He takes about ten minutes to compose a text message.

"Maggie." Dad lifts the phone to his ear and rises from his chair. He walks towards the bay window. Whenever he's on the phone, he always paces up and down. Even in the days of wired phones, he would go as far as the cord allowed. "Where are you?"

Pause.

"Why are you lying to me Maggie? I'm at Fiona's right now. Which is where you're supposed to be?"

Shit. It's all unravelling. She must have told him she was still here. He doesn't look angry, more confused.

"Lunchtime. And it's a good job I did. She'd have been going through this on her own otherwise."

This is a dad I have heard little from before - standing up to Mum. Maybe it's because he feels safer over the phone, whilst she's miles away in Devon. Whatever it is, he needs to do more of it. He's had enough years of being henpecked and under her control. I'm getting to where I don't care if she cuts me off, as long as she doesn't come between me and Dad like she's threatened to. She managed it when I was a teenager. Rob was right. I'm a grown woman now and she can't hurt me anymore.

"That still doesn't answer why you're saying you're here, with our daughter and grandson, when really I know you're in Devon."

Bloody hell. She'll know that I've told him. There's only me he could have found that out from. But I haven't told him who she's with. The proverbial is really going to hit the fan now. I don't know how I'll cope if Dad goes off the rails again.

I've got a funeral to arrange, Jack to take care of and I haven't even thought about finances yet, although the questions that DI Green asked have reinforced the need that I should see what I can find out about the money I invested. And the money Rob invested. There's the other stuff that Denise has plagued me about too, the will, life insurance - what a nightmare.

I do a mental reckoning of support I might call on. I wish I had siblings. Even friends. I've a couple of cousins from Mum's side, but I'd most likely walk past them in the street, it's been so many years since I saw them. Other than Dad, I've only really got Christina and the AA support group. I guess there's a few of the other mothers who might take the load off with Jack, like Lynne. But I don't enjoy asking for help. If you don't rely on others, then no one can let you down.

"I'm not stupid Maggie. I've suspected for a while that you're carrying on with someone else again. Though why you had to drag Fiona into it makes no sense at all."

Even above the TV, I can hear the rise of Mum's voice, though I can't make out what she's saying. It's probably just as well. I was stupid thinking there was a possibility that she might have been on her way up the M1 last night. She's the most selfish person I've ever known.

"No, I've worked it out for myself."

I leave the room to get some water. When I return, Dad's still pacing.

"I don't want to discuss this any further." His voice is calm, considering. "I'm going to get back to looking after our daughter, whose husband has just been killed."

Pause.

"Don't bother. I'm here. You might as well stay where you are now." He presses the end call button on his phone and looks at me. I think he looks more worn out than I do.

"Your mother claims to have ended whatever relationship she's been having." He lets a long breath out.

The chill of the water hitting my stomach is comforting. "What's she gone all the way to Devon for? Surely she could have ended things with him by telephone and saved herself a trip."

"You could've told me what was going on." He sinks into the armchair next to the window.

"I knew it would fizzle out."

"I had a right to know love."

I follow his gaze. He seems to be staring at the last of the daylight. "How could I tell you Dad? Look what happened last time." My voice has risen without me realising. I lower it again. "I'm sorry to bring that up. I wanted to tell you – loads of times. But it worried me how you'd take it? Or if you'd even believe me."

"Of course I would."

I swallow, once again feeling like a young girl, fearing my mother's wrath just as much as I did then. "Mum threatened me. She said I'd lose her, and she'd ensure I'd hardly see you if I got involved." For now, I'm consumed by all this. I realise that with what's going on between my parents, I've hardly thought about my predicament for the last quarter of an hour.

"I can't speak for your mother, but you'll never lose me." Dad reaches across and lays his hand on top of mine. "She could never come between us love. You're my daughter." He sighs. "Look, I know things are horrendous right now, but somehow, we'll get through this."

"But she's your wife." I can't tell him of the real reason mum doesn't want him to find out about her dodgy behaviour. Perhaps a small part is her concerned about his welfare. But knowing her as I do, it is more because she risks losing her entitlement to life insurance, and other financial compensations if he were to commit suicide.

"You must try not to listen too much to your mother. I don't think she really means it. Perhaps she makes such hurtful threats about cutting you off, *and* cutting us off, because she's trying to bring you down to the level she's at." He pulls a sorry-looking hanky from his pocket. "Maggie feels so crap, that she wants others to feel the same way. It makes her feel better somehow." He blows his nose, sounding like a trumpet. Normally that would be something I would laugh at too. "I'm proud of you, you know Fiona."

Dad never says things like this. For a moment I forget Mum. And Rob. And even Jack. I'm not on my own. For the first time since yesterday, I think perhaps I can get through this. Without Mum. And without brandy. Dad's taken the finding out of Mum's affair unbelievably well.

My phone beeps. *As if you have told him Fiona. After all we agreed. Just you wait.*

I show the text to Dad.

"Delete it."

* * *

Once the funeral is over,
it will be like it never happened.
The flowers will wilt,
and everyone will return to their own lives.

Chapter 15

I switch the engine off and reach for Jack's hand. "You don't have to do this, you know. You can have a few days at home. Grandad's sticking around."

"I want to see my friends." All the sparkle from Jack's eyes has faded. I must respect his decision to carry on going to school. It's his way of dealing with things. Besides, it gives me a break as well. I seem to have retreated into a numbness.

"I'll come in with you Jack." I press the release button on my seatbelt. "I want a quick word with your teacher."

"Why?" He looks nervous, possibly worried that my presence will attract more attention. He's always been a reserved lad at school, and more interested in other kids than the limelight being on him - it's probably one thing that makes him popular.

"I just want to let her know what's going on and ask her to keep an extra special eye on you."

"OK."

He lets go of my hand as soon as we enter the playground and runs towards a group of boys who are playing football. I stride towards the entrance and ring the bell, ignoring the sideways glances and mothers not-so-subtly nudging one another as I pass them. I'm so sick of being playground gossip fodder.

"How are you doing Fiona?" I glance back. It's Sam's mum. I've forgotten her name again.

"Erm, I'm OK." I call back over my shoulder as I'm buzzed into the school. What does she expect me to say? *I'm falling apart and would give anything just to drown my sorrows.*

It's true. It comes in waves. Usually I'm fine, then suddenly a craving takes hold of me. When I return to the car, I ring my AA sponsor. This is, after all, what she's there for.

She gasps when I tell her about Rob. "I've seen the story in the news, but I didn't know it was your husband! How on earth are you coping?"

"It's as though it's happening to someone else, but I can't lie… I keep feeling as though I need to drink. To take the edge off, and maybe to help me sleep. I keep waking up and what's happened hits me again. Last night was terrible. My brain was going round and round all night."

"It's natural you'll feel like a drink." The good thing about the AA sponsor arrangement is that she's been exactly where I am. But she's further along the path of sobriety. "But you do recognise, don't you, that to give in, and to have a drink, even just one, will make the problem even worse than it already is. You've done so well up to now. You must keep reminding yourself of that."

I watch as the other mothers flood through the school gates, many clad in gym gear, others dressed to begin a day at the office. I look down at myself. Jeans which need a belt. Trainers. Baggy t-shirt. At least I've brushed my hair today. I washed it, so I had to. I'm losing weight after barely eating for two days. Dad keeps trying to force food down me, but I feel constantly sick.

"I don't see how my problems could get any worse than they are right now."

"Fiona, if you were to add alcohol to the equation, you'd have all the physical and psychological repercussions of drinking again thrown into the mix. Headache, guilt and regret, to name but a few."

Obviously, she's right. I tell her about the situation between my parents and the crushing loneliness I'm feeling. Once upon a time, Rob was my best friend. It was never the bells and whistles sort of romance, but we got on well and had a laugh together. I've always got on better with men. This is probably a reflection of the bond I didn't have with my mother. Somehow, I always feel threatened by other women. Apart from my wonderful grandmother.

In the early years of getting together with Rob, I didn't feel as though I needed anyone else anyway. I let a lot of my friendships slide. Most of them weren't particularly deep ones, anyway. Then I failed to nurture the ones I had left. After Jack came along and Rob became more immersed in his work, the bottle became my closest friend again. And my greatest enemy, as my sponsor keeps reminding me.

"I suggest you get along to the next meeting." Her voice cuts into my miserable reminiscences. "It's tomorrow evening."

"I will." However, I struggle to think beyond the next five minutes. "If my dad is still here to look after my son, I'll come."

"Have you got anyone else who can watch him if your dad can't? I think it's important that you come. Especially now. Let us look after you."

"My neighbour might help. I'll do my best to get there. I do like the thought of being looked after."

"I'll keep in touch with you Fiona. Is it alright if I ring you later?"

"That's fine." When she rings me, I feel listened to, so I'll welcome her call. It's like she really cares about me.

"Is there a time that's best? When you're on your own?"

"That doesn't matter. I don't care who I talk in front of." I don't broadcast it but I've made no secret about the issues I've faced and overcome. In fact, from where I was, to where I am now, I'm proud of myself. Some people I was knocking about with in my late teens and early twenties are dead or pretty far gone on alcohol now, or worse.

I knew I'd feel better after ringing my sponsor. I always come away feeling a new sense of motivation. Then reality returns to slap me around the face. Rob's dead. And I probably will be when Mum gets her hands on me.

As I go to slide my phone into my bag, it buzzes. *Friend or foe*, I think. There's a new text message, and two earlier ones. I flop onto a wall. All around me life continues. A toddler trotting alongside her mother. A woman pushing a pram along as she laughs into her phone. A pair of teenagers hand-in-hand.

This is the Co-Operative Funeral Service, the first message says. *We have had notification that your husband is due for release later today or tomorrow. Please telephone at your earliest convenience to confirm arrangements.* Bloody hell. That was quick. They must have nearly done everything they needed to.

The next one is from Christina. *Are you OK? You know where I am if you need anything.*

And lastly, the mortgage company. *We have tried without success to contact you. Please get in touch as a matter of urgency quoting reference three seven one five.* I don't like the sound of this one. I can't understand why they would ring me. I paid my half share of the house with one lump sum when we bought it. Although I had agreed to act as guarantor for Rob's half as he was already financially over committed. I hope to God that he's been keeping up his payments. I'm realising now that I handed over far too much power to him. But it worked for us. I kept the house nice and cooked for him. He worked hard and handled the finances. We both took care of Jack.

I can't face ringing the mortgage company back yet.

By the time I set off, the playground has emptied and most of the other mothers have driven away. There's a couple left, leaning towards each other at the school gate. It's now day three since I lost Rob and life around me is going on as though nothing has happened.

The women glance towards my Jeep as the engine starts with a roar. I'm glad of the blacked-out windows so they can't see me from the outside. *That's her.* They'll be saying. *The one whose husband was a victim of a hit and run.*

That's the headline now. *Hit and run.* Although it's more a case of send a person hurtling into the air at sixty miles an hour, see how they fly, and drive off. If it hadn't been for the farmer being nearby, Rob could have lain dead for hours in the field. The police are appealing for people to be on the lookout for a possibly damaged car. They're saying that you can't hit a cyclist at that speed without damage, even though they don't seem to have recovered much from the scene. They've also expressed surprise that the driver could regain control so quickly after the impact and drive away.

The farmer didn't see the car. I watched this morning, as he gave a brief interview to a news reporter. The car, he said, was long gone by the time he'd got to where he could see the road. He only heard the noise which he said wasn't even loud enough to raise too much alarm.

Eventually, I'll contact him. Thank him for ringing the ambulance and trying to resuscitate Rob. It's comforting to know that in his final moments, Rob wasn't alone.

Without ever intending to, I find myself, once again, at the crash site. Not that there's much evidence of it being a crash site; the wall is intact, and the only clue that someone has died here are the bunches of flowers that have been laid. I park up and walk towards them.

Simone has left some. The card says 'Daddy.' At ten years old, surely she's a bit old to have still called him Daddy.

A bouquet of lilies has been left by the cycle club. The card reads. *RIP to our friend Rob. Our outings will never be the same without you.*

White roses have been laid beside them. I flick the card over *Bx.* No prizes for guessing who's left that one. I'm going to give it another day or two to see if the police turn anything up and then I am going to pay the husband-stealing bitch a visit.

It's another scorcher today, but I can't get warm. I must be the only person in Yorkshire to be wearing jeans and a jumper. Rob always used to call me a reptile. I'll miss being able to warm my cold feet on him in the winter. Well, at any time of the year. As I look again at the flattened patch of grass where he finished up, I shiver. I remember a saying Grandma used to come out with, *it's like someone has walked over my grave.* I don't know why I came here. It will not change a thing.

As I return to the car, I notice a sign the police have left. It's one of those *Accident. Please help* signs. *Monday 8th June. 10:30 am. Contact 111.* I have only seen them before at the scene of fatal accidents. They've always stopped me in my tracks, compelling me to consider the human tragedy behind them. I could never have imagined that one day they'd tell a story I'm a character in.

This is partly why I keep myself to myself in life. If you don't get close to anyone, you can't get hurt. Grief is the price you pay for love. I could go further than that and say, betrayal is the price you pay for trust, and abandonment is what you pay for loyalty, but that would show how cynical I've become. With a life like I've had, it's no wonder.

I'm certainly worse since I had Jack. I struggled to bond with him at first. But luckily, I had an insight into myself and knew I was suffering from postnatal depression. I told them about my mother's experience of it, so they kept a close eye on me. They told me that Mum must have suffered from a severe form – postpartum psychosis.

Thank God I never got that bad, but I really thought either something would happen to Jack if I got too close, or that someone might take him away from me. I was obsessed with the idea that he might die from cot death and would check on him constantly, even though I had one of those alarms. I don't think I'll ever have any more children. Besides, I'd have to get close to a man for that, and I can say, hand on heart, that I never will.

It's unreal that I'm even thinking these thoughts here, at the spot where Rob died. I glance at my watch. Quarter past ten. This time, forty-eight hours ago, he was still alive.

* * *

I didn't notice anyone else around.
Luckily, the side of the car took the impact,
resulting in a mere well-placed clip.
Not much damage at all.

Chapter 16

A police car crouches like a panther alongside the garden wall. My heart seems to fill my throat as I consider what new information they might be about to impart. Dad's watching my arrival from where he sits in the lounge window. I see him rise from his seat, and he's at the front door before me.

"The police are here. Where've you been Fiona?" Concern is etched across his face. "I thought you were dropping Jack at school and coming straight back."

"I *can* see they're here." My voice is a hiss. Does he think I'm blind or something? "I went for a drive to clear my head. Or is that a crime now?"

He gives me a look that says *wind your neck in.* "Do you want some tea? I've already made them some."

I resist the temptation to make a wisecrack about tea. He means well. "Yes. Thanks Dad. Sorry for snapping."

He squeezes my arm as I pass him. "It's OK love."

"Morning Fiona." DI Green gives me a weak smile as I enter the room and take the seat Dad's vacated. I swivel it around so I can face them.

"How are you doing this morning?" PC Robinson nods at me in acknowledgement, squinting as he gets an eyeful of the sunshine behind me. They seem nicer than in the interview room yesterday.

But I don't trust them one bit. They're probably here to try to trip me up.

I tilt the blind. "OK, I suppose. I've got my son to keep me going, and my dad's looking after me."

"Good. I'm glad to hear you've got some support. Anyway," DI Green takes a sip from her cup. "We've made some more inquiries which we'd like to speak to you about."

"OK. Did you get hold of Bryony?"

"Who's Bryony?" Dad passes me a mug, then sits in the armchair at the other side of the room from the police, so we're all at right angles from each other. It's stuffy in here this morning, but the cat looks happy. It's enough to make me smile, although I don't, to notice her stretched out in the sun on the windowsill. I'd swap lives with the cat right now.

"Rob's ex-girlfriend. She kept trying to ring him on the day he died."

Dad frowns but says nothing. I expect he might later. It appears he and I have been unknowingly going through the same thing.

"We haven't spoken with Bryony yet." PC Robinson sets his mug down on the coffee table, ignoring the strategically placed coaster.

I frown.

"We've tried ringing and calling round to her house but haven't got an answer. We'll keep trying."

"We have been in touch with his ex-wife," adds DI Green. "She's coming in today to make a formal statement. We're also here to ask if you've had any clarity about your location at the time of your husband's death?"

"I was here, ironing, like I told you."

"We need to take your mobile phone. Obviously, we'll return it as soon as we've inspected it."

"Why do you want my phone? You've already seen the messages I sent Rob. We didn't even text each other very often."

"It's procedure." PC Robinson leans forward so I can see the whites of his eyes behind DI Green's head. "It's more to rule you out, than to attempt to implicate you. Whichever signals your phone was picking up, will verify your whereabouts on Monday."

"There doesn't appear to have been much love lost between Robert and his ex wife, does there?" DI Green raises her gaze from her notepad to mine.

"Surely that's normal when people get divorced." I wonder what they're getting at here.

"Denise tells me your marriage was in trouble." DI Green glances at our large wedding photo above the fireplace. We look so happy. The photographer had said something funny but still – she really captured something between us. Who'd have thought things would end up where they have?

"Denise wouldn't know something like that, even if it was true. The only relationship Rob had with her these days was as a co-parent."

"That's not how Denise saw it. She said Robert never arrived to pick up his daughter. And apparently, she's been struggling lately to even get maintenance from him. It's forced her to start a claim with the Child Support Agency."

"That's total rubbish. She's lying. He's always gone to Simone's parents evenings, sports days, and paid maintenance. I'll find his bank statements and prove it to you."

"That would be helpful. It will hopefully turn up other information too. Do you know anything about your husband's money problems Fiona?"

What are they on about? Even Dad's looking worried now. "He didn't have any, as far as I know."

"What bank accounts do you have, Fiona?

"Just our joint ISA, and my current account," I reply. I don't spend a great deal. It's been months since I even bought myself new clothes. I used to love clothes shopping, but not anymore.

"We'll need to have a look at the transactions for the last six months from your accounts?"

"Why?"

"Again. It's procedure."

"I've got nothing to hide. I'm happy for you to look at my accounts, but I want to know more of what it's about."

"All I can tell you at this stage is that it's in connection to an ongoing investigation with Bracken Furniture."

"But what's all this got to do with my son-in-law's death?" Dad looks baffled.

"That's what we're looking into. I'm sorry to be hazy but we're at the early stages of an ongoing inquiry." DI Green puts her cup down. "Thanks for that. We don't normally get offered a drink when we do home visits." She straightens herself up. "Looking at accounts is just one line of enquiry we're pursuing."

"Do you know someone called James Turner?" PC Robinson looks at me. "We believe he's the *JT* in your husband's phone."

Momentarily, I feel relieved that I don't have another woman to worry about. That he's been having anything to do with Bryony is bad enough. "I don't think so. Why?"

"Could he be a friend of your husband's?"

"His name rings a bell." James Turner. James Turner. I turn the name over in my mind. "Why? What's he got to do with anything?"

"If and when we can tell you more, we will," DI Green says. "At this stage, we're just asking whether you know him."

Dad stands. "If you will not be clearer with your line of questioning, I suggest you get on with finding out who killed my son-in-law, and in the meantime, leave my daughter to grieve and get on with helping my grandson cope with all he's going through."

DI Green and PC Robinson also stand.

"I'm sorry we can't tell you much." She gives me a look I don't like. "But I promise you, we're following some substantial leads and conducting a thorough CCTV investigation. It's only a matter of time before we get to the bottom of what's happened."

"I'll see you out." Dad heads towards the lounge door.

* * *

The story is riding high in the media.
But soon,
it will be yesterday's news.
Just a couple more days,
and then I'll be able to breathe again.

Chapter 17

My head is killing me. I open a window, watching as the police car turns in the cul-de-sac and drives away.

"You've said nothing about money troubles." Dad sits back in the chair, spreading the newspaper across his lap.

"We haven't got money troubles."

"What's happened to the money my mother left you?"

"Dad, that was nine years ago."

"It was over half a million."

"Money doesn't go anywhere these days. Besides, that's why we were investing."

"Investing in what?"

"Well, that's what I need to look into. Rob's had some of my money which he said would be returned ten times over."

"Do the police know about this?"

"Of course they do. They've been through all of Rob's text messages and bank accounts. I hate all this. All this poking into my private life."

"If you've nothing to hide…"

Dad's getting on my nerves today. He's always got to be the voice of bloody reason. "I haven't."

"How much did you give him?" He folds the newspaper into quarters.

I sigh. "Thirty grand." It sounds like a lot of money said out loud.

"With no idea of what Rob was doing with it?"

"Not entirely. There were two things. But you know me, Dad – financial stuff goes over my head."

"So what did he tell you?" Dad folds his arms and peers over the top of his glasses at me. "Go on. I'm interested."

"One investment was with a company of property developers. All I know is that it was something to do with a new shopping centre in Harrogate on some very sought after land. They'd been granted preliminary planning permission, Rob said it was a go-er."

"That shouldn't be too difficult to find out more about." Dad raises his feet onto the pouffe. He always wears socks with a diamond pattern on. I've often bought him novelty socks for Father's Day or his birthday, but have never seen him wear them. "What about the other one?"

"That one's more complicated. It's a Chinese company. Some sort of *data miner* that diverts to other operations. It's financial technology."

"Like a block chain?"

"I don't know."

"Can you find out?"

"I'm going to poke about in Rob's office. You can help me if..." I avert my attention to a crunching sound as Mum's car arrives on the gravelled driveway.

"Were you expecting her?" Dad appears to pale beneath his beard as he puts his newspaper down.

"No," I reply. "She made it perfectly clear to me she was staying in Devon." I rise to let her in, but she's already standing in the lounge doorway. Dad must have left the porch door unlocked after seeing the police out.

"We weren't expecting to see you Mum," I try to keep my voice light. I'm relieved that I tidied up on Sunday. She's one of those people who runs their finger along surfaces to check for dust, even in someone else's house. Although that's the least of my worries amongst everything else.

"I thought I'd better come back. Help you out."

"There's no need," Dad looks at the floor. "Like I said on the phone, I'm taking care of them. You might as well go back to where you came from."

"Don't be like that love," she replies, without looking at him. "I'm here now, anyway."

"I'll leave you to it." I start towards the door. I can do without being piggy in the middle of their domestics. I make a coffee and carry it through to the conservatory, keen to escape their raised voices. I remember I opened the lounge window and regret it – the whole neighbourhood will hear them. I slide the conservatory door behind me, relieved that it muffles them out. They must sort it for themselves. I haven't got the energy to get involved. All I know is that if I was in Dad's shoes...

The conservatory is my favourite room in the house. I turn the fan on and settle on the wicker sofa with my coffee. Everything around me looks familiar and unchanged. But my life has been rocked to its core. It all feels out of control and I've no idea what's going to come next. The cat slinks from under the sofa and lands in my lap. I'm glad of her company even if it's always on her terms.

My head's spinning. There's Bryony, then there's this Turner, or JT. There's Rob's ex-wife with the accusations she's making, and *also* the fact that he's not even been going to work. Somebody knows more than I do. I decide that as soon as Mum and Dad have sorted their crap out, I'm going to look deeper into Rob's business and personal relationships. I need to look through his office.

Jostling me from my thoughts, Dad slides the conservatory door open with Mum hot on his heels. I can't even have five minutes' peace.

"We can't both stay here." Dad takes the step down into the conservatory and looks at me. "Fiona. It's your call. You know what's going on between your mum and I – send one of us back to York."

"Come on Dad. You're effectively asking me to choose between you both. That's not fair."

"I'm sorry, love. You're right." He sits on the chair next to mine and looks at Mum, framed in the doorway, looking calmer than she did when she first arrived. "I'll leave you with your mother. I can't stand to be in the same room as you." He glares at her. "Look after her Maggie, and Jack. Because if I find out that you're issuing any more of your threats or ultimatums, I'll…"

"You'll what?" Mum's eyes narrow.

"I won't be responsible for my actions."

"Just go home Roger. And don't ever tell me how to be with my daughter."

I know it's all Mum's fault – the situation between her and dad, but I can't help but feel slightly warmed at her referring to me as her daughter. It's an unusual term for her. It almost gives me a sense of belonging.

* * *

Driving normally clears my head.
But I can't think straight at the moment.
I'm looking over my shoulder,
and jumping every time the phone rings,
or there's a knock at the door.

Chapter 18

We're sitting in the conservatory. Dad's gone, and she's barely looked up from her phone since he left.

"So why did you come back Mum?"

"I'll talk to you about it later." She still doesn't give me her attention. "I've got to be somewhere at two o'clock."

"Where?" *What are you up to now?* That's what I really want to say. I'm still baffled why she's back. Something must have happened with Shane. That must be who she's madly texting.

"The police station. They just want a quick statement from me. Because I was here the other morning - before Rob had his accident. It shouldn't take long."

"Yes, they told me they wanted a word. I guess it's checking the times and any information that I've given them. Have you heard they're treating his death as a hit and run?"

She slips her phone back into her handbag and gazes out over the garden. "I heard it on the news on the drive back up. You seem to be bearing up well, considering. You must be made of tougher stuff than I give you credit for." She doesn't look at me.

Not as tough as your décolletage, I want to say, bitchily. Someone should tell her that's she's too old to wear the low cut tops she does.

"How's Jack doing?" She's still staring at the garden and is definitely not herself.

I follow her gaze, noting that the lawn needs mowing. Rob's always done that. I don't even know how to switch the lawnmower on. "Pretty upset. He idolised his dad. I'm just taking it one day at a time. It's not as though I haven't known awful times before."

"Have the police got any ideas yet? Have they said anything to you?"

I take a sideways glance at Mum. She suddenly seems genuinely interested in my awful situation. Perhaps I even detect a glimmer of sympathy in her expression. We're having a normal, adult conversation about me for a change – not about her. It feels like a miracle.

"There's a couple of lines of enquiry they're following up." I sip my coffee. "Sorry I didn't make you a cuppa – you were busy with Dad. Obviously, the police won't say too much to me with things being ongoing, but there seems to be suspicion around one of Rob's business associates. There was something untoward with his former employers as well."

"His former employers? What do you mean? I thought he'd been with Bracken since he left university?"

I wonder for a moment whether I can trust her, but decide to give her the benefit of the doubt. "He's been pretending to go to work, but it sounds like he was sacked a month ago." I hope she doesn't use this information to fire back at me. "His boss won't tell me what it's all about. I'm hoping the police might turn something up."

"And you have a go at me for being dishonest! I've always said there was something shifty about your husband."

"I haven't had a go at you about anything, Mum. I just didn't want dragging into your bloody affair. I felt bad about Dad as well."

"Well, it's all over, anyway. It doesn't matter."

"What is?"

"The thing with Shane. It feels as though my life is as over as Rob's. Shane's decided to go back to his wife and kids. I couldn't talk him round."

So that's why she's back up here so quick. He's dumped her. No wonder she had a face like a bag of spanners when she arrived.

But I don't want to talk about her relationship woes. No chance. Maybe she might want to make a go of things with Dad now. That's if he can forgive her. Again. I decide to change the subject. "So when did the police get in touch with you?"

"Last night. I was in a state after Shane had gone, so I didn't talk to them for long. They offered to let me do the statement in Devon, but when they rang me this morning to arrange a time, I told them I was driving back up to you. There's not exactly a lot I can tell them though."

"Do you want a sandwich before you go?" We've always been like this. Me looking after her. As though I'm the mother. She looks rough though.

"No thanks. I'd better be off. Get it over with. I'll see you when I get back."

I need to take control of things. Rob's office is a good place to start. I generally keep the door shut on the room, as it's always an absolute tip.

Once upon a time, this, our spare room, might have been where we would put a second child. Somehow, we lost our way with that plan.

I don't think it's hit me fully yet that Rob's not coming back. And the only time I've *really* cried has been when I was first told, and in response to Jack's pain. When I was a *drinker*, I'd cry at the drop of a hat. Now, it's as though my emotions are injected with anaesthetic.

"How do you find anything in this mess?" I'd said to him at the weekend when I took him a coffee. Only *now* can I recall him jumping as I entered the room. He'd slipped whatever document he was looking at into one of his file trays. I feel sure that whatever he had in his hand is going to lead me to more information about what's gone on with his job, or who this James Turner is.

"Organised chaos." He'd grinned at me, accepting the coffee. "I'll be downstairs shortly. I've got a couple more things to sort out." In times gone by, he'd have drawn me onto his knee and invited me to distract him.

In the end, it had been a further two hours before Rob had joined Jack and me in the garden. By the time he surfaced, I was feeling annoyed and resentful. He had been out at work all week, or so I thought. It was the first day of lovely sunshine on Saturday – we should have been going out somewhere as a family. Instead, I was left to occupy Jack, whilst Rob did whatever was so important in his office. And now I'm determined to find out what it was. I start by sifting through the papers in his middle tray. The same one I watched him slide a sheet of paper into on Saturday.

All that seems to be in here are bank statements. But a closer look shows they're not from our joint account, or from Rob's own current account. I didn't even know he had an account with Nat West. The transactions are uniform, except for a huge payment which was made to James Turner. I gasp as I realise it's three hundred and seventy-five thousand pounds. The statement is from six weeks ago, around the time when I gave Rob thirty grand towards his supposedly cast iron investments. Where has he got the rest of the money from? Other than what I gave him, as far as I know, we only had around forty grand in our ISA. I need to check whether that's still there.

Rob's always worked hard, and with my inheritance, we've been comfortable, but monies were depleting. I was toying with the idea of getting an office job or setting something up myself where I could work from home. I didn't realise we still had that sort of money between us. 'Had' being the key word. However, this James Turner seems to be the one who will provide some answers.

I rifle through one of the other trays. It's a pile of bills, all addressed to Rob. Council tax, gas, electric, water, internet. He always dealt with the money side of things – occasionally thrusting a piece of paper under my nose to sign. I never questioned it. As far as money went, I trusted him, and have always had what I need in my own personal account.

The sunlight illuminates the surface of a notepad. Though it's a clean page, there's the imprint of something that's been written on the torn off page above it.

* * *

This is the worst bit.
I've got to hold my nerve
until they release his body

Chapter 19

I go into the next room and pluck one of Jack's fat crayons from the art box on his desk. I make his bed and open his window before returning to Rob's office. As I rub the crayon over the imprint, the words reveal themselves to me. *If you don't have my money by 6pm, there will be consequences.*

It doesn't look like Rob's handwriting, but then Rob's is fairly standard. His half lower case, half upper case scrawl is replicated by men half the world over. But two things are clear. I need to find out who would have been on the receiving end of these consequences, and I need to find out who James Turner is. I wonder if he's anything to do with the loss of Rob's job.

Evidently, I didn't know my husband as well as I thought I did. And it's not just the financial side of things. There's the situation with his ex-wife and daughter, not to mention the rekindled relationship with Bryony.

The landline rings, startling me.

"Where are you?" It's Mum. She's never one for social niceties, like the word *hello*.

"I'm at home. Where else would I be?" I look up at the smiling photograph of Jack at two years old, hanging on the wall above Rob's desk. We were happy then.

"Why aren't you answering your phone?"

"I just have."

"Your mobile?"

"The police are looking at it."

"Why?"

"For evidence, I suppose."

"Where are you?"

"Upstairs. In Rob's office."

"What are you doing?"

"Gosh Mum. It's like being on Question Time. I'm sorting a few things out. Bills and stuff."

"You should leave that for now. You've enough to be dealing with."

"It's OK." I'm amazed by her sudden concern. "It's good to keep busy."

"I thought I'd see if you wanted me to pick Jack up from school whilst I'm out. What time does he finish?"

That she wants to help me out provides a momentary lift. I glance at the clock, my eyes falling on a letter from *Bracken Furniture*. My gaze returns to the desk. "In twenty minutes," I tell her. "He'll be pleased to see you."

"Right. I'll hang around for him then."

"How did you get on at the station?"

"In and out. It was procedure, they said. Though you might want to know that they were asking questions about your relationship with Rob."

"Like what?"

"You know. Were there any problems? That sort of thing."

"What did you say?"

"The truth. That it seemed alright to me. That you'd had your ups and downs, but who doesn't? I didn't say that I don't know what you ever did to deserve such a secure life with a half-decent husband." That's Mum all over. She builds me up slightly, then tears me back down. Probably to make sure that I fall from a greater height.

I end the call, then ring school to allow for her to collect Jack. The receptionist asks if I'm OK.

I'm grateful for the extra time I've now got to poke around in here. I don't know if it will give me any clues as to where our money's gone, or what Rob has been up to, but it's worth a look.

I turn my attention back to the letter, signed by Phillip Bracken.

Without prejudice

I refer to our meeting of last Friday 4th June at 3pm, attended by myself, David Myers, Deputy CEO and yourself.

As you know, you are under investigation for the disappearance of monies totalling £122,000, which were found to have been paid into your personal bank account. You are also being investigated for fraudulent documents found in the drawer of your desk.

Following your failure to explain the situation, or return the funds, I am left with no alternative than to bring formal proceedings against you.

I am writing to inform you that these will be instigated immediately.

You were suspended without pay on Wednesday 6 May and must continue not to enter the premises of Bracken Furniture, nor must you contact any employee or customer of the company, directly or indirectly.

You can, and are advised to, seek legal counsel as we look to be compensated for our losses. We request, in the meantime, that the sum of £122,000 is repaid to us.

Sincerely, Phillip Bracken, Managing Director

I pick the phone up again. "Good afternoon. Can I speak to Mr Bracken please?"

"Certainly. Who's calling, please?"

"It's Fiona Matherson."

"Erm. I'm sorry. He's not available."

"I really need to talk to him. Can you tell him it's urgent?"

"I'll pass a message on. That's the best I can do, I'm afraid."

I've no choice other than to accept the best she can do. However, I know for a fact that she was about to put the call through, until she discovered it was me.

"Mummy." Jack's voice echoes through the house.

I decide to leave all this for the time being and head down the stairs to see him. I still need to speak to James Turner, but I want to see what else I can find first.

"Granny Maggie picked me up from school." He's smiling, and it's good to see. "Everyone was looking at her. I had to tell them she's my Grandma."

"You know I don't like being called that."

I glance at her as she slides her feet into mules, expecting her to be smiling, but she's not. "Have your friends taken care of you today?" I'm still not sure that he should have been at school, but it does appear to have done him some good. He looks brighter than this morning.

"Yes. Sam could sit with me all day. Sometimes he has to sit on a different table for literacy and numeracy, but today, he didn't have to. His mum came to talk to me at the end of school too to see if I wanted a sleepover again."

"She seems really nice," Mum adds. "Plenty of money too, looking at her. What does she do?"

"I'm not sure."

"More than you, I would expect."

I resist the temptation to laugh. Mum's lived off Dad's hard work for the whole of their married life. She lets the bun out of her dark hair, and it swings above her shoulders. Her grey roots are coming through; it won't be long before she's at the hairdressers. It's the length I'd like mine cutting to, but I would fear looking too much like her. I used to be pleased when I was told we were alike. However, since I've become a mother myself, I recoil at the chill that exists within her and am scared of being anything like her, looks or otherwise. I can't understand the indifference she's always shown towards me.

"Someone called Bryony said hello to Jack as well." Mum smiles.

The hairs stand up on the back of my neck. *Bryony.* What was she doing at school?"

"She's Ella Partridge's auntie," Jack explains. "But I've been to her house with Dad before."

"You have?" I feel a crawling sensation over my skin. Rob's taken Jack to her house?

"I saw her at the station earlier as well. Pretty, isn't she?"

"At the police station?"

"Yes. I was in the waiting room when she arrived. I got called in then though."

"So you didn't find out why she was there?"

"No."

"Would you mind looking after Jack for an hour? I could do with a walk. I need to clear my head."

"I suppose so. As long as you're not long. I've got some calls to make."

I slide my feet into flip-flops. I've got to get out of here.

"Where are you going, anyway?"

"I need to find out what she was doing at the police station."

"Let it all go," Mum calls after me as I open the first door onto the porch. "There's no point acting on anything. With Bryony, I mean. Not now."

I look back at them. Jack looks puzzled but seems happy to be left with Mum.

109

"I'll be back shortly," I say, grateful to exchange the cool hallway air for some warm sunshine. Even so, I shiver. I must look a right sight. Shapeless jumper, baggy jeans, and flip-flops. I rake my fingers through my hair. I should have probably tidied myself up. Particularly in view of the person I'm about to face. But maybe I'm past caring.

* * *

The police will accept they're not going to find out who hit him.
Two and a half days have passed.
If they suspected me, I'd have been arrested by now.

Chapter 20

There's no answer when I ring the bell. I can hear voices so tiptoe up the driveway and push the gate into the back garden. A girl is running in and out of a sprinkler. I recognise her as being a couple of years above Jack at school.

"What are you doing here?" Bryony jumps to her feet as I close the gate after me. "You can't just barge into my garden like this."

"You wouldn't take my calls or reply to my messages." I step towards her. "What was I supposed to do? I want answers."

"Ella, go inside," she says to the girl. "Put the TV on for a few minutes."

"But Auntie Bry, I want to play in the water."

"Just for a few minutes. Until this lady goes."

"I want her to go now." Ella scowls at me as she flounces past us into the house.

"I want to know what was going on between you and my husband." I'm stood right in front of her now. Mum's right. Bryony is very pretty. She looks cool and elegant in a long sundress and blonde hair which effortlessly cascades down her back. Without meaning to, I tuck mine behind my ears, feeling ugly and unkempt in front of her.

"Nothing was going on. Just yoga and meditation."

"Is that what it's called nowadays?"

"Rob and I were friends Fiona." She looks straight at me with the green eyes which I imagine have stared into Rob's. "It is allowed, you know."

I hate her. And I hate him as well. Since I spotted them in a coffee shop a couple of weeks ago, it's been hounding me. Now that he's gone, I should let it go. But I can't.

"You were together once. You and him. You shouldn't still have been seeing each other. He was married to me. I thought all that had stopped, anyway."

"All what?"

"Meditation." I spit the word out like a fishbone. I know meditation was part of their connection to one another. Something spiritual. Something they couldn't turn their backs on. I never had that with Rob.

Once, when Rob and I were having a heart-to-heart, he described Bryony as having too much of a bohemian attitude towards money. I really think that's why he married me – the huge inheritance from my grandmother would've attracted him. I'd only just received it when we met in the park, back in 2011. Though now it sounds as though Rob's been having the best of both worlds. Me and her.

"Look," Bryony glances towards her patio doors. "Rob and I were close, I don't deny that. But we weren't having an affair. He was having trouble and confided in me, that's all. And the yoga and meditation were helping him."

"What sort of trouble?" He's confided in her. I should have known.

She seems totally unruffled with the situation. I bet she doesn't have to find her calm in the bottom of a snifter of brandy or glass of wine. "Have you been in touch with his work?"

"Yes. They won't tell me anything."

"That's where you'll find your answers. And with that friend of his."

"Do you mean James Turner? What do you know about him?"

"Nothing really. Rob only came to me to find some peace. I'm only sorry that it obviously didn't work."

"Why didn't he talk to me? I'm his wife."

"And I was his friend. He should have been able to be friends with whoever he chose." Her expression darkens. "Without worrying about repercussions from you. Do you know how scared he was that you'd find out he was here? Love is not a possession, you know."

"Don't start with your psychobabble. I wasn't possessive. I just wouldn't have wanted him hanging around with his ex. Who would?"

"You didn't trust him at all, did you?"

"It would appear I had good reason not to." We fall silent for a few moments. She knows more than she's letting on. "Since he's spent so much time confiding in you," I say, "I want to know what you know about his money troubles?"

"I've told the police everything I know."

"I've got a right to hear it too."

"You haven't got a right to anything from me. Ask the police to tell you if you're so interested. I'm sure they'll be in touch anyway."

"Have you got an alibi for the other morning?"

She laughs now, a tinkly sound which makes my fist ball in my jeans pocket.

"They will not be looking at me when they look into you. And his ex-wife."

"What's that supposed to mean?"

"You're the ones with the history. The form. The reason. Anyway, I'm looking after my niece. I'd like you to leave. And if you come back, I'll have you done for harassment."

I stare at her. "Why are you being so awful? What on earth has Rob said to you about me?"

"Enough. You've put him through the mill over the years, haven't you? He should have stayed with me."

"Well, he didn't, did he? He married me."

113

"Ask yourself why." She rubs her index finger against her thumb in a gesture that says money, then jerks her head towards the gate. "Please leave. Now."

I open my mouth to respond, but tears sting my eyes. I don't want to give her the satisfaction of seeing me cry, so I do as I'm told and lurch away from her house, back onto the street. She's lucky I haven't got a drink inside me. I'd have punched her if I had.

I can't face going home yet. I walk around aimlessly for a while. My face is burning in the heat of the sun. It's typical. The weather has been shocking so far this year, then as soon as I'm going through this shit, we get given a heatwave. Mum barely sees Jack, so I've no qualms about taking advantage of her presence. I can't imagine her being around for long before she hot foots it back to patch things up with lover boy.

Without planning to, I find myself in the town centre and sit outside a café, too hot to carry on walking. I slide the menu from its holder. I've eaten an apple and a piece of toast today. It's no wonder I feel sick all the time.

"Can I take your order, madam?" I hate being called madam. It makes me feel much older than my thirty-six years. "It's last orders now. We're closing up at five."

Last orders. It's like being in the Black Bull. I wish. *No, I don't.* "I'll have a toasted teacake and a chamomile tea please." It might calm me down.

"Will that be all, madam?" I want to shout at him. *Don't call me madam.* He thrusts the payment machine in front of me and I present the card for our joint account.

"I'm afraid to tell you that it has declined the transaction." His voice is loud enough for a couple walking past to look at me, and three people at the next table. He rips the receipt from the machine. "Would you like to try an alternative method of payment madam?"

"There should be money in that account." I flush to the roots of my hair as I fish around in my purse and pull out the card for my current account, which normally doesn't contain more than pocket money. Most of what I had left should be in the joint account. I was happy with our financial arrangement. With my drinking being as it has been, Rob liked to keep hold of the purse strings and monitor what I was spending.

Luckily, my personal account payment works, and the waiter leaves me alone.

I feel lost without my mobile phone and wonder how long the police will have it for. Surely not for long. Luckily, I've still got my Kindle Fire, which I slide from my handbag. At least I can get onto the internet and check our joint account. But it's so long since I was on it I can't remember the login details. I flick through to Facebook and try to ignore the thirty plus notifications that are there. At first glance they're the condolences everyone feels compelled to leave, most saying the same thing and I can't bear to read them right now. There'll be time when we get to the funeral to face all that.

For now, I've got to hold it together. And not give into drink. I click onto Rob's profile page to see if he's friends with this James Turner. He is. I click to the page, disappointed to find it inaccessible apart from when he's changed his profile or cover photo. I need to find some contact details for him.

All his pictures relate to cars or football matches. He's about the same age as Rob. There's some information on his *about me* page. Lives in Manchester. Self Employed. Supports Manchester United. James Turner doesn't sound interesting. I think again of the huge transaction in the bank statement I found in Rob's office – I hope to God my money is safe.

The words *if you don't have my money by 6pm, there will be consequences,* swim back into my mind. I must do some more digging around in Rob's office. I've got a bad feeling in my gut about this. And the mortgage company. And our joint account.

* * *

I'm devouring every news report and every bit of social media.
When his body has been released to the undertakers,
I will know I'm in the clear.

Chapter 21

Mum raises her eyes from her phone. Her face is pinched with fury as I walk towards the garden table. "Where the hell have you been?"

"I told you. I needed some time to myself."

"You've had all bloody day whilst Jack's been in school." She looks awful. I'm not used to seeing Mum without a face full of make-up. Even her hair is a sweaty mess.

"Where's Jack? Is he OK?"

"I sent him to his room. His noise was driving me to distraction."

I feel guilty now for leaving him. She's hardly *granny of the year*. I turn back towards the house. I need to keep busy and out of Mum's way. "I'll put some dinner on. Chicken and salad if that's OK?"

"Don't take advantage of me again Fiona. I've done my time. With you. If I wanted to look after children, I'd open a nursery."

Ignoring her, I walk across the patio.

As I chop salad, I hear her through the open window. "Please Shane." She's crying. In my garden. I hope the neighbours aren't in their gardens, listening to her. "We're wonderful together. She can never give you what I can."

Pause.

"But they're getting older," she wails. "And before long, they'll leave home, and what will you be left with? Her?"

Pause.

"No, you don't love her. If you did, you'd have come nowhere near me. Happily married men don't have affairs."

Pause.

"I wish I'd never told you now. You can't make threats like that."

I wonder what he's threatening her with. It definitely sounds as though she's better off without him. And not just for Dad's sake.

"Do you know how that makes me feel? After everything we've shared. As if you're treating me like this. You bastard!"

"Mum, enough!" I stride through the conservatory doors towards her. "You're not using that kind of language in my garden." Her phone is still lit up on the table. She reaches into a bag and pulls out a bottle of wine.

"Get us a glass, will you? The plan now is to get drunk."

"I'd rather you didn't. Not here. You know what I've been through Mum. I find it really hard to be around people who are drinking. Especially when they're drinking to get drunk."

She twists towards me, squinting in the early evening sunlight. "Well, tough. Don't you stand there, judging me. Just because you're an old soak. If I want to drown my sorrows, no one, especially you, will stop me."

I march towards the house before I blow up with her. "You OK Jack?" I call up the stairs, trying to steady my voice. I should have sent her away this morning, whilst I had the chance.

"Yes, Mummy. I'm playing with my train set."

My heart sags. That's something he and Rob always did together. They'd be at it for hours. "Dinner won't be long, sweetheart."

I pause as I hear Mum clattering around in the kitchen, presumably finding herself a glass, and wait until I hear her footsteps fade back towards the conservatory. I know every nuance and creak of this house. It will be too big for Jack and me. Particularly when I get around to clearing it of all Rob's stuff. That's a daunting thought.

I can hardly believe how much life has changed in less than three days. It's Wednesday evening, and it's totally unrecognisable from the start of the week. I glance out of the window. Mum's drinking wine from a tumbler. This is going to be a fun evening. She's typing into her phone – probably another begging message to Shane. I wonder again what threat he was making. Possibly to tell Dad.

I used to crave Mum's time and attention, no matter what. This probably went on until Jack was about a year old. But now I wish she would leave. My husband has just died. I'm a recovering alcoholic, and she's sat in my garden, crying, and getting sloshed. Rob, if he were still here, would probably throw her out on her ear.

"Dinner's ready, Jack."

He bounds down the stairs. I hand him a plate of bread to carry into the garden whilst I balance chicken, salad bowls, and the dinner plates. He seems less burdened than he did yesterday. The normality he'll have felt from his usual routine must have helped him.

When I was still drinking, eating would take the edge off the desire to drink. Rob would have to coax me to eat. Which I now find myself doing with Mum.

"I'm not hungry," she snaps. "I'm too upset to eat, can't you see?"

"Is it because of Daddy?" Jack bites into some bread. "Because he's gone to heaven?"

I bite my lip. "We're all sad, love." I reach for his hand. "What do you want to do after dinner?"

"Can I watch TV?" He looks at me hopefully. He's easily pleased.

I know I should spend some proper time with him but haven't got the energy. "Yes. Just for a while and then I'll run you a bath."

"Will you bath me Granny Maggie? And read me a story?"

"Another time," she says. I watch Jack's face fall. I know how he feels.

Mum's onto her second glass of wine as Jack races back into the house, the lure of the TV stronger than anything else.

"What am I going to do Fiona?" She looks at me through teary eyes and takes a large drink.

"About what?"

"Shane. I need him to come back to me. He's gone and bloody returned to his wife."

"You can't control the behaviour or decisions of someone else Mum." Gosh, I sound like Bryony now. "Why don't you let him go - make a go of things with Dad?"

"Your Dad? You must be joking."

"Why?" I want to tell her she doesn't deserve him, but I'd never dare. "If it's that bad, why don't you go to Relate?"

"It's like I said to you the other night. You've got no idea."

The next thirty minutes pass with me letting her rant and wail. I watch her become more incoherent as she empties the bottle. I'm relieved I don't drink anymore and am possibly coping with Rob's death better because of this. She'll probably wind herself into more of a knot, then she'll go to bed. However, I watch in dismay as she pulls a second bottle from her bag.

"I'm off to run Jack a bath and get him settled." I rise from my spot opposite her, pitying this now aging and pathetic excuse for a wife, mother, and grandmother. She thinks about nobody but herself.

I hear her on the phone to Shane again, as Jack splashes around in the bath. She's louder now that she's drunk. I hope my neighbours don't think it's me. Dad once said our voices are similar when on the phone. Jack decides he no longer wants to play, reality seemingly dawning that Daddy won't be tucking him in again tonight.

He's tearful when I take him to his room. I wish my dad was still here to help me. I lay at Jack's side until he falls asleep, dropping off myself for a while. When I wake with a jolt, the light is fading.

I slide from the bed, and glance out of Jack's window to see Mum slumped where I left her. I can't face returning to her, so wander into the room I've shared with Rob for the last nine years.

I haven't opened the blinds all week. Clothes, mine and Rob's, litter the floor. I walk into the en-suite, trying to ignore Rob's shower gel, toothbrush, and comb, and wash my face, grateful for the warmth of the water against my tired skin.

Tomorrow I'm going to find out as much as I can about his dodgy dealings and try to put things right. But tonight, I'm going to grieve for my husband, and all we once shared. I open his side of the wardrobe and touch one of the shirts which hangs there. It's the one he always used to wear when we went out. Not that we've been out together much lately. I pull it towards me and inhale the scent of his aftershave.

Then I feel something rustle in the top pocket and pull out a receipt. It's textbook affair stuff. Rummaging through my husband's pockets. A receipt from the Queen's Hotel in Leeds. The Thursday before last. When he said he was at a conference in the Midlands. I now know they had suspended him from his job. It's for a meal. A hundred and nine pounds. Wine. A king room. I stare at it. It must be Bryony.

* * *

I'm doing what I can to get through it.
The guilt is seeping in occasionally,
but when I focus on the bigger picture,
I know it will be worth it.

Chapter 22

J ack spoons rice crispies from his bowl to his mouth. "I don't want to go to school today Mummy. I only want my daddy." He's reverted to referring to us as mummy and daddy again. He'd started calling us mum and dad before all this, like his friends do, he had said. At the time, I'd felt a pang that he was growing up.

"I know, love. But I think you should go to school. It'll do you good to be around your friends. Keeping busy will help you feel better – I promise. I'll take you today."

I need him to go to school if the truth be known. I've planned to spend the day tearing Rob's office to bits. The police have taken his laptop and phone, where I reckon a lot of the information will be, but there's plenty of paperwork to go through and some phone calls I can make.

I also plan to get rid of Mum. I can't cope with her here. Thankfully, she's sleeping the wine off. I've moved the empty bottles from the garden table. It feels strange, dumping drink bottles in the recycling after a year of not doing so. I'm going to ask Dad if he'll swap places with her. The police investigation is ongoing, and I've got a funeral to plan. I'm much better with *him* around.

I don't owe my mother a thing. And if she thinks she can pour all her bloody boyfriend woes out to me whilst getting slaughtered, she's very much mistaken.

122

"How are you doing Fiona?" Lynne appears at my car window as I pull up at the side of the school gates. "Are you coping OK?"

"As one does when their husband has been killed in a hit and run."

She pulls what can only be described as a sympathetic face. "I can't imagine what you must be going through. But as I've said before, if I can help with Jack at all?"

Everyone trots out the same lines to me. But Lynne's getting on my nerves, constantly asking to take Jack. I'm sure she means well, but it's the fourth time in as many days. Does she think I can't cope with him?

"Thank you. But his place is with me right now, where I can help him come to terms with things."

"Well, the offer's always there. As you know, Sam loves having him around. We can keep his mind off things."

"Thanks, but right now, he probably needs to face the fact that he's lost his dad. In his own surroundings." I try to muster a smile. "Honestly, I really appreciate the offer. I must go, anyway. I've got loads to do."

I should be grateful really. She's one of the few mothers that speaks to me, but I can't understand what she wants from me. It's not as if she's short of a friend, or a chat. She probably goes back to them with the gossip from my sad life.

I'm glad Mum is still sleeping when I arrive back at home. I head straight for the phone in the lounge.

"Dad. It's me." He always recites his full telephone number when he answers. York, seven, six, three, one, eight, two. He's so old-school. He even drives a Ford Sierra. It's a relic now, but he says it's economical and still goes. Apart from recently, when the petrol tank fell onto the forecourt when he was filling up. That was hilarious. I wonder what car Shane drives. Whatever it is, it's turned Mum's head.

"How are you doing, love? Is it all sinking in?"

"Yes. I guess so. I still feel really out of it though."

"How's Jack?"

"Up and down. It's his reaction that's getting to me the most. I can kind of keep going, but supporting him is hard."

"It'll all take time. You've had a massive shock. What about, dare I ask – your mother?"

My hesitation probably says it all. Eventually I say, "I could really do with her going home, to be honest Dad."

"Is it that bad? Have you told her?"

"She's still sleeping. She drank two bottles of wine last night."

"You're kidding." There's a slight pause before he says, "I'm coming over."

"No. Dad. It's…" She's going to kill me for this.

"I'm on my way." He rings off. I am pleased really. After all, this is what I wanted.

There's still no sound from upstairs. I don't want Mum to wake until Dad gets here. Hopefully, he'll stay then, and send her home. At least he'll help me out with Jack, without telling me he's already done his time, bringing me up.

I make myself a coffee and take it up to the office, closing the door softly behind me. The letter from Bracken Furniture is as I left it on Rob's desk, with the bank statement beside it. I wonder whether the police know anything about this yet. I guess if there is anything relevant to discover, they'll find it.

He's somehow embezzled a hundred and twenty-two thousand pounds. It's a sizeable amount, but not exactly earth shattering. We could have scraped that together between us. I'd already given him thirty grand to invest. And he had some of his own. There should be forty grand in our joint account as well. My heart rate quickens as reality dawns. I think back to the refused transaction at the café yesterday and dash into the bedroom for my laptop.

I don't need to search through his papers for this, I simply need to open up the banking app on my computer. I scan down the three accounts I have. There's only a few thousand in my personal current account. There's a minus balance in our joint account and just over a hundred pounds showing in our ISA. I stare at the numbers, a chilly hand of fear clutching at my chest. *Where the hell is all my money?*

I sift through papers in the bottom tray on his desk. Perhaps he's done some transfers to an account with a higher rate of interest. Yes, that's what it will be. Or to one with a reward, as an incentive for switching bank accounts. I pull out what looks like an agreement from the Yorkshire Building Society who we have our mortgage with. It's a re-mortgage agreement. Oh, my God. He's re-mortgaged the house. He can't have done – they would have needed my signature. I jointly own it and paid my half at the start. My blood runs cold as I spot my signature and printed name, clear as day, at the end of the document. He's taken a hundred grand out of the house. But I didn't know about it. *Could I have signed it when I've been drunk?* I check the date. It's only three months ago. The mortgage repayments will be much higher now than they were when we moved in nine years ago. And according to that message that was left – we're behind.

But there's more. A joint loan for fifty grand – again sporting my signature. I haven't agreed to any of this. He's been forging my signature. What on earth has he needed all this money for? I don't get it. But more importantly, what the hell am I going to do to get it back? He's totally cleaned us out. And I can't confront a person who's dead. I've still got his funeral to pay for which will potentially wipe out what's left. That will be me, done. Finished.

I Google *James Turner, Manchester.* There are several profiles on LinkedIn. One has the same profile picture as was on Facebook. I click through. It lists his profession as Financial Adviser. Looking further down his profile, I see he was at the same university, at the same time as Rob. That must be where they know each other from. But he doesn't look familiar.

I press on a hyperlinked phone number. My chest palpitates as I wait for a connection.

"Is that James Turner?"

"It is." Even with those two words, I detect an arrogance in his voice.

"You don't know me, but you know my husband, Robert Matherson."

Silence. At least he doesn't deny anything. Nor has he hung up. Yet.

"Have you heard what's happened to Rob?"

"Yup." There are no condolences – nothing.

"I'm getting in touch to discuss some financial discrepancies I've discovered whilst going through Rob's papers. There seems to have been a large payment made to yourself. Three hundred and seventy-five thousand pounds. What's that about?"

"I've absolutely no idea. Sorry. I can't help you."

"But I've got the statement in front of me. Three hundred and seventy-five thousand pounds transferred last month to James Turner. I need to know where my money is."

"It must be a different James Turner. It's not exactly an unusual name, is it?"

"You and Rob were at university together. You're friends on Facebook. It must be you. Perhaps you could check your accounts if you're not sure."

"Don't you think I'd know if three hundred and seventy-five thousand quid had hit my account?"

"I have to know where our money has gone. My husband's dead, and this situation has left me with nothing." I try to breathe through the panic I'm feeling. "I can barely cover the cost of his funeral. Can you at least check for me? I don't mind waiting."

""Look, love." He really sounds smarmy. "I don't know what you think you're doing, ringing me out of the blue, but I know nothing of any three hundred grand, nor any discrepancies."

"Well, I'll be giving the police your details. If you..."

"I haven't been in touch with Rob for months." He cuts in. "Don't bother me again, do you hear?" With a click, the line goes dead.

As I try to gather my jumbled thoughts, the phone bursts back into life. The phone's display says *No Caller ID*. I snatch it up from the desk, wondering if James Turner has taken pity on me and has decided to tell me what he knows. But it's a female voice.

"Is that Mrs Matherson?"

"Speaking?"

"It's Elaine Watson here from the Co-Operative Funeral Service in Otley. Did you get our message yesterday?"

"Erm yes. Sorry for not getting back to you. I'm all over the place."

"I understand. It must be a difficult time."

They'll have a stock of phrases, these funeral people. "I've had better weeks," I say.

"I'm ringing to let you know that the post-mortem report has now been passed to the police, and Mr Matherson is ready for collection from the hospital." She's so brisk, so business-like. "Do we have your authorisation to proceed as you initially instructed?"

I want to tell her I don't know how I'll pay for their services with only a few grand in my current account. But I won't. I'll have to manage. I haven't a clue what I'm going to do. There's Bryony who won't tell me anything, Phillip Bracken, and now James Turner. It's like a conspiracy.

"Mrs Matherson?"

"Sorry. Yes. Do whatever you have to."

"Can we make an appointment for you to come in? So we can start making the necessary arrangements?" I hear a rustling of pages. "Is tomorrow at four o'clock any good?"

"Yes. I think so. I'll get back to you if it isn't." I've lost track of what day it is. I think it's Friday tomorrow. Someone will collect Jack for me. Mum won't be here with a bit of luck, but Dad hopefully will be. I could ask Christina, or there's always Sam's mum, Lynne. She always seems desperate to help.

"There's just one question I need to ask you." She pauses. "Do you wish for us to undertake the embalming process with your husband?"

"Whatever. Do what you would normally do." Right now, I don't care what they do. They can bury him in a ditch for all I care. Not only was he most likely carrying on with Bryony, he was lying to me about his job. Not to mention embezzling and thieving money, including mine, by forging my signature. My head is throbbing.

"Right, I'll be in touch if we need to know anything else, otherwise we'll see you tomorrow. Oh, Mrs Matherson. Sorry, there is just one more thing."

"What?" I realise that my voice is sharp, but I want her to get lost and leave me to work out what I'm going to do next. I've got things to get my head around other than the funeral. I can hear Mum moving about. Great. That's all I need.

"If you could bring an outfit for your husband. Something you'd like him to make his last journey in."

What a cheery thought. A cloth sack, I think to myself. I'm so angry. But mostly, I'm panicking. Unless I can find out what Rob has done with all our money, I've got nothing left once I've covered this funeral. He's got no other family to take it on. His parents had him late in life and his mum died when he was in his twenties. At least his father got to meet Jack. Rob was bereft when he died. What am I thinking about all this for now? I haven't even found out what the mortgage arrears are yet. God – we could end up homeless as well! There has to be a way out of all this. And an explanation for it.

"I'm sorry about last night, love." Mum squeezes past me in the kitchen to pull a glass from the cupboard. "I don't know what got into me." I smell soap and shower gel on her. She certainly looks better than she did.

"Too much wine. That's what got into you." I try to smile, despite my misery. "I can't talk, some of the states I've got into over the years. Pot, kettle, and all that. How are you feeling?"

"Rough. Look I *am* sorry."

She must be. Mum never apologises. Twice in less than a minute is a record. "What are your plans now then?"

"Oh, I don't know. Stay here for a few days. Help you out with Jack. Keep trying to talk Shane around..."

"What about Dad?" I'm not going to tell her he's on his way.

"What about him?"

"Shane, or whatever his name is, is making a go of his marriage. You said so yourself. Don't you think you should do the same?" I glance at the clock above the cooker. I don't know how the morning has slipped away so fast.

"If I wanted a lecture, I'd ask for one." She fills her glass with water and takes what looks like paracetamol. She deserves every ounce of her hangover.

"Mum, I'm not lecturing you, but I've got enough problems of my own. I can't cope with yours right now."

"I get it. Your husband has died. I've got sympathy with you for that. But you're young. You'll get through it. You've got a beautiful home, an easy life, lots going for you. Look at me." She tears off a piece of kitchen roll and blows her nose. "Life has passed me by."

"You haven't got a clue about my life Mum," I begin, poised to blurt out everything, but I'm cut off by calls of Fiona echoing around the hallway.

"What's he doing back here?" Mum hisses.

129

Dad strides into the kitchen. "I'll leave you to it," I say to them, much the same as I did twenty-four hours earlier. Only now, so much more has changed. Then, I thought I had enough money to get by with. I knew I would have to chase my thirty grand investment back, but I didn't know that Rob had wiped everything else out and plunged us into debt. What the hell am I going to do? Who do I tell? Where do I go with this?

I fill a glass of water then walk past Dad, out of the kitchen, and towards the conservatory.

* * *

Everything seems to have gone quiet.
He's been released.
Well his body has.

Chapter 23

I'm getting a migraine. I've been turning the money situation around in my head all day. I need more on this James Turner. I'm going to speak to the police tomorrow. But tonight, it's more important that I attend the AA meeting. My sponsor rang me again to check I could make it.

Mum's gone home, thankfully, and Dad's staying, so that's one less thing to stress about. She can mope to her heart's content in the comfort of her own home. She can drink herself into a stupor for all I care. I swallow. Hard. I might not have a home soon. One neighbour from two doors down left a casserole on the doorstep for us tonight. It's the sort of thing my Grandma would have done when she was still alive. Dad made me have some. I'm so glad he's back. And if he's struggling with his marital situation, he isn't letting on to me.

I need the AA meeting tonight. Without it, I may well have found a pub and got blitzed. I don't know how much more I can cope with. I remember the words of my midwife when I was expecting Jack. Rob was working away and I was lonely. Mum had been a right cow to me, telling me how I didn't have the patience or the maturity to make a decent mother. I had broken down at my antenatal check-up and my wonderful midwife said, "God won't make you carry more than you can bear." That's always stayed with me.

On my way to the meeting, I find myself at the 'spot.' I don't know how I've ended up here – I hadn't even planned to come this way. I slow down as I pass, realising that I can't even recount the journey I've made so far. I keep doing this – zoning out. It's dangerous really. If I can't recall my journey, I probably shouldn't be on the road. I guess that I'm just trying to hold everything inside my head.

More bunches of flowers have been added to Rob's roadside memorial. I have laid none, and don't feel inclined to. Not with everything that is coming to light. Somehow, I have to piece it together and try to reconcile everything with the husband I thought I knew. I don't have time to stop and inspect the flowers. If you don't get to the meeting on time, the door is closed. They're strict on that.

We only know each other by first names here. When I first started coming, I worried I may be recognised, or know someone else. That's why I joined a group in Ilkley, rather than Otley. Still, it's not exactly a million miles away. There are one or two people who look familiar, but I can't place them.

The heatwave has broken today, which I'm glad about. It was almost taunting me, the beautiful sunshine, clear blue sky and cheery people dressed in summery clothes. It's been too much at odds with my own darkness and my struggle to keep putting one foot in front of the other.

"Would you like a hug?" My sponsor approaches me as I make myself a drink. The familiar warmth pricks at my eyes again as I allow myself to be momentarily enveloped in the warmth of another human being. Lately, even Jack's not as cuddly as he normally is, seemingly preferring the company of his grandad. Somewhere in my psyche though, I'm aware he's detaching from me, perhaps because he fears losing me as well.

Nobody here seems to know anything about what's happened to me this week. I guess that even if they've heard the news, they won't make the connection with me as they'll have only heard Rob's name. They only know me as Fiona, a recovering alcoholic, not Fiona Matherson, wife, mother, daughter, and woman.

We all sit down, and the usual introductions pass around the circle. I want to scream out, *how can you all be so trivial? Do you want to know what's happening to me?* I've got a lid on my temper these days though, so I keep schtum. I used to lose it readily when I was in my twenties. I've lost count of how many jobs I walked out of, and how many arguments, to the point of brawling at times, that I got into when drunk. I'm relieved I'm not that person anymore.

We chant AA's cornerstone twelve steps, church-like. At each meeting, a member takes a turn to be the main sharer about an aspect of their recovery from alcoholism. We're not allowed to interrupt, but we can add comments or ask questions once they've finished speaking.

I sit through a rendition of the man's three instances of being banned for drink driving. He stopped drinking on the third occasion, after knocking down and killing a pedestrian. It really is close to the bone right now. He'd been three times over the limit and served nearly two years in prison. He's found God since being released, he says, and subsequently has to be reminded by this week's chairperson that Alcoholics Anonymous is not affiliated with any religion.

I look around the room. Everyone appears to be listening intently. My sponsor keeps looking at me. She's the only one in here who knows what's happened. There's a strong stench of feet combined with an overpowering deodorant smell. Cloth is draped over boxes of toys and musical instruments, and the AA's posters have been temporarily pinned up around the room. All is normal and familiar in here. Except it's not.

The man's voice drones on. He's had his driving licence returned this week and knows he will never lose it again. He's thankful for what the period of sobriety in prison, along with AA, has done for him. It's all about him. I want to shout, *what about your victim? What about their family?* I wonder if they, too, have been left with empty bank accounts, and secrets which are crawling out of the ashes of the person who died. I can't sit in here, I really can't. I push my chair back with a scrape and lurch towards the door.

"Fiona!" I hear my sponsor call as I slide into the car. "Come back."

My wheels screech as I reverse the Jeep, and again as I lurch forwards. I drive away from her then pull up in the road once I've got far enough away. I don't want to talk to anyone.

"Bastard!" I shout into the void of the car. "Bastard! Bastard! Bastard!" I thump the steering wheel in time to my shouting until my fists feel as though they might bleed. I don't know who is the *bastard*. Rob, the AA man, Bryony, Mum, James Turner, Phillip Bracken, or the bloody lot of them. "Bastard." I thump the wheel, less enthusiastically this time, and my body dissolves into tears. I cradle the steering wheel in my arms and let my head rest on it, sobbing so hard that my body shakes. "Bastard!" I howl into the silence.

"Are you alright?" I hear a muffled voice from the pavement and a tap on the passenger side window of the Jeep. Without looking at the man, I turn the key and quickly drive away, tyres screeching again.

* * *

I'm in the clear,
I'm sure of it.
I can breathe again.

134

Chapter 24

"Do you fancy a bit of company?" Christina pops her head through the open conservatory door, making me jump. "You should keep this locked when you're in on your own, you know. Anyone could sneak up on you."

"I'm not on my own. My dad's here. He's just got back from taking Jack to school."

"Was it your mum and dad that were shouting yesterday?" She sits beside me on the wicker sofa and places a hand on my arm. "I've been thinking about you, you know."

Her sympathy warms me. "They've been having a few problems. My mum's gone back home now though."

"That's all you need. Playing referee to your parents. I don't know how you're still standing."

"Neither do I. And you only know the half of it."

"Are you looking after yourself? Eating? Sleeping OK?"

Her concern brings tears to my eyes. "No, on both counts. But I'll be fine. I had a meltdown yesterday, but it probably did me good."

"I'm glad to hear it." She squeezes my arm on which her hand still rests. "You need to let it all out."

"I'm trying to. Everyone's been great around here. I've had bread and milk left on the doorstep, flowers, casseroles. I'm so glad to live amongst such good neighbours."

"Everyone keeps asking about you – and Jack, of course. People just want to help."

"I know, and I'm grateful. It's just there's so much - hang on, I'll be back in a moment." I rise as the doorbell echos through the house.

"I've got it," Dad calls from the hallway.

I sit back down, ears pricked up in readiness for the identity of the caller. Probably salespeople at this time of day.

Moments later DI Green and PC Robinson appear in the conservatory doorway, with Dad behind them. I glance sideways at Christina.

"OK Fiona. We need to ask you some more questions. Under caution, this time."

"What – what do you mean?"

Without responding, DI Green continues. "Fiona Matherson, we are arresting you on suspicion of causing death by dangerous driving. You do not have to say anything, but anything you do say may be given in evidence."

"Death by dangerous driving?" Dad echoes. "What are you on about? You should be out there, looking for the real culprit who did this. You're clutching at straws here."

I catch Christina's expression, a cross between shock and suspicion.

"We're going to take you down to the station," PC Robinson says. "We've got the car waiting."

"You can't do this. My daughter has done nothing wrong!" Dad steps towards us.

Christina stands and places her hand on Dad's arm as though trying to placate him.

"Don't worry love." There is panic in his voice. "I'll get a solicitor organised and pick Jack up later. You don't need to worry."

As we pass through the hallway, I grab my cardigan which is hung over the banister. Not that I'll need it in that sweaty hell-hole. I've had one shower already this morning, but I'll need another one after I've been in there. The filth of the place gets into the pores of your skin.

As I'm guided into the back of the police car, I worry about how long I'll be there. They've actually arrested me. What evidence they could have gained, I do not know. Thank God Dad is around to sort Jack out. DI Green sits alongside me, and PC Robinson gets into the driver's seat. I look back at the worried faces of Christina and Dad as they stand in the porch. Christina folds her arms and looks down at her feet as she notices me watching them. *Innocent until proven guilty,* I want to shout at her. *I thought you were my friend.*

It's a whole different scenario this time around. I'm not ushered into an interview room and offered a cup of tea. Instead, I'm treated like a criminal; swabbed, fingerprinted, photographed, and stripped of my jewellery. My engagement and wedding rings are slipped into a polythene bag. Two rings, so carefully chosen, so significant, so loved, now meaningless. Rob never got me an eternity ring, despite me dropping hints more than enough times.

I'm led to a cell to await the solicitor. Dad's hopefully sorting it. I ask the custody sergeant to double check before he locks me in.

There's a clunk of the lock, then the sergeant's footsteps die away from the door. I sink to the concrete slab topped with a skinny mattress and survey my surroundings. It's no wonder people kill themselves whilst incarcerated in these places – it's absolutely dire. I wrap my arms around my legs and curl into the foetal position, scrunching my eyes against the gloom of the cell.

My grandmother's face swims into my mind. I can't imagine what she would say if she could see me here. I was twenty-six when she died, still in the grip of my drink addiction, which I kept well hidden from her. She liked a sherry herself, so would welcome me joining her in one, without realising how much sherry I could get through when she wasn't looking.

Grandma, Dad, and Jack are the only people I've encountered in life who have genuinely loved me. Certainly not Mum. Friends have come and gone, most of them drunken acquaintances, and as for Rob. I would have added him to the list of people who loved me, until these last few days, with all that is coming to light.

"Fiona, we've had a call from the solicitor's office."

I hoist myself up in response to the voice. For a moment I wonder where I am. I must have fallen asleep. It's DI Green.

"Mr Wright has been held up in court." Her voice echoes around the concrete of the cell. "When he spoke to your father earlier, he had expected to be here by now. He thinks he'll be here in an hour, two at the most. He sends his apologies."

"Two hours. I can't sit in here that long."

"Well, you have the option of proceeding without him. It's your call."

I'm no expert on this, but am sure that now I'm under arrest, I shouldn't be answering questions without a solicitor to advise me. Not on a charge like this. But I can't face staying in this cell another minute. I can't imagin I could fall back to sleep.

Plus, I want to find out exactly why they've arrested me. I know from all the thrillers I read, that I can say *no comment* if I'm not sure how to answer. Especially if they're asking questions without proper evidence. That's what I'll do. It's all recorded as well, so if there's any later discrepancies, I'll have some protection. I need to get out of here.

* * *

They must have found who or what they are looking for.
Perhaps there's only me who knows for sure that
they are missing something.

Chapter 25

I feel woozy. I don't know if it's the heat in here, the stress I'm under, or because I've only just woken up.

"The date is Friday June 12th, and the time is 12:05 pm. My name is Detective Inspector Diane Green, and this is my colleague," she nods towards him.

"PC John Robinson."

"We are here to interview - can you state your full name, please?"

"Fiona Mary Matherson." My grandmother pops into my mind again. Mary was her name.

"Your address and date of birth, please?

"7 Orchard Mews, Otley, Leeds. 4th April 1985." They already know this. Why are they asking again?

"Fiona Matherson, you are being interviewed following your arrest in connection with the death of your husband, Robert Lee Matherson, who was killed in a suspected hit and run incident on Monday 8th June. You have had your rights read to you, but I will go through them again." She takes a deep breath. "We have arrested you on suspicion of causing death by dangerous driving. You do not have to say anything, but anything you do say will be given in evidence. Do you understand your rights, or do you need me to explain them to you?"

"I understand." *Just get on with it!* I want to scream at her. I don't feel a hundred percent. I try to remember if I've eaten anything today.

Half a slice of toast. No wonder I feel woozy. I only picked at the casserole last night as well.

"You have declined your right to legal representation. If you change your mind, we can pause the interview until representation is sought." She looks at me, as if double checking I've made the right decision. I know it's reckless to proceed without the solicitor, but I just want to go home.

"If the solicitor my father has arranged arrives whilst you're interviewing me, can we stop and allow him in?"

"Of course. But for now, can you confirm for the tape that you will allow the interview to begin without legal representation?"

"Yes."

"You have declined your right to have someone informed of your detention, and you have also declined your right to access a copy of the Police Code of Conduct. Is that correct?"

"Yes. My father knows where I am."

DI Green raises her gaze from her notebook to me. "We've arrested you in connection with the death of your husband, Robert. Do you understand the charge?"

"Of course I don't. I want to know why you've arrested me."

"We've received information that implicates you in the incident. Before I begin with my questioning, is there anything you'd like to tell me?"

"No, nothing." My heart is hammering. I'm sure if I looked down at my t-shirt, I could see my chest moving beneath it. What the hell is she going to ask me?

"Where were you between 9am and 12pm on Monday 8th June?"

"I've already told you. I was at home, doing the ironing."

"But as you've admitted yourself, no one can verify this."

"I was on my own, so no."

"We've had information from Hill End Garage in Ilkley, to say you presented your vehicle for repair at 11am on Monday 8th June. What have you got to say about that?"

"I know nothing about it. I was at home at 11am."

"What if I told you we have evidence of your presence there?"

"You can't have."

"For the benefit of the tape, I am now showing Fiona Matherson a receipt dated Monday 8th June, for the provision and fitting of a part-worn front nearside tyre."

"That's got nothing to do with me."

DI Green pushes the sheet closer to me. "Can you confirm whether this is your name, address and registration number Fiona?"

"Well, yes it is, but…"

"The garage operative who worked on your car told us of a blown-out tyre. He remembers wondering how you'd driven any distance on the wheel, to even get it to a garage."

"I don't know what he, or you, are talking about."

"Come on, Fiona." She glances down at her notes again. "He gave a description which bears a remarkable likeness to you."

"It wasn't me."

"It's a coincidence, don't you think, that your husband dies on Denton Road after being involved in a hit and run at ten thirty and your car turns up at a garage close by, for nearside repairs half an hour later."

"I keep telling you. It wasn't me. Put me in a line-up. They won't pick me out."

"We may well have to do that Fiona. But first I'd like to ask why you opted for a part-worn tyre? So that it wouldn't look too new and out of place when we had a look at your car as we did on the day of your husband's death?"

"No comment."

"You've been a person of interest to us all week Fiona. We understand from Bryony, is it?" She glances down at her page again. "That you've gone to her house, asking questions and behaving jealously about her relationship with your husband."

"I didn't know about any relationship, until *after* Rob had died, so that's rubbish too."

"Now that's not strictly true, is it? You caught them having a drink in a café together."

"No comment." I glance at PC Robinson, who's busy scribbling things down. I want to take his pen and ram it where the sun doesn't shine. I had thought they were on my side.

"Then there's the financial trouble you're involved in. You're in it up to your neck Fiona. So desperate that you even colluded with your husband to rip off his firm."

"I knew nothing about that."

"That's not what Mr Phillip Bracken believes. Or us. In fact, from our inspections of Robert's computer, it seems the two of you were pretty desperate to lay your hands on a large sum of money as quickly as possible."

"I've already told you about that." God, this is a nightmare. "Can I have some water, please?"

She buzzes through to request some, then slides two pages from a folder and places them gently, one by one, in front of me. One is the loan document, and the other is the re-mortgage agreement. "Is that your signature Fiona?"

"Yes, but he's forged it."

"Who has? Robert?"

"Yes. I found copies of these documents in his desk the other day. And I knew nothing about them. It was the first time I'd seen them. Nor did I know about him being suspended from work for fraud. I've only found out since he died."

"Unfortunately, that doesn't add up Fiona. Not when we sit it side by side with the recent text messages you've sent him. Thanks Sarge." She smiles at the man who brings in a jug of water and three plastic cups. She sets another piece of paper down in front of me. "For the benefit of the camera, I shall re-read them," she says.

Twelve days ago - 30th May. *So what about this money then?????*

And this one from 11th May, one month ago. *Have you paid it in yet? This could change our life.*

"You can't tell me you weren't colluding in your husband's financial dealings when you were sending text messages of this nature to him?"

"I've already admitted to giving him some of the money to invest. But that's where my involvement ends." I rub at my temples. My migraine is getting worse. Great.

"What do you have to say about the fact that the money embezzled from his employers was in your joint account?" She pours water into the cups, passes one to me and one to PC Robinson.

"I know absolutely nothing about it. And it's not there now."

"Do you know someone called James Turner?"

"I know a large sum of money, some of it mine, has been paid to him. I thought he was some sort of intermediary for the two share opportunities Rob told me about." Just talking about James Turner sets my teeth on edge. "But I've contacted him, and he says he knows nothing about it. In fact, he wouldn't even speak to me. He's the man you should look into."

"What did Rob tell you about these share opportunities?"

"All I can remember is that one so-called opportunity was to do with a Chinese company, a block chain thing. The other was a shopping centre that's opening in Harrogate. He told me that anything I put in would be multiplied tenfold. I've already told you this."

"Which explains why you'd want to lay your hands on as much money as possible."

"Why do you say *so-called opportunity* Fiona?"

"Because, as things stand, I do not know where all my money is. In fact, you've no idea how stressed out I am about it. It's James Turner you need to be questioning. Not me."

"We've been told you're a recovering alcoholic."

I see distaste swimming in her eyes. "What's *that* got to do with anything?"

"I imagine it's cost you a lot over the years. Eaten away at your inheritance. No wonder you wanted to get your hands on some easy money."

"Has Bryony told you about my past drink problem? Which by the way, is in the past." My voice is strong and steady, but inside, I want to weep. How much has Rob told his bloody ex about me? He's laid on a slab in a hospital mortuary, well by now, he might be at the chapel of rest, and he's managing from wherever he is, to take me down. *Why?* "I'm not saying anything else to you without a solicitor present."

"That's fair enough. That's about all we've got to ask. For now, anyway."

"So I can go then?" The tension in my shoulders sags as I contemplate getting out of this hellhole.

"Not just yet. I'm sorry." She doesn't look sorry at all. "We must return you to your cell whilst the Crown Prosecution Service decides whether formal charges will be brought against you."

"Charges for what?"

"Murder, or manslaughter. Causing death by dangerous driving, fraud, embezzlement. Quite a list for starters, don't you think?"

Sarcastic cow. I regret saying a single word to them without waiting for a solicitor to be present. I thought it would get me out quicker. I've can't go back in that cell.

They return me to a different cell, this time it's one that reeks of urine. I perch on the edge of the concrete slab. "It's disgusting that you're treating me like this," I shout at her. "You won't be getting away with it. This is a violation of human rights. Have you smelt it in here? You can't lock me in!"

She half smiles as she closes the door. It's like a bad dream. I'll be sick if I have to stay in here for long. I close my eyes and bring my t-shirt over my nose. Breathing deeply to calm down, I try to take myself out of where I am, if only just inside my mind. But the problems won't stop swirling. My head feels as though it is being squeezed in a vice. I can't cope.

I don't know how long I sit there, still as a rock, too numb to cry, too shocked to process what's happening. Eventually, there's a click as they release the door.

"You're free to leave Fiona," a different police officer says.

"Free?"

"We're releasing you on police bail." She's a young woman, petite and pretty, making me even more aware of my unkemptness.

"I'm not being charged?"

"Not yet. That doesn't mean you won't be though. Your case is pending enquiries. DI Green and PC Robinson have a few more people to talk to."

"Like who?"

"It's their case, so I'm not sure. I wouldn't be able to say, anyway. I shouldn't tell you this but I understand some analysis is due to be carried out on an old tyre that was taken into a garage. So once that comes back, they may want to speak to you again." She steps further into the cell. "Gosh, it doesn't smell too fresh in here, does it?"

"I've already complained. It's not fit for a dog."

"I'll make sure it gets sorted. Anyway, my advice to you would be to get yourself some legal representation. Like I said, you're on police bail and you're required to report back here a week from now."

"Why?"

"It's the condition that's been set. You'll be notified in the meantime if they lift bail, or alternatively, you could be rearrested."

I will not argue. I sign to accept the bail conditions and am beyond grateful to also have my phone returned to me.

* * *

The flattened grass has sprung back,
and they have removed the accident sign.
The only evidence that anything ever happened is
the pile of flowers
at his final resting place.

Chapter 26

I slide my purse from my bag. "A double gin and tonic, please." It's the middle of the afternoon and the town centre pub is already half full of daytime drinkers. There are a few people with food, but most are here to make the most of the happy hour prices. Happy hour lasts from three until six pm in here.

Over the last year, I've convinced myself that the smell of an alcoholic drink would repulse me. However, as I raise it to my lips, this isn't the case. The liquid seems to infiltrate my being, and it feels like coming home. A warmth spreads through me and I'm immediately calmer. Within a minute, the glass is empty.

"You look like you needed that." The young and exceptionally good-looking bar man smiles at me. "Can I get you another?"

"Well, with an offer of two-for-one measures, it would be rude not to." I smile back and slide my glass towards him. Though what I have got to smile about, who knows? I feel almost normal, whatever that is, since I came in here. "Make that two," I say. "I'm expecting my friend shortly." For a moment, I feel sad. I wish I was expecting a friend. I could certainly use one right now. Instead, I'm pretending one is on their way just so I can buy two doubles without looking like a complete alcoholic, as Mum so nicely calls me.

I enjoy the familiar sound of fizz as I empty the bottles of tonic water into each of the double gins over the ice. I've never been one for all these fancy fruity gins. Straight London gin, that's me. As I make my way over to a secluded table in the corner, the ice clinks against the glasses. I feel hazy after just one drink - it has been a year. I promise myself that I'll order some food soon. I'll be blotto if I don't.

Now that I've got my phone back, I should let Dad know that they've let me out of the police station. He would expect me to go straight back though. I can't face home right now. The walls are closing in on me. Dad would be heartbroken if he knew where I was. Besides, he'll be picking Jack up from school about now. I need some me time. I'll eat. And then I'll go home.

I make the next two drinks last longer. I've got plenty to mull over, although the effects of the gin quickly affect my ability to contemplate anything clearly.

I'm on bail for causing death by dangerous driving. As soon as I sober up, I'll get some proper advice. I shouldn't be in here, but I can't take any more crap this week. If this is the only escape on offer, I'm having it. Tomorrow's another day.

There's never any music in this pub, but I've always found it to be atmospheric. It's a pleasant building and everyone seems to be enjoying themselves, gearing up towards Friday night, and the weekend. I expect most of them will spend it continuing to drink.

Not me though. I'm better than that now. As I raise the glass to my lips, I know I'm not, really. I'm on my third double, and I might as well have another one when I finish this. What's that saying Grandma had, *you might as well get hung for a sheep as for a lamb?* The more I look around at the conversations and enjoyment occurring around me, the lonelier I feel.

I've got to find this James Turner. He's got our money – and he's ripping us off. I hope Rob had some proper paperwork drawn up for these investments. I wonder why the police aren't getting on to this man. My signature has been forged at least twice, and there's all that money that's gone missing from Bracken Furniture. The huge transfer has got his guilt written all over it. Why are they blaming me for everything?

I don't feel able to walk to the bar again but fumble around with my phone and download the app to receive table service. I order another two doubles, this time vodka and coke, and a plate of chips to soak it all up.

By the time I've drained the last of my gin, my order has arrived.

"Just one plate of chips?" the barman asks. "Doesn't your friend want some?"

"She's just popped out," I say. "She'll order some when she gets back."

"OK. Enjoy."

I pick at the chips. Drink has always stripped me of any desire to eat. And today, I'd rather drink. After the week I've had, I think even my AA sponsor would understand.

I recall DI Green asking me about being a recovering alcoholic. Bitch. And Bryony has evidently told her. Who the hell does she think she is? Clearly, she and Rob have had some in-depth conversations. She thinks she knows my husband better than I did. I bet she's been telling him to leave me, that he'd be better off with her. If I know Rob correctly, he'll have been having his cake and eating it. He's not been at work, and he's hardly been at home lately either. I can't imagine he would have found it easy to leave Jack, but he's so financially motivated that he would have got beyond any guilt soon enough.

Maybe once Rob had completely fleeced me of every penny I had, he'd have left, and started again with Bryony. She might even be in on it all too. I wouldn't put it past her.

As I take a huge swig of vodka, her face swims into my mind. That smug and knowing look on her perfect face. I imagine Rob being up close and personal with her and running his fingers through her perfect hair. Perfect figure, perfect clothes, perfect voice – I hate her.

And she's out to cause trouble. To make things worse than they already are. I bet she knows where I can find what's his name, James Turner. She knew Rob when he was at university – with James Turner. She knows something and I'm going to get it out of her. When I've drunk my vodka. My thoughts are tumbling over one another now. I might have another one.

I find myself on Bryony's street. The more I try to recall how I got here, the more muddled I feel. As I approach her gate, I'm surprised to find myself swigging from a near-empty bottle of wine that I don't even remember buying. I'm going to know about it tomorrow. I'm not even sure if I can remember the way home from here. I might have to ring Dad. I might just have enough phone battery left. I fumble around in my bag. No, I can't. He'll kill me. I'm best sneaking in later. Like I'm twelve or something. A couple walking arm-in-arm past me are staring. Smug bastards.

"Yeah?" I shout. "What the hell are you looking at?"

They laugh and I resist the urge to wipe the smiles off their faces. Twenty-two-year-old Fiona is back, with full awful temper. I let myself through the same gate as the other day and towards the patio door at the back of the house. I hammer on it with my fist, noticing lit candles inside. I imagine Rob turning up here, tapping on this back door to be let in. The shape of Bryony moves behind the blind, then she slides the patio door across.

"What the hell are you doing here?" Her hair is piled in a bun on top of her head. She's wearing skinny jeans, a flowing white blouse, and has nothing on her feet. "God, look at the bloody state of you."

"You!" I know I'm slurring, but I don't care. "I want a word."

"I've got nothing to say Fiona. I think you should go home."

"What have you been telling the police about me?" I point my finger at her.

150

"Just go home Fiona. I mean it."

"Get fucking out here and face me. Now." I don't normally swear that much but anybody would in these circumstances.

She steps through the patio doors towards me. "If you don't go now, I'll ring them."

"You'll be in no fit state to ring anyone by the time I've finished with you."

"Are you threatening me Fi…"

I grab her by the scruff of the neck and slam her against the wall, the force making her gasp. "I want to know what you know about James Turner."

"Get your bloody hands off me." She places her fingers over mine, bending them, probably trying to prise them from her neck. If I squeezed harder…

"Bloody hell. You reek. Have you peed yourself?"

I let her go. I stumble back as I raise the wine bottle to my lips. *I can't have done. I'm not that drunk. Am I?*

"God, you have. You're soaked. You dirty cow. You're so drunk you've lost control of yourself. No wonder Rob wanted out."

"What did you say?"

"You heard. He was here the day before he died."

Her words have a slightly sobering effect. She turns from me and steps away, that awful self-assured expression on her face.

In that split second, I drain the wine bottle then hurl it to the floor. "I don't care anymore if you were shagging my husband. But I do care about getting my money back. I want to know about James Turner." I grab the broken bottleneck from the floor and lunge towards her.

"Get away from me. Put that down. Help me someone. Help!"

I push her against the house wall, holding the broken bottle towards her. "I'm getting done for causing a death." I lift the glass closer to her neck. The edge is pressing into her skin. Just a little more pressure will pierce it. "I might as well add you to my list."

"Please, put the bottle down. I'm begging you Fiona."

"Then you'll tell me what you know?"

Footsteps hammer behind me. I'm being dragged backwards and downwards. Suddenly, I've got several pairs of hands holding me to the ground.

"Get your fucking hands off me." I writhe to get free, but they're too strong.

"The police are on their way," a male voice says. "Are you OK Bryony? We heard what was going on over the fence."

"Yes." Bryony's hands press around her neck. "She didn't cut my throat like she was threatening to. Thank God you came when you did."

"Who is she?" One man releases his hold slightly and looks at me with disgust in his face, before averting his gaze towards Bryony. More people have appeared in the garden. All fight has drained from me. I'm shaking on the ground and feel nauseous.

"She's nobody."

"So this nobody has just appeared in your garden and threatened you with a bottle? Why?"

"She's married to that man who died in the hit and run on Monday. The one on Denton Road. She did it to him. And because she thinks I was carrying on with him, she's here to do me in as well."

"Get off me!" I try to sit up. My mouth is watering. My stomach lurches and bile burns the back of my throat. As I gurgle on the floor, the men let go of me. I hoist myself up and puke all over the grass.

"Dirty bitch," one of them sneers.

"She's pissed herself as well." Bryony's voice this time.

"Just you wait." When I've done retching, I look at her. "I'll be back, and next time…"

My voice is drowned by an approaching siren. "In here," someone

152

shouts as van doors bang and heavy boots thud up the drive. "I don't think you'll have much trouble taking her in. She's in a right state."

"Blimey. You don't smell too good," one officer says as he pulls me to my feet. I'm made to face the shed as they snap handcuffs on me.

* * *

I've never known nights to be as long.
Turning thoughts over and over.
Sometimes I regret what happened that morning.
But I can't change anything now.

Chapter 27

I wake to the sound of banging doors and raised voices. I lift myself from the thin mattress and attempt to open my eyes.

The barren room swirls around me and I lean over the side of the bed, if I can call it that, to be sick into a metal bin which has been left there. I've spent all night in a stupor, periodically waking and retching. I lay back on the mattress, tears leaking from my eyes and down the side of my head. How could I have been so stupid?

Not only have I got myself wasted after an entire year of abstinence, I've allowed the cocktail of drink to turn me into a violent thug. I used to get into fights when I was younger, if anyone challenged me whilst I was drunk, but this... I've never threatened anyone with a bottle.

Rob is dead. I'm on bail for causing his death, and all my money has gone. I think of Jack and Dad and wonder if he's been told anything. Of course he'll know. He would have phoned the station by now to see where I am. Why didn't I just go home when they let me out?

I lean over again and retch once more. Nothing is coming up now. My throat burns and my head feels as though someone is hammering at it from the inside. I don't think I've ever felt so ill. I've certainly never been as low as this.

I hope more sleep will permit some further escape, but closing my eyes makes things spin even more. I need some water. I haul myself to my feet and bang on the door.

There's a beaker of water, a cup of something masquerading as tea, and some limp toast waiting for me on the table of the interview room when I'm called in.

"I must warn you," I say to the policeman. "I've been throwing up all night. If this," I point to the toast, "doesn't stay down, is there a loo nearby I can get to quickly?"

He points at a bin. Charming.

"Look. I know I've done wrong, but you don't need to treat me like an animal."

"Let's just get on with this, shall we?" He nods towards another man who enters the room. "I'm going to start the recording." He waits for the beep. "I'm DI Thornton and this is my colleague..."

"DI Langton." The other officer sits down and pulls a cap from the top of his pen.

"And we are here to interview..."

"Fiona Mary Matherson."

"Could we have your date of birth and address, please?"

Here we go again. "7 Orchard Mews, Otley, Leeds. Date of birth 4th April 1985."

"Thank you. Well, we would have preferred DI Green and PC Robinson to have interviewed you, as they've been dealing with you up to now, but they're both on a day off."

Lucky them. I fold my arms and look at them both. God knows what they must make of me, stinking of urine and vomit, having done what I've done last night. I would give anything to turn the clock back to yesterday, and certainly to a few days ago. How I would make sure things were different.

DI Thornton runs his finger down a page in front of him. "We've been brought up to speed with your ongoing investigation, and though I'm sure it is relevant to the current allegations against you, we're here now just to question you in relation to the allegation of aggravated assault against Bryony Rose." He looks at me again.

I nod.

"You do not have to say anything when questioned, but anything you do say may be given in evidence. Do you understand?"

I should do by now. I'll be saying the police rights in my sleep. "Yes."

"You've declined the right to legal representation, despite being advised to the contrary. Is that correct?"

"Yes." I'm not risking slowing things down again like yesterday. Besides, what can a solicitor do for me today? It's cut and dried. Bryony's neighbours heard what was happening. There's nothing I can do to get out of it. They won't send me to prison. Surely they know I've got a son to look after?

Then, as if reading my mind, he says. "You've got a son, haven't you?"

"Yes."

"We've had a call from your father this morning. He knows you're here."

He'll be so disappointed in me. But I can't even contemplate that right now. "Do you know whether my son is alright?"

"He never mentioned that. But I'm sure he will be. The sooner we get this done, the sooner you can get back to him."

"I'm going to get bail?"

"Not necessarily. Let's just see how the interview pans out."

I want to tell him to hurry. I take a huge gulp of my water. I really don't want to be sick in front of these two police officers. I smell bad enough as it is.

"You were arrested at an address in Otley, the residence of Bryony Rose, at 6:20pm yesterday evening, for aggravated assault. What have you got to say about it?"

"I was really drunk." I look down at my hands, which are trembling. "Usually I go to Alcoholics Anonymous, but my husband has died this week. Then I find out that he's been seeing Bryony. I've also found out that he's lost all our money and been lying to me about everything. I lost control. I couldn't take anymore."

"You're saying that gave you a reason to go to her house, push her about and threaten her with a broken bottle?"

"Of course not. I barely remember doing it. I hadn't eaten much, and I'd been drinking gin, vodka and wine after a year of not drinking at all."

"I'm afraid that being drunk and out of control will not stand up as a defence in court."

"I know. I can't stand the woman, but I had no right to do that to her. I would never normally behave so dreadfully. I'm really sorry."

"Well, your remorse is noted and might have a slight impact in terms of how you are viewed. Miss Rose is very shaken, but otherwise OK. We've already been in contact with the Crown Prosecution Service, which has authorised us to charge you with aggravated assault."

"So what now?"

"It's up to them whether you are granted bail. I have to say though, that because you're already under investigation for causing death by dangerous driving, I think it's unlikely."

"But I haven't been charged with anything there."

He and his colleague look at each other. "Let's just see what they say."

"Please." Tears leak from my eyes. "I need to get back to my son. I didn't kill my husband. I was at home that morning. I loved my husband. I need help to find someone called James Turner." I realise I'm gabbling, but they seem to be listening. They wait in silence as I take a gulp of water. "He's the man you should speak to. He knows something. It's all being pinned on me, and they've got it wrong. I'm a victim here too. This man has got all my money and I feel sure that he was involved in my husband's death."

"Let's just allow the investigation to be carried out. I promise you that every relevant lead will be thoroughly investigated. DI Green is an experienced detective. If we charge you, then you'll have every opportunity to build a defence and will get a fair hearing."

"I have to say, though," says the other one. "You've done yourself no favours with what you did last night."

"I know."

* * *

I've always recognised the anger and vengeance
that exists inside me.
I knew one day there was a risk I might act on it.

Chapter 28

I hurry along my street, hoping none of the neighbours are watching. They've all rallied around since Rob died – I'll be so embarrassed if I'm seen. I've never looked, felt, or indeed smelt worse.

They gave me police bail. I've to return later with my passport and report to the station each week until my court appearance. I've got to sleep at home every night, though it's not like I'm going anywhere else anyway. I've not to contact Bryony directly, or indirectly.

"Mummy! Where have you been?" Jack pokes his head around the lounge door as I step into the hallway.

"Just let me have a shower, honey, then I'll come and see you."

Dad emerges from the kitchen, disappointment all over his face.

"I'm sorry Dad."

He shakes his head. "I don't know what to say to you. Get yourself cleaned up. Then we'll talk." The look on his face is far worse than anything he could say to me.

"Did anyone let you know where I was?"

"Yes. Go in there, Jack. Grandad will be there in a minute." When Jack has gone, he looks me up and down with an expression that makes me want to shrink down to nothing. "Thank God I was here, to look after your son, that's all I can say. What would have happened to him otherwise?"

"I'll be down shortly." Fighting back tears, I take to the stairs, desperate to get away from Dad's scrutiny.

A shower makes me feel more human and at least I don't stink anymore. The clothes I was wearing can go in the bin. I never want to see them again. Reaching into the bedside cabinet, I swallow a migraine tablet, followed by an anti-emetic. Whilst being a non-drinker, I haven't needed either of these. But today, I feel lousy, with no one to blame but myself. I fill a pint glass with water in the en-suite and down it, feeling slightly better straight away. I must have been dehydrated.

Even though it's a warm June day, I feel cold, so pull on clean jeans and a jumper. I slide a pair of Rob's socks over my feet and head downstairs to face Dad.

He's clattering about in the kitchen and the strains of *Phineas and Ferb,* which Jack is hooked on, echo from the lounge. Dad glances over his glasses at me, as I sit at the breakfast bar and pluck an apple from the bowl.

"Tea?" he says. He can't be that mad if he's offering me a brew.

"Please." The tablets I've taken are starting to have an effect, thank God. I can say, hand on heart, that I'd rather die than touch an alcoholic drink at this moment. I'm going to ask the doctor for some Antabuse tablets to ensure I keep completely away from it. For good.

"So why, Fiona? Aren't things bad enough?"

"I was drunk. I'd had enough of everything. I couldn't cope anymore."

"I get that. I really do. But to get so drunk that you have pushed and threatened another woman. *My daughter* doesn't normally carry on like that. Why didn't you come and talk to me?"

"Please Dad. Stop going on at me. You don't know how much I regret it."

"I don't understand why you would lose it like that. Who is this woman anyway?"

"Bryony. Don't you remember the police mentioned her the other day. It looks like Rob had been having an affair with her."

"I really don't think he would have done that to you. Or Jack."

"I know you got on with him Dad, but you don't know the half of it. I think they've been putting their heads together to take all my money. It's gone Dad, *all of it.* Everything that Grandma left me. After I've paid for the funeral, there'll be nothing left."

"What are you talking about? *Nothing left?*"

"The bank accounts have been emptied. Before Rob died. Plus, he's forged my signature to re-mortgage the house and taken a loan out. That's all gone as well."

"On top of the fraud thing that's come out with his work?" Dad's expression changes to one of concern. "Bloody hell. There's a hundred grand there, isn't there?"

"And the rest."

"We'll come back to the money stuff love. What I want to know is, how did you think that getting drunk was going to help you?" He turns his back to me to butter some bread. "Why didn't you come to me?"

"I wasn't thinking *anything.* I didn't plan to get drunk. I just wanted to take the edge off the stress. Like I said, I wasn't coping."

"Yes. I can see that. But you still haven't answered my question. Why didn't you come to me?"

"I just wanted to be on my own after I got bailed yesterday. And I got myself wound up. I was in that much of a state, I don't even remember getting from the pub to where Bryony lives. You'd have killed me if I'd turned up here like that." I stare at the photograph of Rob, Jack and me, pinned to the fridge. A fresh wave of misery washes over me. "Especially in front of Jack. Besides, you've got enough on with Mum right now."

"Let me be the judge of that. I would've done anything to stop you hitting the self-destruct button yesterday." He looks around at me.

"Look Dad. I know you mean well, but what's done, is done. They've charged me with aggravated assault. There's nothing you can do to change anything." Tears jab at my eyes. I can't bear how he looks at me. It's a cross between pity and shame.

"Here. Get that down you." He lifts a sandwich onto a plate and slides it towards me. "You look bloody awful."

"I feel it. My head's banging, even though I've had a migraine tablet." I squint against the sun that's streaming into the kitchen. One reason we fell for this house was because of the sunny kitchen. That feels like another life now.

"Get that eaten, then have a lie down." Dad nudges the plate closer to me. "We'll talk more about this when you get up."

"What about Jack?" Guilt seeps into me. "I've not seen him properly since Thursday."

"What are grandads for? Anyway, it's hardly been a normal set of circumstances these last few days, has it?" He reaches across the breakfast bar and pats my hand. "The time will come when you'll be able to make it up to him."

"Why are you being nice to me?" Fresh tears spring to my eyes. They're part grief, part self-pity. "I don't deserve it."

"No matter what happens, or what you've done, you'll always be my daughter. Somehow, we'll get through this." He sits on the stool opposite me, and pauses for a moment, as though gathering his thoughts. "I'm not sure how your mother will react when she hears of your latest escapade though."

Over a year ago, I got drunk and let rip at Mum, big time. In front of all her neighbours. She warned she would disown me if I behaved like that again. "Why does Mum have to know anything? You won't tell her, will you?"

"She'll find out soon enough." A darkness crosses his face. "You'll be in court soon, for God's sake. They've charged you, haven't they?"

"Yes, but what..."

"Just go to bed Fiona."

His abrupt tone stuns me. It's as though the thought of Mum has changed his mood. No way can I face Jack in this state, even though I should acknowledge him. No, I'll go upstairs, pull myself together, then spend some time with him. It's really like I'm ten again, being sent to bed by my father. And it has a while since he has used the word *escapades* to describe my behaviour. I can't remember how long it's been since I've received threats of *wait until your mother finds out*, either.

The bedroom is cool and inviting, the curtains still drawn. As I crawl under the duvet, I make a mental note to change the sheets later. The bed still smells of Rob's shower gel and aftershave. Part of me wants to nuzzle into it, the other part feels like ripping the sheets to shreds.

I wake up feeling groggy. I always feel rubbish when I sleep in the daytime. A reminder of current events steamrolls over me. I got rip-roaring drunk last night. After a year of sobriety, I went and got blasted. I hate myself and deserve to feel like I do. At least the feeling that I'm going to throw up has gone. So has the migraine. I just feel hollowed out. And so ashamed.

The house is in silence. Either Dad and Jack are asleep, or they've gone out. Probably the latter. There's only so long a seven-year-old can be cooped up inside. Especially Jack. He'll need to let off some steam.

I slide the Apple Mac from the bedside table, and balance it on my stomach. The police missed taking this to examine. It's mine, mainly, though Rob was always after it. He'd tell me I had no need for a laptop of this quality, as all I did with it was *mooch about on the internet.* He ended up using it a lot of the time.

I log into my personal bank account. £4529. That won't get me far. Not with a funeral to pay out of it. I need to find Rob's will. Hopefully, he'll have kept up his life insurance payments. There will be something. I feel slightly more optimistic at this thought. However, guilt and depression soon chase the positivity away and I'm swiftly reminded that he's dead, and it's me who's suspected of killing him.

Dad was right. There was more than enough to deal with, without me getting wrecked and turning up at Bryony's last night. Maybe if I apologise, she'll drop the charges. There was no real harm done. It's not as though I whacked her over the head with the bottle, or slit her throat, however much I felt like it. In hindsight, I'm not sure what stopped me. My temper had totally gone. A younger me might be on a murder charge.

An ad flashes on my screen for an unsecured loan. I swear there's computer intelligence that's somehow sniffed out my desperation for money. It's not like we're going to starve, but I'm not used to living this near the knuckle. Not anymore.

I click on the ad. It's only seven and a half percent APR. I'll go for ten grand. At least the funeral costs won't completely wipe me out then, and I'll have breathing space until I get hold of my money from James Turner. I go through the application process, pausing at the status section. Eventually, I select widowed. There's nothing I can enter for employment as it's years since I last worked. I haven't needed to. It dawns on me I might have to address that. Perhaps that's what I need. But it's a decision for when all this is over with.

I hit submit. Within two minutes, I've received an email notification from the loan company. *Thank you for your recent application. We're sorry to inform you...*

Shit. As if they've knocked me back. Rob's dodgy dealings must have affected my credit rating too - by financial association. Or maybe I should have chosen *married* and put Rob's former income down. But that's fraud. It puts me in the same league as him. Another email drops into my inbox. Like I said, they can smell desperation. *Apply for a credit card today. Pre-application check.* I might as well look at that. I've not had a credit card since my twenties, so I'm bound to get accepted. I type in the information, then quick as a flash I receive an acceptance and an invitation to complete the whole thing. They'll only give me an initial credit limit of £1200 though. Shit. Shit. Shit. That's not going to scratch the surface.

Lying back on my pillows, I turn it all around in my mind. However, I'm struggling to think clearly. If I don't find out what Rob did with my money, then I'm done for. James Turner is the one I need to find. The situation I've found myself in is unbelievable. I was having more fun as a twenty-something lush. The bang of the front door jolts me out of my miserable thoughts.

I swing my legs over the side of the bed and rake a brush through my hair. I'm sweating, a combination of alcohol withdrawal and having slept in my jeans and jumper, so I change into denim shorts and a floral t-shirt. That, in itself, makes me feel better. As I descend the stairs, Jack's sat on the bottom step, untying his shoes.

"Why didn't you come to the park with us Mummy? We've fed the ducks, had an ice-cream, and everything."

"It sounds as though you've had a lovely time, you and Grandad. I'll come next time." And I will. I've been a pile of crap as a mother this week. I just can't get it together.

He drops one trainer and looks down. "We kind of had a lovely time.

But I can't have a properly lovely time anymore. Not now that Daddy's in heaven. I feel sad all the time. I want to play trains with him."

"I know." I step towards him and ruffle the top of his head, making a promise to myself in that instant that I'm going to fight, tooth and nail to make him happy again. Apart from Dad, because Mum can't really be included, I'm all Jack's got. I've got to make sure I get our money back, get free of these police charges, and hang onto the house – even if it's by the skin of my teeth. "I'm going to have a word with Grandad, then I'll come and play a game with you."

He brightens slightly. "Promise?"

"Pinky promise." I wiggle my little finger.

"OK. While I'm waiting, I'll draw a picture for you." He walks towards the lounge.

He's such a good kid. What I ever did to deserve him, I don't know. With the all-too-familiar tears stabbing at the backs of my eyes again, I head off to find Dad.

He's coming through the conservatory with the kitchen bin. The expression he wore before I went to bed is still etched across his face as he notices me.

"I know you're not happy Dad, but I promise, I'm going to sort myself out. Starting with getting some tablets to make sure I can't drink. Antabuse, they're called."

"Never heard of them." He lowers the bin to the floor and sinks onto one of the wicker chairs.

"If I'm on Antabuse tablets and go anywhere near even a drop of alcohol, it will make me violently sick." I sit on the sofa opposite him. "People at AA have tried them so I know they work."

"Right. Well, if you think they'll help you."

"Look, I've had a blowout. And now I need to focus Dad. I've so much to sort out." I look at him, relieved that the sharpness in his face has softened. "I've just been knocked back for a loan and only approved for a £1200 limit on a credit card. I don't know how I'm going to pay for Rob's funeral."

"Did he not leave provision for it? When I depart this mortal coil, there's a funeral plan to cover it."

"I don't think so. He was too busy fleecing me to be bothered about any sort of provision. Besides, I don't suppose he was expecting to die just yet."

Dad sits back in his seat and moves the bin to one side with his foot. "If he was having some sort of relationship with this Bryony one, and if he has manipulated funds by forging your signature, then I don't see why the responsibility of his funeral should fall solely to you."

"Well, who else is going to be responsible? People are hardly lining up. Rob was an only child and his parents are dead. He might have done me over, but I'm still his next of kin. And the mother of his son."

"I get all that. And I also get the impression that you're asking me for help?"

"I don't know. Maybe. I just don't know what to do Dad." God, the bin reeks. I pick it up and put it outside the conservatory door. My sense of smell is always heightened after a migraine.

"I, erm, it's your mother… She's got hold of the purse strings, as you know, and I'm not sure what's happening with me and her yet."

"I know." I also know Mum's as tight as a duck's bum, and in all honesty, I don't want her knowing anything about my financial situation. She'll use it as another stick to beat me with.

"How come you've been knocked back for a loan? You won't have any bad credit, will you?"

"Probably because I don't work. I don't know. But I definitely need to find out if there's anything else that Rob's been financially implicating me in."

"Are you absolutely sure you've known nothing about it."

"I hate that you don't trust me Dad."

"I do. It's just... what does your solicitor say?"

"He never came the other day. He was held up at court. He left a message with the officers who interviewed me."

"You never said. Why on earth didn't you wait for him?" He leans towards me. "You were being questioned for causing death by dangerous driving, and you let them interview you without a solicitor. Are you mad?"

"I think he's been trying to ring me" I can't argue with Dad. " I just wanted to get out of there. You should see the inside of those places."

"Surely you got in touch for help with the assault charge? Don't tell me you faced that one on your own as well?"

"I felt too ashamed Dad. Besides, there's no solicitor that can get me out of that one, is there?"

"Oh, Fiona."

"Look, I'll give him a ring now." I walk into the dining room, where I've left my phone, scroll to the messages he's left, and hit call as I walk back into the conservatory.

"Well, thank God for that."

"It's Fiona Matherson," I say. "Is that Alan Wright?"

"Ah, I'm glad you've got back to me Fiona. I had DI Green on the phone a short time ago, wanting to make an appointment for us all to meet at the station." His voice is warm. Trustworthy. "She wants to go through the allegation of *causing death by dangerous driving* in more depth. The sooner we find out what we're dealing with, the better."

"They're saying I took my car in for a tyre repair after my husband was killed. But I didn't. I was at home."

"Right OK. Because I didn't get to your initial interview, they've agreed to provide a space where we can go through the allegation before they interview you again. They're suggesting tomorrow?"

"But it's Sunday tomorrow."

"Like I said, the sooner the better. We must go through some paperwork as well. Formalise the fact that I'm acting for you."

I raise a hand to my aching head. "Have you been told about the other charge yet?"

"Yes. DI Green mentioned it. We can talk more about that tomorrow as well. They can see us any time until two o'clock. Does eleven am sound OK?"

"Just a second." I lower the phone. "Dad. I've got to go back to the police station in the morning and meet the solicitor. Are you still going to be here? Will you look after Jack?"

He nods.

"I'll see you there." Dread pools in the pit of my stomach at the thought of another police interview. "I must go. I've got another call coming through."

"Great. It's the funeral director," I say to Dad, closing my eyes as I raise the phone back to my ear. "What a fun-filled few days it's been. Hello?"

"Mrs Matherson. We're just ringing to rearrange yesterday's appointment. We were expecting you at 4pm?"

I won't tell them I was too busy getting slaughtered, before going off to threaten Rob's ex, or whatever relationship he and Bryony classed themselves as having. Instead, I apologise and make an appointment to go in on Monday morning, after I've taken Jack to school, assuming the police let me go again tomorrow. At least I've got a solicitor this time.

It's probably best to send Dad back to Mum after I've been to the station. Whether she'll agree to helping with the funeral fees, I don't know. As if I am having to go cap in hand. Hopefully, Mum won't come back here before the funeral. I really can't cope with her.

She must be telepathic. As I hang up from the funeral director, Dad's phone rings. It's obvious from his face that it's her. I can read Dad like a book. "Don't tell her anything yet," I hiss, walking to the kitchen door. Not wanting to overhear their conversation, I distract myself from my hangover and other woes, by keeping my promise of playing a game with Jack.

* * *

As he awaits his funeral,
accusations continue to fly
Speculation is rife.
Who knows what really happened?
I do.

Chapter 29

J ack's voice rings through the house. "Mu-um! Simone and her mum are here." I sit up in bed, surprised that I've slept the entire night without waking and glance at the clock. It's nine o'clock so I should be grateful that they've woken me as my appointment at the police station is in two hours.

Though what Rob's ex-wife is doing here, first thing on a Sunday morning is anyone's guess, and I could do without it. I can't find a belt for my skinny jeans, so slide a long cotton top from its hanger. It will hopefully stop the gaping waistband from being visible. The weight is tumbling from me. I managed to eat a little of the stir-fry Dad cooked last night – his signature dish, but even now, the after-effects of Friday's binge haven't left me. It feels like I poisoned myself.

Before I have to deal with Denise, I should try to be more groomed, but can't be bothered. Who cares what she thinks of me, anyway? I pass the spare room. Dad's having a shower in the en-suite. I head down the stairs to where Denise waits at the bottom. Her expression is one of utter revulsion.

"I still can't believe you ended up living in a house like this. Whilst we got what we did."

"What! Oh, I'm not getting into this with you Denise." I stand in front of her. "Where are the kids?"

"Jack's taken Simone into the lounge to draw."

I hate the thought of them spending time together, but it's probably for the best that they're not around to overhear any discussion we're about to have. No conversation between Denise and me has ever been over friendly.

"I'm here about Rob's will and life insurance." Denise's eyes are cold, her voice accusatory. In contrast with me, she's piled weight on lately. She must be a comfort eater when the going gets tough.

"At nine o'clock on a Sunday morning. You're kidding?" I fold my arms.

"I've had no money out of him for months. You owe me." She points at me.

If anything is guaranteed to make my heckles rise, it's someone pointing at me. "I owe you absolutely nothing Denise. Your daughter is not my responsibility." I resist the urge to add *thank God.*

I took a step back from Simone a couple of years ago, after becoming exhausted from trying to get on with her. I got sick of her whining possessiveness of Rob whenever we were all together. She wouldn't even allow him to sit with me. It became easier to leave them to it. I guess we didn't stand a chance as stepmother and stepdaughter, not with her mother dripping poison into every orifice.

"She's your *husband's* responsibility though." She spits the word *husband* out, like a piece of gristle. "And I don't care if you have to put your posh house on the market. As long as my daughter gets what she's entitled to."

"You've always hated me, haven't you? As if you've turned up like this. Rob's not even cold on the slab yet." I'm going to have to make her leave. I've no control over my temper right now. I'll end up thumping her and to assault someone else less than two hours before I'm due at the police station, wouldn't be a wise move.

"I want what my daughter is owed Fiona." Her usually ruddy face is pinched white. "It's disgraceful how you and that selfish sod of an ex of mine have treated us. You will not get away with it, you know."

"I'd like you to leave. Now." I turn towards the closed lounge door where I can hear Simone and Jack laughing together. They get on well – it's me she doesn't get on with. "Simone - your mum's leaving. Come on, please. Now."

"What about our money? I mean it. I'm not letting this go."

Every line and crease is visible on her face. She's only a few years older than me, but looks more late than early forties. Time has not been kind to her. "When I find Rob's will and life insurance, if either of them even *exist*, I'll let you know if *she's* entitled to anything. But let me get past the funeral first if you don't mind."

She points at the lounge door this time. "*She* has got a name. And I want to know about the money now, not after the funeral."

"Tough." I reach past her and open the door. I need to get ready for this police interview. I want her gone.

She steps towards me. "You stole my life you know. This," she sweeps her arm in a circular motion as her eyes scan the hallway. "This should have all been ours."

"Out. Now."

Simone emerges from the lounge. She looks just like Rob. Long, wiry limbs, pointed features and the same slant to her eyes. I can't bear to look at her.

"Why do we have to go Mum? I want to see Jack. He's my brother."

"Half-brother." The words leave me before I plan to say them.

"You're such a bitch," Denise snaps.

"I hate you," Simone says as she passes me. "You should be dead, not my dad."

"Simone, get in the car. She's not worth getting upset with." She points her key fob towards the door. Her car is parked across my driveway. I watch as Simone stamps through the open door towards it and notice there is no nearside wing mirror. It's been snapped off.

173

Not only that, there's some considerable damage around the headlight. It's dented right in.

"Before you go Denise, I want to know why you were sending texts to my husband on the day he died?"

"Who do you think you are, the Gestapo?" She laughs and folds her arms. I once read about body language. Folding arms is defensive. "I was texting him because he wasn't fulfilling his obligations as a father."

"Did you see him on Monday morning?"

"I don't answer to you. I've already given a statement to the police."

"So what happened to your car?"

Her gaze follows mine. "I had a bump." Her tone suddenly softens. "A while ago. I haven't been able to afford to get it fixed. It's hard, you know, bringing a child up on your own." A smirk crosses her face. "You're about to find that out for yourself."

"Just get lost, will you? And don't turn up like this, at my home again."

"I've got every right…"

"Look, I've got to get ready to go out. I'll be in touch when I've got something to tell you. *After* my husband's funeral."

I don't catch her reply as I turn away. I don't want to hear any more. Shit – I need to get a photo of her car before she drives off. I shoot upstairs to find my phone. By the time I've found it and got to the window, she's already gone. I'll certainly mention the damage when I go into the station. If that doesn't take the focus off me, nothing will.

* * *

Everyone harbours a darkness of some sort within them.
Some can suppress it.
I couldn't.

Chapter 30

The solicitor, not dissimilar in looks to my dad, stands from behind the desk and shakes my hand. "Fiona Matherson? I'm Alan Wright. It's nice to meet you."

I'm not going to return the sentiment as to meet a solicitor, in this sort of situation, is far from *nice*. I'm back in this wretched interview room for the fourth time in less than a week.

"Have a seat." He gestures to a chair as though it's his office or something. "DI Green would like us to get started within the hour, but we've got plenty of time to discuss everything."

"Has she told you anything else? About their evidence, I mean?"

"We need to get this paperwork signed first. In order that I can act for you. Without that, I get told very little." He slides a sheet of paper towards me.

"How will I pay for your services?"

He peers at me, as though silently assessing my socio-economic status. "Because this is a criminal matter, my costs can be partially covered on a sliding scale, depending on your income, by Legal Aid."

I shrivel under his gaze, knowing how unkempt I am right now.

"Do you feel as though you may qualify for Legal Aid?"

I laugh, though it's an empty sound. "Since my husband seems to have squandered all our savings somewhere, yes I think I might."

He slides another form towards me. "This can be completed at home, as facts and figures will be required. Try to get it back to me the next time I see you."

I sign the first form, which he slips into his briefcase, and folds the other one into quarters. I notice again that my solicitor looks like Dad, apart from the beard. I feel it will help me to trust him. "It was my Dad who organised you to act for me. Do you know him?"

"Not on a personal level. He's done some work at my house though. A pleasant man, as I remember. Anyway, we must get on with this. The clock's ticking." He glances at his watch whilst I consider he's probably being paid a tenner a minute." We'll start with the clear cut part," he says. "The aggravated assault. You've been bailed for this." He says aggravated assault like it's an item on a shopping list.

I can't meet his eyes. "Yes. I got drunk. I don't normally drink. Not anymore. And I got myself into a situation with my husband's ex. They'd been seeing each other again. Plus, I think she knows something about my money which has gone missing."

"We'll come back to the money side of things in a moment." He clasps his hands together on the table. "Bryony Rose wants to proceed with pressing charges. So that charge will probably end up in court. Were there any witnesses?"

"Some of her neighbours overheard us arguing and pulled me off her." I'm surprised I remember that moment so clearly, the mess I was in.

"That's pretty straightforward then. But from the little I know of the situation from your father, the strain you've been under may go in your favour. We can argue diminished responsibility. However, the court will take a dim view of you visiting her house."

"I know."

"What happened whilst you were there?"

"We argued. I pushed her into a wall. Then I smashed a bottle and threatened her with it." I stare at the graffiti-etched table. *Let me out*

176

is scratched into where my hands rest. I'm glad it's not as hot in here as it was last week. Nor do I feel as sick. I ate some fruit on my drive over. I've got to start looking after myself.

"How did you threaten her with it?"

"I held it towards her throat." I keep my gaze cast down and lower my voice. This isn't one of my finer moments. "What will I get?"

"I take it you'll plead guilty? Especially with there being witnesses?"

"I can't really do anything else, can I?"

He shakes his head. "Have you been in trouble before?"

"A bit of scrapping when I was young. I was drunk then too. I've had a problem with it. Drink, I mean."

He writes something on his notepad. "A lot will depend on the magistrate when we get to court. I think it will be sent to magistrates. However, if you end up having to account for the other charges, we could be looking at Crown."

The enormity of what I'm facing creeps over me like a fever. *Crown court.* The promises I made to myself that I'm going to be the best mother possible for Jack, and put what I can right, have turned to dust. "Will I get sent to prison?" My voice is smaller now. It's the first time I've seriously contemplated it, since getting arrested two days ago.

"You could. However, if it's the assault charge, and you show remorse, which you evidently feel, they'll be more lenient with you."

"I'm thinking of starting Antabuse tablets to combat the drink addiction, once and for all. AA hasn't worked."

"That will go in your favour." He writes something again. "The best-case scenario will be a suspended sentence. They might make alcohol rehabilitation part of the conditions. There could be some victim awareness and community service as well."

"It's better than going to prison. Now that my husband's dead, I'm a single mum."

"I know, and that too will be in your favour. Like I mentioned, I took some information from your dad when I spoke to him the other day." He slaps his pen on top of his notepad. "Right, that's that. They probably won't say too much about the assault today. You've already been interviewed and charged. Though, you should have been in touch with me to attend that interview with you."

"I know." We both glance towards the door of the interview room in response to an altercation going on in the custody suite.

"Get the fuck off me, you fucking pervert," a male voice yells. There's a load of banging and further raised voices. I glance around the putrid green walls and once again, long to turn the clock back. Just one week. Things could be so different.

Alan clears his throat. "Anyway, we are where we are. If you get charged with the other matter, all the charges will probably get brought and dealt with together."

We are where we are. He makes it sound as though we are in it together. I pick at the fragments of polish on a mis-shaped fingernail. I look a right state at the moment. It feels as though there's no point in anything anymore. There wasn't that much point before either. Rob never noticed me anyway. How could I ever compete with Bryony Rose?

"I understand from your dad that you don't have an alibi for the morning your husband died? Last Monday at ten thirty?"

As he says *last Monday* out loud, I can hardly believe that nearly a week has passed. "That's right. I haven't. I was just at home, ironing. I always do it on a Monday."

"Is there anyone who knows this is your normal routine, even if they can't vouch for that day?"

"No, not really. I've only got one real friend on the street. I only really know the neighbours to say hello to. I prefer to keep myself to myself."

"OK. At this stage, I'm unsure what evidence they have on you in relation to your husband's death. I guess we'll get the full picture during the interview."

"DI Green was accusing me of having taken my Jeep into a garage in Ilkley. It was at eleven o'clock that morning, to replace a tyre. Apparently the mechanic took *my* details for the service invoice. But is wasn't me who gave them."

Alan frowns. "I see. Do you think someone could be setting you up?"

"I've absolutely no idea. All I know is my Jeep was parked up outside my house and I was busy at home."

"Do you have any CCTV at home, or a dashcam perhaps?"

I shake my head. Rob, who always liked gadgets, had been on about getting both.

"What about your neighbours? If we can prove your car was outside your home at the times in question, you've nothing to answer."

"I doubt it."

"Well, it's worth asking them. You never know. We'll see exactly what evidence the police have got when they come in. Until we know that, you are at liberty to make *no comment* responses, if they're making accusations without evidence, particularly if you can't defend them."

"Won't that go against me, saying no comment?" I feel calm, despite the circumstances. "I thought I could only say that *without* a solicitor." I should be a nervous wreck. I still feel anaesthetised.

"Not at all. It's better than blurting something which you later regret. These police interviews can be highly pressured. Of course, if you want to discuss a question prior to answering, you can request time to talk to me alone. The police will have to pause the recording and leave the room."

"Will I be able to leave here after the interview?"

"Hopefully. It depends on what new evidence they've got. You're not here under arrest."

"Well, they didn't have enough on Friday to charge me. So hopefully that's still the case."

* * *

No alibi.
A tendency to drink.
A charge of violence.
An anger over lack of return on investment.
The evidence is stacking up.

Chapter 31

DI Green does the interview preliminaries for the recording. I feel reassured by Alan Wright's presence. Less alone.

"Fiona, when we spoke last week, you denied all knowledge of having taken your car to Hill End Garage in Ilkley for a nearside tyre replacement. This is despite a statement being made, giving details of a woman being there on the Monday, seventh of June at eleven am. She matches your description, and gave your personal details, right down to your registration number."

I don't like the way she repeatedly uses the word *your*. I'm unsure how to answer, or whether to say no comment. Luckily, Alan wades in.

"I take it," he says, "that it would have been the nearside of the vehicle that hit Mr Matherson, when the incident in question took place, if he was cycling on the left of the road."

He's got such a way with words, Alan has, describing Rob's death as *the other matter, or the incident in question.* I don't know whether to be annoyed or amused by him. This is no time for either. This is serious stuff.

"That's correct. Both Mr Matherson and the car were travelling towards Ilkley. The garage is the closest to where the incident happened."

"Does it have CCTV?"

Many of Alan's questions centre around CCTV. I guess it's what's needed nowadays to nail someone. And forensics. Doesn't he realise though, that he's in the tail end of nowhere here, where half of the neighbourhood comprises sheep and cows?

"Unfortunately not. It's a small, back-street garage. But we're satisfied that the mechanic's description of Fiona, and the fact that they took her registration number for the service receipt, are proof of her attendance there."

"What about other CCTV? Around the garage, perhaps? Or in the vicinity of where the incident took place. Surely you have to prove her presence beyond all reasonable doubt."

"Both areas are in rural locations – the accident site and the garage." PC Robinson echoes my earlier thinking. "We were hoping for some dash-cam or farmhouse footage but so far, we have turned nothing up."

The glee in my solicitor's face heartens me. It's the first glimmer of hope I have felt all day. "And there are no eyewitnesses to the accident?"

"I've got two statements here, one from the farmer who stayed with Mr Matherson at his time of death, and the other is from the garage operative."

"Is there any firm evidence in either of those statements to definitively place my client at each scene?"

DI Green appears to skim read the page. "The farmer reported seeing the roof of the car that drove away. He described a four-by-four vehicle, like the Jeep Fiona drives."

"The garage operative has given the description of a woman, aged around forty, with long, light brown hair and medium build," PC Robinson adds.

Alan laughs. "You're going to have to do better than this to make the charge stick to my client. It sounds to me, that with nothing more concrete, you're trying to make her a scapegoat."

"Do you know about his ex-wife's car?" I'm trying not to be perturbed that my age has been estimated to be four or so years older than it is. "I saw it this morning, and it's damaged. Front left headlight. It's got a dent in it too." I feel a surge of satisfaction as PC Robinson writes this down. "Denise Matherson. It's not a four-by-four that she drives, more of a people carrier, but it could easily be mistaken for a four-by-four if only the roof was seen."

"You say you saw this damage today?" PC Robinson writes something else.

"Yes. She came to my house, carrying on about money. Making threats of what will happen if her daughter doesn't get what she is entitled to." I draw air quotes in the air, resisting the temptation to garner some sympathy for the financial mess I'm in.

"That may well be," DI Green continues. "But it still doesn't explain your own tyre replacement, only thirty minutes after your husband had been mown down, just a few miles along the road."

"Especially when you haven't got an alibi," PC Robinson adds.

Are they even interested in what I'm saying? "You know about Denise contacting Rob to do with money on the morning he died as well, don't you?"

"Isn't that what's behind this mess?" DI Green says. *"Money?* For the benefit of the tape, I'm now showing Fiona Matherson and her representative copies of four documents. They are as follows:

A joint agreement signed by Robert and Fiona Matherson, in acceptance of a loan of fifty thousand pounds, dated 10th May.

Secondly, A joint agreement signed by Robert and Fiona Matherson, in acceptance of a re-mortgage agreement, dated 11th May.

Next, a statement for a joint account in the names of Robert and Fiona Matherson, showing a credit for one hundred and twenty-two thousand pounds from a subsidiary account of Bracken Furniture Limited.

And a transcript of text messages, taken in the month leading up to the death of Mr Matherson. There is a demonstration of volatility in their relationship, particularly a mistrust of her towards him. If I could draw your attention to three messages in particular. They're marked with a cross in the margin.

Alan and I bow our heads over the page:

15.5.21 *Where the hell are you Rob? It's the middle of the night. It's no wonder I used to turn to drink.*

18.5.21 *You said you were working. So how come I've seen your car in the middle of town?*

20.5.21 *I need to talk to you. You've been seen.*

"What do those messages relate to, Fiona?"

"Nothing. I just got insecure sometimes."

"What did you mean by *you've been seen.*"

"He was in a coffee shop with Bryony. Look, no wife wants to put up with their husband meeting an ex for a cosy drink in a café."

Alan raises his eyes from the page towards DI Green. "I hardly think this is what I'd call concrete evidence against my client."

"I agree, to a point." DI Green places another page on top of the first one. "It's more about the accumulative effect of it all. These next messages prove you were in it up to your neck, by that I mean, financially, with your husband. Again, I've highlighted the messages of interest with a cross."

13.5.21 *Have you paid it in yet? This could change our lives.*

23.5.21 *So what about this money then???*

24.5.21 *You said it would all have come good by now. If I find out you've risked everything on a whim, I'll make sure you're left with nothing.*

"So?" DI Green sits up straighter in her seat.

"I've already admitted to putting thirty grand into Rob's investment opportunity. But I didn't agree to him also emptying our ISA. Nor did

I agree to him taking out a loan or re-mortgaging our home. He must have forged my signature. And I didn't know *a thing* about him taking money from his employer's business."

"Phillip Bracken disagrees. Having worked closely with Rob for many years, he believes you would have been the driving force behind your husband's embezzlement, particularly since the gains went into your joint account. To say he's upset is an understatement."

"What was the subsidiary account these monies were paid from?" Alan glances up from his notebook, pen poised.

"Two accounts - both opened by the company and fed through their books over a six-week period. One was operating under the guise of paying a supplier, and the other, a contractor."

"I see. But if it's only Mr Bracken's *hunch* that Fiona was involved, I'll reiterate my previous point. It isn't enough to warrant a charge. Or even an arrest for that matter."

I'm so grateful for his presence here. I'm stupid for sitting through my previous interviews without him.

DI Green shifts in her seat. "We're here to find out facts. Your client is not under arrest for fraud charges -*yet.*"

"I knew nothing about any suppliers, or contractors. Nor did I know about any loan or re-mortgage. Rob handled everything to do with money. And I trusted him." More fool me.

"It doesn't sound like you knew *nothing*, not from these texts."

"Are you intending to charge my client with anything, Detective Inspector, or are we here to share text messages and suppositions, which frankly, amount to not very much at all?"

DI Green ignores his question. "For the benefit of the recording, I'm now showing Fiona Matherson and her representative, photographs, along with email correspondence between Robert Matherson and James Turner, which have been forwarded by Robert Matherson to Fiona Matherson. They are dated May 8th."

One-by-one she produces the photographs Rob forwarded to me last month, which he'd sent to exemplify the lifestyle one of his 'associates' was enjoying, because of the investment decisions he had supposedly made. A red Porsche, a house that makes ours look like a shed, and a foreign villa. Topped off by a smiling, balding man with an extremely glamourous woman on his arm.

"Like I've told you before, Rob promised me the investment deals would be winners."

"It's no wonder you wanted to contribute as much as possible. No matter what you had to borrow, legitimately or otherwise. That would explain the transfer for three hundred and seventy-five thousand pounds made on 12th May."

"Yes, I admit Rob made them sound like good investments, but I didn't know he invested that much. I thought it was just my thirty grand, along with any money Rob had scraped together. I left it up to him. He worked as a financial director, after all."

"Did you not think to do any research into these 'get rich quick schemes' yourself? There's no way I'd hand that sort of money over without looking more closely first."

Alan jumps in again. "I cannot see how your hypothetical musings could have anything to do with my client's decisions."

I answer anyway. "Rob was at university with this man. They went back a long way, so Rob said. He'll have had confidence in what he told him. As I did. So yes, if being naïve is a crime, then I'm guilty of that. But nothing else."

DI Green runs her finger down another sheet of what looks like messages. "Judging from the attempts that Rob made to contact James Turner in the week leading up to his death, I'd say he was beside himself with anxiety, as anyone would be, worrying where all this money might have ended up. Not to mention angry at being ignored."

"I didn't know about any of it."

"You must have been angry and anxious too. Especially with your husband. That he could have transferred such a huge sum, without personally overseeing its administration. Perhaps he had other things on his mind?"

"What are you saying?"

"Bryony Rose, losing his job, potential fraud charges from his employer." She pauses. "Have you been in contact with James Turner?"

"Yes, I tried a few days ago. I just want our money back. But Turner denies all knowledge of ever having received it, or even having contact with Rob recently. Why haven't you approached him yourselves yet?"

"We're not at liberty to discuss that with you."

Who does PC Robinson think he is? We're not at liberty…

"Then we move onto the morning of Rob's death." DI Green places another sheet on top of the previous two. "Again, a cross marks the message of interest."

8.6.21 You carry out your threat and I'll make sure you regret it.

"One hour before his death. What was that about Fiona?"

"It's not what you think. My mother was having an affair. Rob was threatening to tell my dad."

"So enlighten me. How did you plan to ensure he *regretted* it?"

"Not by running him over! I don't know. How do women show they're mad at their husbands? I'd have ignored him, had a row with him, left him, I don't know."

She writes something. "We'll obviously be checking that *story* out."

She's a cow. It's the way she says the word *story*.

She puts her pen down slowly. "I have to say Fiona, that you're our number one suspect here. Even more so after the violent conduct you displayed the other night towards Bryony Rose. Therefore, if you've anything you'd like to tell us, you'd be saving everyone a lot of trouble by just coming out with it now."

"I've got nothing to tell you."

"The investigation has got a way to go yet," PC Robinson says. "By helping us understand things more quickly and easily, the court would show more leniency when sentencing. And we'll get to the bottom of things. With or without your cooperation."

"Whoa." All eyes turn to Alan. The word is out of place in a police interview room. "Don't you think you're getting ahead of yourselves? You're talking *sentencing?* You've not even charged my client yet."

"I think we've got everything we need - for now. Don't venture too far away Fiona." She gathers up her papers as she speaks. "As this inquiry deepens and we receive full CCTV from everywhere we've requested it, we'll *definitely* require you to answer some more questions." She tucks the papers into her file. "We're expecting the results back today from the tyre that was removed from your vehicle."

"It wasn't my vehicle!" God, they won't leave this alone. "Anyway, what about James Turner? When are you going to question him? And Denise Matherson. She didn't have an alibi for last Monday either. Plus, I've told you now about the damage to her car."

"We are talking to them. Right, I'm ending this interview at 12:30 pm. We'll be in touch Fiona."

"Can I have a few minutes with my client, please?" Alan looks up from the notes he has been making.

"Certainly. We'll leave you to it."

As the door clicks behind them, I take a sip from my water bottle and look expectantly at Alan. "Well, at least they haven't charged me."

"Their investigation is all over the place." He pauses for a moment, then says, "I can't understand why they haven't impounded your car, and those text messages prove nothing. But it's true you do appear to be the one with most motive in their eyes, and the person who would have had most cause to have taken revenge on your husband." He runs his finger down the notes he's been making. "However, they've got to prove with no doubt, that it was you that took the car for repair."

"How can they do that when I was at home?"

"With a lack of CCTV, perhaps the garage staff would have to choose you out of an identification parade."

"I said that to the police in the first interview. That would sort it once and for all. But let's say they did pick me out, that still wouldn't put me on Denton Road at half past ten, would it?"

"True. Let's wait and see what their car forensics and CCTV investigation throw up. Then, once they've spoken to this James Turner chappie, we'll see if you're looking at fraud charges."

"For what?"

"The monies that have been embezzled from Rob's former employers. If they've shown you to have accessed your joint account or made any transactions, that could be aligned with you knowing about what was going on."

"I don't see how they can pin any of that on me. Just because it went into our joint account. I hate that man, his boss. He's always looked down his nose at me."

"Just sit tight Fiona. Over the next couple of days, it sounds as though they'll receive further results, and will be asking questions of James Turner and Denise Matherson. Let's wait and see." He slides all the papers into his briefcase and fastens it with a click.

"But if you think of anything, or find something out, get in touch with me straight away. And in the meantime, for goodness sake, stay away from Bryony Rose."

* * *

All is quiet and still.
Especially Robert Matherson.

Chapter 32

I've been told to stay away from Bryony Rose, but not Phillip Bracken. When I drive past Bracken Furniture on my way home, and spot his huge car outside, I pull up. It's definitely his. PB 1001. Bastard.

Rob often commented about him working on Sundays. Since his wife left him, he's become a complete workaholic. It's how he's got to where he is. I cross the road towards the main entrance. It's set back from the rest of the businesses, in between a hair salon and a sandwich shop. Rob used to rave about the sandwiches from there and sent his secretary most days. Before he got fired.

I stand in front of the double doors, noticing a security camera bearing down on me. I can't get into trouble for simply being here. I'm not committing any crime by merely talking to the man. But there's no denying that I'm more infuriated after the police interview and hearing DI Green categorically stating how Phillip Bracken credits me as being the brains behind Rob's fraud.

I've been to this building several times. Never right inside though. I'd usually just drop something off at reception. Rob's cycling shorts or his golf clubs – something like that. I never saw Rob's upstairs office in all the years he was here. The car park at the front is normally heaving, the road heavy with traffic, and a buzz of conversation emerging from the office floor. Today, all is quiet and still.

"Hello?" I call into the silence, my voice probably bearing traces of surprise at finding the door unlocked. There's a whiff of furniture polish and a blank space where a photograph should be within the management gallery. The *Director of Finance* sign still hangs there. My stomach twists. There's a rectangle of brighter paint where Rob's photograph once hung.

On hearing a creak from the upstairs landing, I straighten up. As I catch the sound of footfall on the steps, my chest quickens and my breath catches. He's coming. I've always found Phillip Bracken intimidating, but normally I've had the benefit of some Dutch courage before having to deal with him. I've been able to give him as good as I got. From what I can remember, anyway.

"What are you doing here?"

The distaste in his voice couldn't be more apparent. My anger immediately flares, but that's not the way. He's not better than me. I've got to face him as an equal. It's the only way this conversation will go anywhere. I've never seen him so casually dressed. He's wearing combat shorts and a Levi t-shirt. I'd be surprised if he'd met no one else since his wife left him. I guess he's quite a catch. Even if he's an arsehole.

"I saw your car outside."

"That still doesn't explain what you're doing in my building." He arrives at the foot of the stairs and faces me. "You weren't invited, therefore, you're trespassing."

I shrug and gesture towards the entrance. "The door was unlocked."

"What do you want, anyway? And make it quick."

"Why do you have to be so unpleasant? You always have been towards me."

"Do you really want me to answer that?" He folds his arms and surveys me as though I'm something he stepped in.

Tears prickle the back of my eyes. I get so sick of being judged and blamed. Especially by people who hardly know me and can't see beyond the drinking. "I've just come from the police station." I try to keep my voice steady. "I want to know what grounds you think you have for blaming me for Rob's fraud."

"I'm not discussing that with you. It's a police matter."

"What proof do you have, to drag my name into it, Mr Bracken?"

"I know what type of person you are Fiona." He uncrosses his arms – the veins in them and in his neck bulge.

Nobody, not even Mum, has ever looked at me with so much venom in their face.

"You're manipulative, devious, and grasping. I've watched over the years, as you've brought Robert down to your level."

"That's not true." Being evaluated in this way is not doing me any good. Maybe it was a mistake to come here. But if I can get him to drop me off his radar, I have a chance of getting my money back. We could even join forces against James Turner.

"I've seen your behaviour with my own eyes. Your sort is capable of anything. Especially when it comes to ripping others off."

"Yes, I've been drunk a few times." I sink to a seat in the waiting area. The little girl that wants to be liked is surfacing. It's the way he looks at me. Like he can see to my core. He's making me feel like a piece of crap. "That doesn't make me party to fraud."

"You might not have committed it yourself. But I've worked with Robert for many years, and this is not the sort of thing he could or would have acted alone with."

"So you assume I put him up to it."

"The funds have gone into your bank account."

"That still doesn't implicate me." I hold eye contact. "And I resent the insinuation that because you believe Rob wouldn't have acted alone, that it had anything to do with me. Anyone could have helped him. That's if anyone else was involved."

"He didn't have the gumption to have dreamt this up himself. It definitely has a woman's touch. He's betrayed me in the worst way possible."

"So he's taken you for well over a hundred grand. Why didn't you have him arrested?"

He looks thoughtful, as though he's considering what to divulge to me. "I wanted to deal with it internally. To keep it quiet and out of the local media. This sort of thing can blow a business apart."

"My heart bleeds. Maybe when you go around treating people like you do, it's bound to come back and haunt you."

"Look. I don't want you in my building. I've got nothing else to say to you."

"I'm not leaving till I have some answers."

"You can either walk out or I can throw you out. And I won't rest until they have charged you for what you helped your husband to do. You'll do at least a couple of years for that sort of money."

"You've no proof, and if you don't stop trying to blacken my name, you'll have more to worry about than your precious company."

"What's that supposed to mean?" The top of his lip curls.

"You had far more cause to run my husband off the road than me, Mr Bracken."

The tension in his shoulders visibly softens. "I was here. My staff have already accounted for me. You'll have to do better than that."

I rise from my seat and stand in front of him again. We're nearly nose to nose. I can smell his sour breath. "Keen cyclist yourself, aren't you?"

His face darkens, and he's quiet for a moment. "Are you threatening me?"

I smile. "Stop throwing your nasty false accusations around, Mr Bracken, then maybe things can return to normal."

"I just want my money back."

"Don't we all? I've lost nearly everything too."

Something in his expression changes towards me. "If you don't get off my premises now Mrs Matherson, I'm going to call the police. And I will, of course, be informing them you've been here."

"It's a free country." I walk out into the sunshine. My next port of call is the garage which I've Googled and learned is open seven days a week.

I pull into the last space on the forecourt. As I lock the car, I notice a young man bent over a computer in the office at the front of the building. I press the button with an *Attention* sign above it and the man jumps at the sudden disturbance. Normally, I'd make a joke in such circumstances, but say, "remember me?"

A puzzled look crosses his face. He's very tall, about six foot three, and gangly. He looks like how I'd imagine Jack to look when he gets older. "No. Should I?"

"Were you working last Monday morning?"

"Yes, why?" He stretches as though he's been sitting for a long time and rubs his neck, smearing oil onto it.

"At eleven o'clock?"

He frowns and seems to appraise me more closely. He's in his early twenties, if that. Then a look of realisation appears to come upon him. "You're the woman that…" He seems to glance around the garage then, as though looking for backup.

"That what?"

"I fixed your tyre." He looks worried now. Out of his depth. "It had a blowout. My boss. He'll be back any minute."

"Was your boss around last Monday morning?"

His eyes dart from me, to the doorway, to the clock, then back to me again. "No, he was out on a recovery."

"I asked you when I arrived if you remembered me and you said no." This is good. I just need to get him to tell that to DI Green. All of this trouble I'm in is a load of crap. They will not pin it on me. Except maybe they will. If it all stacks up enough. I was such an idiot going around to Bryony's like I did. Bloody drink. How could I have been so stupid?

"I couldn't place you. But you look familiar. We get loads of customers in here. And I'm useless with faces. My mum…"

"I don't really care about *your mum*. You've got me into a shitload of trouble, telling the police I was here on Monday."

"I-I'm sorry. I don't remember."

"Look." For a moment, he looks so out of his depth that I almost feel sorry for him. *Almost*. "All I want you to do is give the police a call. Tell them you've made a mistake."

"I can't. My boss. He's already unhappy with the police sniffing around. And I don't know that I did make a mistake. I just took your details, didn't I?"

"Look you." I step towards him. "You either let them know that you don't recognise me, and that you got it wrong, or I'll *make sure* you lose your job."

"*How?* You can't do that."

"Watch me. I'm warning you."

"But I'm not even sure whether it was you now. I just fitted the tyre."

"So you remember doing that?"

"Yeah. It's a quick job. I had a car on the ramp in here, so I nipped out to do it. You were in a rush. I thought I was doing you a favour."

"It wasn't bloody me. How many times do I have to tell you?"

"But you gave me *your* details." There's a squint in his eyes as he seems to look more closely at me. If there was to be a line-up, as Alan speculated, this lad would definitely pick me out now.

"I didn't give you any details. It wasn't me!"

"You need to go. My boss is due back. He'll ring the police."

"For what?"

195

"They've done you for killing your old man, haven't they?"

"You little…" I step towards him, but he's too quick. He's back inside his cabin before I can get near him, and he's sliding a bolt across. I wanted him to look at me, admit he didn't recognise me, and agree to go to the police. That's all gone pear-shaped.

I'd better get out of here before he rings them, or his boss turns up. I'll probably get done for interfering with witness testimonies, or something. I've had enough for one day. And enough drama to last a lifetime. It's time to go home. Back to Dad and Jack. Back to normality. I can face all this again tomorrow.

* * *

Sunday.
A day of rest.
For everyone except me.

Chapter 33

I t's Monday. Another week begins. Starting with my appointment with the funeral director. "Thanks for coming in Mrs Matherson. I'm Emma Rowlings and I'm going to be taking your instructions today."

I accept the handshake she offers. "Hello."

"Have a seat. Can I get you a drink?"

I accept gratefully. Jack had a meltdown this morning, so I didn't have time for a coffee before taking him to school. Dad was still in the shower, so I had to deal with him myself. It feels like I've already done a full day's work. I sink into a seat at the polished oak desk as she leaves the room.

I notice the tissue box in the centre. There's a painting accompanied by the words, *Look for me in rainbows, high up in the sky.* I wouldn't want to look for Rob right now. I can't forgive him for the situation I've found myself in. However, I'm fully aware that there's only me that can make these arrangements, and he's Jack's dad if nothing else, so I owe him a reasonable send-off for that alone.

There's a big question mark whether I'll even make it to his funeral. Maybe I'll be locked up? I have heard nothing from the police as to whether they have paid a visit to either Phillip Bracken or that toerag at the garage, but it's still early days.

Dad has said yes, subject to Mum's agreement, to lend me the funeral fees until I get this fiasco sorted. They have a joint account, where both need to approve withdrawals over a thousand pounds, so there's no getting around her knowing about my situation. I think it's fifty-fifty whether she'll agree to it. She'll either use my situation to dramatically refuse my request for help, or she'll use it as another bullet to fire back at me in the future. Either way, she'll enjoy me having to go cap in hand. It's certainly a first.

Luckily, she was unaware of Rob's threat to tell Dad of her antics, nor was she aware of how much Rob disliked and disapproved of her. She'd definitely say no to the funeral fees if she knew that. She seemed at a loss to understand what he saw in me, other than my former financial situation. I doubt she'll ever forgive me for my inheritance. It's her own fault though. She shouldn't have been such a cow to Grandma.

"Coffee, no sugar." Emma returns to the room, halting my scattered thought train. She places a cup on the coaster beside me and a plate of biscuits next to it. It's a strange touch from a funeral director. Who feels like eating biscuits when they're arranging a funeral?

"Thank you."

"I'll start by saying how sorry I am for your loss. It must be a dreadful time for you right now."

"Thank you. It is." My eyes fill up. Tears are coming more frequently now. Especially when someone's nice to me. Which, isn't all that often. I think back to yesterday, to the altercations I had with Phillip Bracken, then the lad at the garage.

"I'll start by going through your husband's details and then we'll go through the arrangements to prepare for his funeral. When are you hoping to hold it?" She reaches into a shelf beneath the desk and pulls out a huge diary.

"As soon as I can." It's true. I want to get it over with as fast as possible. The police released his body sooner than I thought they would, having taken all the evidence they needed. He's been laid here, in the funeral home for four days already. It's strange to think he's only a few feet away from me. The thought of his funeral is hanging over me as much as these criminal charges. It's something else to survive.

I'm sure Dad can talk Mum around in terms of the costs. If not, I'm going to have to use the last of my money. Or try to access what's in trust for Jack. I feel guilty for even contemplating that, but I'm running out of options. That's if Rob hasn't had it already. I must check. He'd have needed to forge my signature again, but he clearly wasn't averse to doing that.

Emma thumbs through diary pages. "We've got an eleven thirty am slot this Friday for a cremation, if that's any good? Is that long enough for you to inform everyone who might want to attend?"

"I can't imagine there'd be that many people." My voice sounds hostile, even to me.

She looks slightly taken aback, so must have noticed it too. Although I'm sure that in that her line of work, she'll have heard everything.

"This Friday is fine."

Well, I wanted to get on with it. I can't imagine anyone coming from his work, given the circumstances.

"We have your husband's full name as Robert Lee Matherson, date of birth, 4th February 1983, and home address 7 Orchard Mews, Otley, West Yorkshire."

"That's correct."

"We have the date of death as the 8th June, the cause of death on his certificate, as a brainstem trauma, and the place of death as Denton Road, Otley."

I nod. I should be bawling my eyes out. After all, I'm sat here, arranging my husband's funeral. The man I adored enough to marry and have a baby with. At one time I would have done anything for him.

And I did, mostly. But now… perhaps I'm just my mother's daughter. Heartless. Cold. Unfeeling.

"Right. I need to get some details to personalise the funeral. First, can you make a choice from these options?"

I'm floored as a brochure full of coffins is slid towards me. What a decision. How does anyone choose a coffin? "That one," I say, letting my finger hover over the cheapest one.

"What about flowers?" She flicks her brochure open to a price list.

"What do people normally have?"

"Lilies or roses, usually. White is a popular choice."

"Budget is a consideration." I hang my head. What must she think of me? I can hardly tell her he's fleeced me of most of my money, and that he was carrying on with his former fianceé behind my back. Nor can I tell her I'm a prime suspect in terms of who finished him. Maybe I should have let bloody Bryony sort his funeral out.

"We could organise a mixture of the two and include some white carnations. That would work out less costly. Is it just a spray for the top of the coffin?"

"Yes." Then I think of Jack. I've seen flowers spelling out names at the side of coffins. He's too young to come to the funeral. Then I remember something. Oh God. It's his birthday on Wednesday. I've not even bought him a present or organised anything. I must sort that when I leave here.

"How much would it cost to spell D-A-D out in flowers?"

She runs her finger down what looks like a price list. "Erm, fifty pounds per letter."

Daylight robbery, I want to say, but I ask her to add it to the bill.

"Have you thought about what you'd like your husband to be wearing for his final journey?"

I hand the carrier bag of clothes I've chosen across the table. It's what he'd normally wear – when not at work, cycling or golfing. Jeans, t-shirt, and trainers.

"When we've got him ready, you're welcome to visit him. If you could call us first."

"Visit him?"

"It often helps with the grieving process. Some relatives report it helps to bring about a sense of closure and acceptance to see their loved one at peace."

Loved one. What does she know? I certainly wasn't his loved one, the way he was treating me. However, this sudden pique of incredulity turns immediately to sorrow. If anyone had told me nine years ago, when we married, that I'd be sitting here now, arranging his funeral, I would never have believed them. I would have somehow ensured that events had taken a different path.

"I don't think I'll want to see him, thanks."

She looks at me, curiosity written all over her face. "Are you getting any support for yourself, Mrs Matherson?"

"Call me Fiona. Yes. I'm OK."

"I can put you in touch with someone if you'd like me to."

"Honestly, I'm fine. If we could just get on."

"Right, OK, onto the service. Will you be wanting a family car to follow the hearse?"

"I'll follow it in my own car, if that's OK. It's black anyway." *That's if the police don't end up impounding it before then*, I feel like adding. My next-door-neighbour, Tim, mentioned he saw DI Green and PC Robinson looking around the Jeep last Monday afternoon, when they first came to give me the news. Come to think of it, Christina mentioned something when she first came over too. Though that afternoon is a complete blur. Obviously, there was nothing on the car for them to see. I must mention this to my solicitor. It's why they haven't impounded my car. At least that makes sense.

"You will not drive yourself, will you?"

"No. I'll probably go with my dad." I imagine Mum will come too unless she has plans to reunite with lover boy. I'm struggling to cope with all the crap that's flying around my head. Maybe I should take up the undertaker's offer of being put in touch with someone and try to let it all out. Although it would take a unique specialist to pervade and help make sense of my thoughts and feelings right now. I feel like I could explode. And if I start to open up to someone, who knows what state I'll end up in.

"Can we make an appointment for the funeral celebrant? For a chat about the service content? Is Wednesday afternoon any good?"

"Erm, yes, so long as it's before I collect my son from school. It's his birthday, so I'd want it done and dusted well before then."

"Shall we say 1:30 then? At your home address?"

"Yes. That's fine."

"His name is Joseph Alexander. He's really nice." She smiles.

"Good. Thanks."

"Do you want us to set up a newspaper announcement? With the basic details of your husband's passing, and of the funeral details?"

"Can do."

"We'll just put, beloved husband of Fiona, and father of… what's your son's name?"

"Jack. You'd better also include his daughter from his first marriage - Simone."

"Does he have other significant family that need a mention?"

"No. He was an only child and his parents are both dead. You could put son-in-law of Roger and Maggie." He and Dad were close, after all. I don't know what he'd make of Mum being given a mention though. Eventually her belittlement of me, and my fear of her, had made him despise her. And look down his nose at me.

"Right. Leave it all with me. I suggest you put an announcement on social media as well, as not everyone looks at the newspaper. And let me know if you would like to arrange a viewing time. You can change your mind up to the day itself."

She makes him sound like a house. "Is there anything else I need to do?"

"Just have a think about the service. Whether you'd like it religious or spiritual. What songs or readings you'd like, if any? And whether you'd like a photo carousel displaying throughout the service – it's two pounds fifty per photograph. There's a minimum of twenty photographs, or you can have a static one displayed throughout for twenty pounds."

She shakes my hand again. I turn and head along the carpet's thick-pile towards the exit, appreciating the exchange of the chilly funeral home, for the comparative warmth of the June Monday.

* * *

No news is very good news.
As the days go on,
I can make plans.

Chapter 34

I slide into the Jeep, grateful to be on my own again, with the chance to gather my thoughts. How I should behave right now, I do not know. God knows how others are perceiving me. But I know that I've had enough funeral talk for the time being. I pluck my phone from my bag and fire off a text to Sam's Mum.

Hi Lynne, it's Jack's birthday on Wednesday but given the circumstances, I haven't got around to organising anything. I wondered if Sam would like to come for pizza and a film with Jack. They could have a sleepover if that's OK with you?" I'm sure Jack will be happy with that. I haven't got the time or inclination to organise anything else.

Quick as a flash, she replies. *He would love that, but I'd rather collect him later, if that's OK. With it being a school night. You and I could have a glass of wine together. Get to know each other more.*

Well, it'll be a cup of tea for me. I don't drink. No doubt that will give her some new gossip to share with her friends.

What would Jack like for his birthday?

His daddy, I type, but then delete it. I'm absolutely all over the place. I'm relieved that there's been no comeback from the visits I made to Bracken Furniture and the garage yesterday, but I still haven't heard a thing since the interview at the station. Part of me hates the not knowing – I'd rather they put me out of my misery.

204

He's popped his football, so he'd love a new one.

I think I can manage that! Sam will be very excited when I tell him.

I'll pick them up from school, then if you could collect Sam at around half seven to eight o'clock, that would be great.

OK. I'll see you on Wednesday if not before. Can you drop me a text to let me know you have picked Sam up safely?

What does she take me for? Someone who's completely inept? She doesn't know that they've charged me with aggravated assault. Word will get out soon enough. Nor does she know that I'm under investigation for causing death by dangerous driving, and being an accessory, if that's the right word, to fraud. I bet she doesn't know I'm a recovering alcoholic either. If she knew the half of it, she'd never let her precious son anywhere near me.

Whilst I'm in an organisational mood, I make a doctor's appointment for Thursday morning. If I've got the Antabuse in my system before Friday, I won't be tempted to drown my sorrows at the funeral.

I feel numb and empty one minute, and full of rage the next. I know grief is a cyclical process so perhaps, by Friday, I might be in the depths of sorrow, or anger, depending on who turns up. Bryony's face flashes into my mind. I wonder how that works out with the bail conditions stating that I'm not allowed to contact her, directly or indirectly. I've got more right to be at Rob's funeral than *she* has.

I expect Denise will turn up too – that's unless it's her who gets charged for Rob's killing. I imagine she'll bring Simone, three years older than Jack. She's too young to attend a funeral but it's not my decision. With Jack though, it is.

I point the Jeep in the direction of the town centre. I'll sort Jack's birthday gift whilst it's in my head. If I don't, it will zip out again and no matter how much he says he's going to forget about his birthday because he's too sad, he'd be devastated if there was no present there for him on Wednesday morning.

He's been raving on about a new scooter and luckily Argos has two left. He's been playing in the street on his micro scooter, then coming in moaning that it can't do the same things as the stunt scooters that the slightly older boys have.

I trudge around the supermarket, throwing in other items for his birthday, small gifts to open; chocolate, a frisbee, a DVD. Then some party decorations, and a birthday cake. I've hardly shopped for over a week, so I fill the trolley up.

The neighbours have been wonderful in leaving the odd casserole and shopping basics on the doorstep, but they don't think about things like Jack's Nutella, breakfast cereal and biscuits.

As I unload the bags into the Jeep, I feel a sense of normality. Outwardly, there's no difference between me and the other women loading their cars up.

I have a flashback to when I used to shop with Grandma. I recall millionaire shortcake, Appletize and Turkish Delight. If I hadn't had her in my life, I'd be even more messed up. I hate being my mother's daughter. A part of me wishes she'd disappear back with that Shane and leave us all alone. She wants the best of all worlds – I've never known anybody so selfish.

I've nearly arranged my husband's funeral. I couldn't feel any less normal. Only when it's over, can any sort of order return.

* * *

The not knowing is killing me.
Pardon the pun.
Things are quiet. Too quiet.
Perhaps this is the calm before the storm.

Chapter 35

I don't know what I would do without Dad. I've woken late, so he's got Jack dressed and breakfasted. He's taken him to school, so the house is in silence.

I'm sleeping like I'm dead. Each morning I have a moment when it could be just another day, then within a minute, reality smacks me around the head. It's nearly forty-eight hours since I was at the police station. I may have to take matters into my own hands if I don't hear from them soon.

I reach for my phone and see that there's nine plus Facebook notifications. It's the usual stuff. *Top man – will be sadly missed ... condolences to Fiona and Jack... Gone too soon. RIP... So sorry to hear this awful news, sending love to the family.* And on, and on. I click 'like' next to each one in acknowledgement, though it's them, they're enabling to feel better with these condolence messages, not me.

I decide I should probably write something. It would be expected. Under all the comments, I put. *Thanks for all the messages of condolence at this awful time – they mean a lot. Funeral details to be announced on Rob's page.*

I go through to his page and type: *Funeral Announcement. A celebration of Rob Matherson's life will be held this Friday, 19th June at 11:30 am. It will take place at Rawdon Crematorium, followed by...*

I haven't even thought about that. I stop typing and think. The golf club. I search for Otley Golf Club and hit call. The lady who answers couldn't be more sympathetic when I say who I am and why I'm calling.

"How many mourners are you expecting Mrs Matherson?"

"I'm not sure to be honest. Fifty maybe."

"Rob was really popular here," she says. "He'll be so missed by everyone. I think there could be at least thirty or so of his golf club friends wanting to be there – they've even had a whip round for you."

"Really?" This brings tears to my eyes. I never expected that. Maybe it'll cover the cost of the wake.

As if she is a mind reader, she says, "And as Rob was such a valued member of this club, I'd like to offer the room for free, and give you a twenty percent discount on the catering. We're so sorry for your loss Mrs Matherson. We've all been so shocked about it."

I gulp. "Thank you. I don't know what to say. You're very kind. I guess I'd better ask you to cater for around seventy then. He was an active member of his cycle club too. He lived for his golf and cycling."

"I'm sure he lived for you and your little boy as well." She pauses. "What time do you think you'll arrive? I'll have everything set up in advance and get extra bar staff on so I can come to the service too."

My ears inadvertently prick up at the mention of the word *bar*. It's an ingrained response. In fact, if I bring to mind the funerals I've had to attend with Rob over the years, I've always ended up sozzled. Even when I attended one for his colleague with him, someone who I'd never even met! I'll never forget the disapproving glare of Phillip Bracken. I'd felt like a naughty schoolgirl. This had encouraged me all the more.

I end the call and return to writing the Facebook announcement.

...followed by a wake at Otley Golf Club. Family flowers only please. A donation plate will be made available to collect funds for Shelter UK.

I don't even need to think about the choice of charity. I know Shelter isn't connected with Rob's death, but it's the charity I *always* support, given the choice. Their outreach service gave me so much help when I was on my uppers in my late teens, even sorting me a hostel place for a time. Then they helped me get my own supported tenancy and put me on a substance misuse programme. I'd have probably been dead without them. I'm lucky I crawled back from that time in my life. No thanks to my dear mother.

Dad and I have since discussed it; he feels dreadful that I sank so low as to have been homeless, and heavily alcohol dependent at such a young age. When I first left home at sixteen, unbeknown to Mum, Dad met me a few times; he'd give me money and take me for something to eat. But when Mum found out, she gave him an ultimatum, *her, or me.*

What I hadn't known at the time was that Mum was pregnant. Dad told me he'd been utterly torn. That's if the baby had been his, of course.

Karma intervened. Mum lost the baby, though it was some time before I found out about any of it. At thirty-seven, they had classed her as having a geriatric pregnancy. She'd have loved that label. She already hated being seen as someone with a sixteen-year-old daughter. However, I could imagine her relishing the prospect of wiping me out of her life completely, and being seen as the mother of a new baby instead.

When I later heard she'd lost the baby, I can't say I wasn't relieved – no doubt she would have treated another kid like she'd treated me. Unless it had been a boy. She has never tired of telling me she'd wanted a boy whilst pregnant with me. She hadn't even thought of a girl's name. I was supposed to be Paul David. Maybe that's another reason she'd never allow me to have long hair or wear dresses as I was growing up.

I didn't see either of them again until I was twenty-two. Dad made several efforts to contact me in between time, but I ignored him.

For a while, I didn't even see my grandmother - I didn't want her to see me in the state I was in. I didn't know what planet I was on half the time and getting off my face was all that mattered. Luckily, by the time I had cleaned myself up in 2007, I still had a few years which I could spend with Grandma. I moved in with her for her last few months, to nurse her. I'll always cherish that time.

She never forgave Dad for what she called his cowardice and hated Mum with a passion. When she died in 2011, it had been seven years since she'd seen either of them. They tried, especially towards the end, but she was having none of it. Hence, she left me nearly everything she had, and only left Dad fifty thousand pounds. She'd clearly done her homework and must have known this gift would prevent him from being able to contest her will, even if he'd wanted to.

The relationship he had lost with his mum, and guilt about me, both contributed to Dad's depression. And though I have never asked him this question, I bet if anyone were to say to him, *have you ever felt truly happy being married to Maggie,* his answer would be no.

I look back at my phone. People have already been commenting on the Facebook funeral announcement. *That's soon... thanks for letting us know... let me know if you need any help with anything... let's give him a good send off, etc.* Then I notice a *Val Turner* has clicked 'like.'

Val Turner. I click through to her page and scan her 'about' information. *Married to James Turner.* Bingo. She certainly looks a different woman to the glamourous, model-type, stood outside a huge house, in the photographs which Rob had previously forwarded to me. Her page isn't locked up, like her husband's is. I scroll down. There's a picture of her, possibly on holiday, with him in the background, at a holiday park in Blackpool. The tower is in the background.

Blackpool, for goodness sake - a far cry from the luxurious villa in the French Riviera, which had also been alluded to. I scroll down some more. Val Turner has posted pictures of dog after dog, and it becomes clear that she runs a small dog grooming business from a shed in her back garden. I can see the modest two-up, two-down behind her and a van in the driveway. Funny looking mansion and Porsche.

If James Turner and his wife are so loaded from his so-called investments, there's no sign of it. I wonder for a moment if it's even the same person. There's a picture of them, on a night out, in what looks like some sort of club. He's there, clear as a bell, balding and paunchy. I click through to James Turner to check. Yes, it's him alright. What's going on? They've had three hundred and seventy-five grand of our money, and there's no sign of it.

I'm relieved to find an address for Klipper's Grooming Services, there on her Facebook business page. I pull on my usual jeans and t-shirt, grab a banana and a bottle of water from the kitchen and head out towards the Jeep.

I momentarily wonder where Dad might have got to. He should have been back by now, but then decide I need to set off before he comes back. He'll only try to stop me if he finds out where I am going. He'll tell me to leave the police to do their jobs without my interference.

It seems I'm easy pickings for the police, and I'll be surprised if they've even bothered to try to contact James Turner, or Rob's bitch of an ex-wife yet. Perhaps it's less of a drain on their resources to pin it on me.

If I get on my way now, I can be in Manchester inside an hour and a half. This might be the only way I see my money again. I type the address into my sat nav and ignore the warning voice that nags inside my mind. *You're going to make things worse.* It's as though I'm developing a split personality as I reply to myself - *how on earth can anything get any worse?*

A loud beep and a screech make me gasp as I find myself in the centre of the road. Shit. I've overshot the junction. I've been so deep in my thoughts, I haven't been paying attention. Thank God the other driver was. I reverse back into the junction and let him pass. I've been driving for around twenty minutes and am about a mile from the motorway. I can't recall getting here. If someone were to ask me, I wouldn't be able to tell them which way I've travelled. It's almost as if I've zoned out. My breathing comes in rapid blasts now. At least the adrenaline rush means I'll be fully alert for the motorway.

*　*　*

I'm grateful
for the moments when my mind
escorts me away from reality.

Chapter 36

I park a couple of doors down from the house, my heart hammering. There it is, the modest terrace with an equally modest front garden. The pebbled drive is long enough to squeeze the *Klippers Dog Grooming* van onto. A battered Volkswagen golf is pulled up onto the kerbside bordering the garden wall. A sign shows the way to the dog grooming shed in the back garden. I take a deep breath and walk towards the front door, hesitating before I knock on the peeling paint. I should not be here but what choice do I have?

"James Turner?" I square up and look him straight in the eye. He's even more balding and paunchy in the flesh. He's got stains on his t-shirt and a hole in his sock. No way is this some hot shot businessman. "I'm Fiona Matherson. I'd like a word with you, please."

"You can't turn up at my house unannounced."

"I just did."

"Well, you can bloody well turn around again."

"You didn't really leave me a lot of option Mr Turner." His name sticks in my throat. "You wouldn't speak to me on the phone."

"My dealings were with your husband, not you."

I'm absolutely sick of people looking at me and speaking to me like a piece of shit. Maybe I'd punch him or put his windows through if I wasn't already on bail.

"You admit to having *dealings* with him, at least?" I will make him talk, even if I have to squeeze the words out of him through his gonads.

"I've already said, I'm not telling you anything."

"Have the police spoken to you yet?"

"I've told them everything they need to know."

"Where's our money?"

He looks thoughtful for a few seconds, then his shoulders seem to sag. "OK, Rob and I had an investment opportunity, but we lost out on this one, unfortunately. You win some, you lose some in this game. That's the way it goes. It's a gamble. You must know that. There is no money. Sorry."

"Don't give me that crap." I look up at his house and across at their car. "Where are the trappings you emailed Rob? All those pictures of - the house, the Porsche, the wife? The wife I've seen through Facebook is nothing like the woman you sent us a photograph of."

He steps from the door and pulls it behind him. "I'm just a salesman when all's said and done. I sell a dream. Sometimes it wins. Sometimes it doesn't."

"Well, if it hasn't *won*, I need proof of that."

"What you need is to keep your beak well out of my business."

I swallow. "Look, I'm not here to cause trouble. I just want my money back."

"It was a transaction between me and Rob. And like I said. It's gone."

"Gone where."

"Gone from your account." The skin of his lip drags across the top of his teeth in his attempt at a thin smile. "I'll enjoy it properly, when all this shit has blown over. All you need to know is, like I said, you win some, you lose some."

"You can't do that to us – you can't take our money."

He lowers his voice. "Look here you thick bitch, I already have. It was your stupid husband who was gullible enough to go along with my suggestions. I didn't force him to transfer me the money."

I glance around, hoping to see one or two of his neighbours. I'm in a strange city at the home of a man who is obviously a nasty piece of work. It's too late to acknowledge how vulnerable I've made myself. "He trusted you. He thought you were friends."

"More fool him then." He folds his arms across his fat chest. "There's no room for conscience in business. It's every man for himself."

I want to cry. This shit is real. He's robbed all our money. "You won't get away with this. I'll make sure of that. I'll…"

"What will *you* do? I don't like *threats,* as your husband found out."

I stare at his pudgy face. "What's that supposed to mean?"

"Look love. I don't want you here. I don't want the police here. Deepest condolences about your husband, and all that, but really, I want leaving alone. By the lot of you."

"Do you know how much trouble I'm in because of you? I'm getting accused of killing him, fraud, and everything. Do you know how much money he stole from his employers?"

He grins. I want to slap him. "Of course I do. I helped him set it all up. I knew I was on to a winner, didn't I?"

"What went wrong? What changed?"

"Nothing. I picked out a couple of companies to invest in. I just decided not to invest in them."

"But they're blaming *me* for it all. If you think I'm going down without a fight."

"You can't prove a thing."

"Watch me. You've fleeced us out of three hundred and seventy-five grand. I will make sure you get what's coming to you." I stare at him, the shock at his cheek, momentarily crowding out my anger. I glance at his dirty fingernails and faded jeans. He's a far cry from the man in the photographs.

"The police have accepted that I invested in legit companies, I've proven it to them, so you've no reason to be here."

"But you didn't even invest it, *did you?* You've admitted to that. You've just put our money in your pocket." My voice rings out into the quiet garden. His wife can't possibly be here – I'm sure she'd have been out by now to see what all the commotion is about. "Where's your wife anyway? Does she know how you've been making your money lately?"

"She's not here."

"Well I'd like to see her. I'd want to know if I was married to someone like you."

"I'm warning you love. You stay away from me and my wife. You can't prove nothing."

"Do you know Rob was coming after you? I saw his note."

"Yeah, on my car windscreen. Not to mention all the threatening messages. He got a bit worked up, your husband." His face breaks into a grin. "In fact, he was an accident waiting to happen."

"You what? What are you saying?" The mist of fury descends on me again. He's lucky I've hung onto my temper so far.

"Right, I've said all I've got to say to you. Get off my property."

"Your property! I'm going nowhere without my money."

"Good luck with that one. Go on, piss off and don't come here again. You can either walk away, or…"

"Are you threatening me?"

"We've said all there is to say here. Business is business. Sometimes you've got to learn the hard way."

"But you've admitted taking our money to invest, and then not investing it. I'm sure the police will be interested in knowing about it."

"Perhaps they would be, if you could prove it." He laughs. "You've got no proof that I haven't invested your money."

"Gotcha!" I back away from him toward my car, waving my phone in the air. What he didn't know is that I had hit the voice record button on my walk from the path to the front door. I've now got everything I need to nail him for all of it.

Quick as a flash, he's after me. Shit – what did I show him the phone for? I break into a run, yanking my keys from my pocket. I'll be in the Jeep before he gets anywhere near me. He's that fat, he won't be able to run. I'm wrong. He slams me against the car. "Give me the phone."

"No chance."

He tries to yank my bag from my shoulder. "I said give me the fucking phone, you little bitch."

"Get the fuck off me!" We're both gripping my bag handle for dear life. His hand tightens around the one I'm holding my keys in. One of them is gouging into my palm. "Get away from me," I shriek, hoping one of his neighbours will hear. He's not getting my phone. It might be the one thing that saves me from everything. Me and my big mouth. But I'd wanted to wipe the pathetic smirk off his face.

He moves the hand that's gripping my shoulder across my throat. "Help!" I yell as he rams my head against the top edge of the car, his grasp on my throat tightening. I've got both hands free. I'm gasping for breath but find the strength to reach between his legs, ready to twist whatever I can get hold of, like they once taught me in a self-defence class, but he's too quick for me and jumps backwards.

"Get your bloody hands off her." A well-built man comes out of nowhere. "Let her go." He lurches towards us. "You arsehole. I saw all that."

I turn towards the voice. Turner takes full advantage of my being suddenly off guard and yanks the bag from my hand. With a sneer on his face, he holds my phone aloft, before bringing it crashing to the ground.

"No." I shout, watching it bounce.

He stamps on it again, and again. Pieces of glass and plastic splinter off in all directions. "Prove it now, bitch." He strides back towards his house.

"I'll be back," I shout after him. "I'll make sure your wife knows what you are."

"Are you OK?" The man who came to my aid gathers up what is left of my phone.

"Thank God you came along when you did." I feel certain that Turner might have choked me to death if he hadn't.

He hands the bits of my phone to me. "Shall I call the police for you? You can wait at my house if you need to. My wife's there."

"Thanks, but no. I'm going to see them in person now. This is all part of an ongoing investigation."

"Are you sure you're OK to drive after that?"

I look at him. He can't be older than his mid-twenties. If he hadn't interrupted, Turner seemed set to throttle me. "I'll be fine. Thanks so much for helping me."

"Make sure you report him. It's blokes like that who give the rest of us a bad name. Here's my card, get the police to call me if you need a witness."

* * *

With still no firm evidence,
I'm nearly home and dry.

Chapter 37

The woman behind the desk looks bored. "Name please?"

"Fiona Matherson. I'm here to see DI Green about the case involving my husband, Robert Matherson."

"Do you have an appointment?" She runs her pen down a list.

"No, but it's urgent."

"I'll see if she's free. Really, you should have made an appointment."

"I'm sorry. I've had my phone smashed so I couldn't ring." I slide the remains of my phone from my pocket to show her.

Her gaze flits to my throat. "Are you OK? Your neck?"

My hand automatically flies to it. "That's partly what I'm here about."

"Take a seat. I'll find her."

"PC Robinson has also been dealing with my case, if DI Green isn't available," I call after her.

I sink onto the metal bench, grateful there's no one else in the waiting room to stare at me. I guess a Monday afternoon will never be the busiest day in a police station. It's nearly two o'clock. I must get this over with so I can collect Jack at three. I feel lost without my phone. Dad may have already planned to collect him, but without being able to speak to him, I can't bank on that. We'll probably both turn up. Dad will go mad when he sees the state of my neck.

It's only half-way through the day. So far, I've arranged a funeral wake, driven to Manchester, had an altercation with that arsehole, driven back, and now this. Not that I recall much of my journey back – my brain was too busy turning the conversation with Turner over and over in my head.

"Fiona. How can I help you?" DI Green opens the door from the custody suite. "Do you want to come through?"

I take a seat in the all-too-familiar interview room. The drive back from Manchester has calmed me somewhat, and I'm able to relay the events with James Turner coherently. "I've got it all on my phone," I tell her when I've finished the story. "Him admitting to taking our money, knowing he wouldn't invest it. Him admitting to being part of Rob's fraud with his company. And in not so many words, it sounds as though he might have been admitting to his role in Rob's death as well."

"Right, you'd better play it to me." She leans back in her chair. "I'll record it as well."

"Well, that's it. He realised what I was doing, recording him, I mean, and he smashed it." I pass the sorry-looking remains of my phone across the table. "It's my own stupid fault. I got cocky and let him know I had his words on record. I thought I could get back to my car in time. Get away from him."

"I see. We should still be able to get access to the recording, as long as it saved onto the hard drive. You saved it, didn't you?"

"It was still recording as I was running away from him. Something might have got pressed on the phone screen whilst he had hold of me which saved it. I really hope so."

She looks at me, sympathy etching her face this time. Over the last week, I've never known what reaction I'm going to evoke in this woman. I've had it all - suspicion, disbelief, respect, and distaste.

She records my version of the episode with Turner.

"Whether this is backed up by the phone recording or not, are you planning to speak to Mr Turner again?" I ask her.

DI Green pauses. "Leave it with me for now Fiona. I'll do what I can with this phone, then we'll see what happens when we talk to Turner again."

"Well, I want to press charges for assault. I've got a witness." I pull the card the man gave me from my bag. "I want the book thrown at him."

I am relieved to find a chiffon scarf in the boot of the Jeep. At least no one at school will have cause for gossip, even though it is too warm to be wearing it. I race into the playground with seconds to spare before Jack will be taken to wait at reception. Dad emerges from the year two cloakroom with him in tow.

"How come you're both here?" Jack looks from me, back to his Grandad.

"I didn't know if you'd remember to collect him," I say to Dad. "And I couldn't ring you to ask."

"I'm hardly likely to forget about my grandson." He pats the top of Jack's head, whilst giving me a look that says, *not like you.* "And why couldn't you ring me?"

"Long story. I'll tell you when we get home."

"Can we go to the park? Pleeeese!"

"Fiona. Hi!" Lynne leaves the huddle of women she is chatting with and hurries towards us, bracelets rattling and hair flowing out behind her. "How are you doing?" She lands in front of us. "I saw the funeral announcement earlier on Facebook." She puts her hand on my arm as though we've been friends forever.

"Hanging in there, I guess. I didn't realise you were friends with my husband on Facebook?"

"Oh yes. Now I'm friends with you. He came up as a suggestion of someone I might know."

But he's dead. I want to say. We shouldn't be talking like this in front of Jack, but he's totally engrossed in a discussion with Sam about what film and pizza topping they should have tomorrow.

"Is this your Dad?"

"Yes, I'm Roger." Dad steps closer to Lynne and holds out his hand. "It's nice to meet one of Fiona's friends."

"Pleased to meet you too." She accepts Dad's handshake. He always has to be so formal. "Will you be there tomorrow when I come round for a glass of wine?"

Worry creeps into Dad's eyes as he looks at me.

"Well, I'll be on tea. I don't drink anymore."

"Of course you don't. You've mentioned it before." She pauses. "Why not, anyway? I don't think I've asked you."

She must know I used to have a problem. Sam only started at this school when they moved here a year ago, but there's no way that the year two mummy in-crowd will have kept a juicy piece of gossip like that from her. I feel like she's fishing for more information to go back to them with. "Health reasons, mainly."

"Ah right. Tea it is then. It will do me good not to drink for a change!"

"I'm glad I've seen you Lynne." At least I remember her name now. "My phone's in for repair, so I won't be able to text you after I've picked Sam up tomorrow. But don't worry – I won't forget."

Dad glances at the boys and smiles. "I doubt these two would allow you to!"

* * *

I shall take my funeral seat on Friday
and then get on
with the rest of my life.

Chapter 38

J ack doesn't normally come bounding into my room at ten past seven.

"Mum! Mum!"

Usually I'm dragging him from his bed after eight. He likes his sleep. But today is his eighth birthday, and I'm happy to see his excitement. It's surprising how resilient kids are. I keep noticing clouds of sadness crossing his eyes, when he's possibly thinking of his Dad, but overall, I'm pleased by how well he's coping. If he shows any sign of not doing, there's grief counselling that can help him. I've already got the number in a brochure from the funeral director.

Dad has been a godsend this week. For Jack, and me. I think the sense of purpose Dad feels from looking after us has kept him from moping about Mum and getting worked up about her affair. It sounds as though her latest extra-marital indiscretion is over. I'm sure there'll be another though. Mum is a person who seems to think that the grass is always greener on the other side. I doubt she'll ever change.

"This is from me and Grandma." Dad slides a card across the dining room table.

"One hundred pounds," Jack shrieks. "I'm rich!"

"He's got a lot to learn." Dad laughs.

He rips the gift wrapping from his new scooter. "Can I show it to my friends?"

I laugh now, for the first time since Rob died. "After school you can, love. But you need to get ready now. I've got you a big bag of sweets to hand out to your friends."

"Maybe my birthday will not be so bad after all." He picks up his money and walks to the dining-room door.

Dad and I smile at each other.

"It's good to see him back to himself," he says. "How are you feeling this morning?"

"Strange," I reply. "I expect things will change after Friday. I just want to get it over with and then get the police off my back."

"I know." Dad sighs and looks up at the wedding picture of me and Rob. I can hardly bear to look at it now. I should take it down. Even on my wedding day, with my beautiful dress, and hair and make-up done, I still felt like a dog's dinner.

Whilst Dad was proud to give me away, Mum had a face like a smashed crab all day – she didn't even make it to most of the night do, claiming she'd fallen asleep in her hotel room after too much champagne. Rob had spent most of the evening with his bike and golf friends. I felt neglected but didn't let on. It seems the writing was on the wall, even then.

Since he's died, I know for certain why he married me. He got everything he wanted. I hope they can prise the conversation from yesterday out of my phone, so I have some hope of getting my money back, and clearing my name. Somehow, I'll pick myself up and start again. I've done it before.

"Your mother and I have been in touch quite a lot over the last few days." Dad scrapes the last of his porridge from the bowl.

"By phone?"

"Well, that Facetime, or whatever it is."

"Oh?" I feel a twinge of jealousy at the thought of their cosy

Facetimes. I want him looking after me and Jack, not going back to Mum.

"She wants us to go away for a week or two." He pushes his bowl to one side. "Wants us to talk, apparently."

"How do you feel about that?" I sniff. He seems to do well enough without her. I thought he'd fall to pieces about the affair, like he did last time. But I'm now thinking that he's better off without her.

"You know me Fiona. Marriage is for life."

"Thanks for the reminder Dad."

"I'm sorry. That wasn't supposed to come across so insensitively. It's just, when I married your mother, I meant every word of my vows." He sips from his mug. "We've been through so much together."

"You mean she's put you through so much."

"Don't be like that. She's still your mother when all's said and done."

"When is she on about going away?"

"I'm not sure. But I got the impression she wanted to set off over the next day or two."

"The next day or two! You know it's the funeral on Friday?"

"I think she might have booked something already." He looks sheepish.

"What mother dearest wants, mother dearest gets."

"To be fair, you haven't allowed a lot of notice for the funeral."

"I took the first available date. What's the point in dragging it out? You can postpone your trip, can't you?" I want to tell him I can't imagine getting through it without him, but something holds me back.

"I'll see what your mother has in mind, and we'll take it from there."

"Dad! You can't leave me to go through it all on my own!"

"I wouldn't miss the funeral for anything love. I'll be there. Even if I have to join your Mum later."

"You mean she's not coming? She's supposed to be my mother. How could she not be there?" I know she's selfish, but bloody hell.

"She absolutely hates funerals Fiona. She's always been the same, you know that. She'll do anything to get out of them."

"Show me a person who likes a funeral. Apart from old people who go for the tea and a get together. What a selfish cow she is."

"Fiona. You've every right to be annoyed, but there's no need for that. Not in front of me. I'm not having you bad mouth your mother."

"Can you take me to school now?" Jack bursts back into the room wearing the *I am eight* badge from his card.

"I'll take you." I push my cereal bowl away and rise from my chair, scowling at Dad.

I do my best as we drive to school, saying yes in all the right places and trying to feign interest in Jack's chatter. It's his birthday, after all. And I've not been present for him over the last week. But I'm so angry. And I've had enough.

I'm glad I've got that appointment tomorrow for the Antabuse tablets as the desire to drink is overwhelming. Even now, on a Wednesday morning. I haven't spoken to my sponsor since my blowout last week. I'm too ashamed. I've ignored the calls both times that she's tried to phone me. I can't bear to hear the disappointment in her voice. And now it's like having to start all over again.

I watch from the school gate as Jack runs across the playground to his friends. He's sociable, like Rob was, not a reclusive introvert, like me. Normally I'd at least walk him through the playground to the space which his year group occupies, but I really can't face the small talk today. Lynne is probably prowling around somewhere.

I've calmed down from the discussion with Dad by the time I turn the corner towards our house. Until I see Mum's car parked beside the gate to the driveway. She's taken the parcel shelf off and I notice the suitcases in the boot. She's either back here to stay, or she's here to take Dad off somewhere. Neither option appeals. A third one is that she's on her way back to Devon. This would be my preferred option.

"I'm back." I step from the porch into the hallway. Silence.

I find them in the conservatory. Dad's doing his usual pacing of the floor.

"Ah Fiona. Did Jack get to school OK?"

"No, I lost him on the way. Of course he did! Alright Mum?"

"Fiona." She nods stiffly, her earrings jangling. The cat is curled up beside her.

"Your mother and I are going away for a few days," Dad says. He always avoids eye contact when he feels uncomfortable. "But we'll be here for the funeral. We'll drive back early. Promise."

"All right Roger. There's no need to go overboard."

"Where are you going?"

"Just to Penrith. It's in the North of the Lake District. It's only a couple of hours away."

"I know where Penrith is." Rob and I stayed at a log cabin there before we had Jack. It was the middle of winter and it had a hot tub. I close my eyes against the memory. "It's a bit sudden, isn't it?"

"We don't need to explain everything to you Fiona."

Whatever I did for Mum to despise me so much, I don't know.

"We've helped you with the funeral money since you've spent everything your grandmother left you. What more do you want from us?

The way she uses *us* makes me feel like an outcast. That's how she operates. But I need to keep her on side, so they don't go back on their decision to pay the funeral fees for me. I'm grateful to Dad. I don't know how he talked her round, but I feel certain she will have put up some resistance. She helps others occasionally, but it comes at a cost, as it does with most narcissistic people. Before the funds have even been invoiced from the funeral director, Mum's already throwing it back in my face.

"You will be there, won't you?" I don't even try to keep the pleading edge from my voice. Dad's been my rock lately. I wish Mum would bugger off. Now I see how well he's been coping, I hope she reconciles with Shane. It's amazing how much my feelings and behaviour have changed towards her over this last fortnight. Until then, I feared her. Especially the threat of her rejection that hung over me, and ultimately Jack too. After all, she's the only Grandma Jack has. A strength I've never had before has fired in me over the last ten days, and I realise I owe her nothing, apart from the funeral money. I guess I'm realising what's really important in life.

"I'm not a hundred percent sure I'll be there Fiona." She won't meet my eyes now.

"Rob was your son-in-law." I open the door to let some air in. I'm burning with anger. "How could you *not* be there? If Dad's coming back, surely you'll be with him?"

"I know what you're saying Fiona. But I'll have to see how I feel on Friday." She strokes the cat as she speaks.

I stare at her. She's wearing a short denim skirt, white low-cut blouse, and flip-flops. She dresses as though she's far younger than she is. Dad always seems pleased to have her on his arm on the rare occasions they go out together. She might look the part, but inside she's dead. I hate her right now and I can't keep this out of my voice. "It's unreal that you're talking about seeing how *you* feel. It's my husband, who has just died. Can't you be there for me, for a change?"

"I will do what I want to, Fiona. If I decide to come, I'll be there. If I don't, I won't."

Something inside me snaps. "Don't bother Mum. It's not as if you'd offer any support, anyway. You enjoy your holiday."

"Wait in the car, love." Dad nods in the direction of the door. "I want a quick chat with Fiona."

"You're packing me off whilst you talk about me behind my back?" Mum pouts, like Jack would. "It's always been the same. You and your little father and daughter unit. Then you wonder why I'm so unhappy."

"God, she's such a witch." I sink into the chair Mum's just left, the wicker creaking beneath me. The cat jumps off and runs into the dining room. Even she doesn't want to sit with me. "As if you're clearing off on holiday Dad."

"She booked and paid for it all before she mentioned it."

Dad looks so beleaguered; I almost feel sorry for him. *Almost.*

"Don't call her a witch. I reckon she wants to apologise for what she's done with that Shane one."

"You're a coward Dad. Grandma was right. You let her walk all over you."

"Don't be like this. Look, I promise I'll be here first thing Friday morning. With, or without your mother."

"Make it without, if you don't mind. I don't want her there."

* * *

This time in forty-eight hours,
it will all be over.

Chapter 39

The thud of the post on the doormat makes me jump in the silence of the house. Now that news of Rob's death has spread, and I have announced the funeral, there are several sympathy cards, mostly signed from people I don't know, then in brackets *cycle club*, or *golf club*.

There's a letter from the mortgage company about the bloody arrears, since I didn't ring them back last week. And there's an interim funeral bill. They haven't wasted any time. Two sodding grand. I must text Dad and let him know. Then I remember, I've no phone.

As if they've gone away. Mum couldn't get away fast enough earlier. I've always known she was cold-hearted, but booking a reconciliatory holiday with Dad at a time like this, goes beyond what even I would have expected of her. It's up there with when she kicked me out of home at sixteen. I'm surprised Dad's gone with her. He must be over her barrel even more than I suspected.

I decide to spend the next couple of hours doing something normal. Housework. My life has fallen apart, but if I can get my house in order, then I might feel slightly better. I've done little since the day before Rob died, when my mother was on her way here. But I no longer care what she thinks of me, or my house. She can write her name in the dust for all she's worth.

As I mop, dust and gather all the clutter together, my mind wanders to solutions rather than despair. It's a better place to be. Perhaps DI Green will have retrieved the recording from my phone by now. She may have even re-interviewed Turner. I've got to stay hopeful about recovering at least some of that money. Even if not from him, there may be some kind of central insurance to help people who are victims of crime. And that's what I've got to prove.

I've still got to clear my name with the hit-and-run allegation, but I think the only reason they haven't let that one go from me, is because they don't have a shred of evidence against anyone else. The charge I've received against Bryony is indefensible, but I'm going to plead extenuating circumstances and grovel my way out of a custodial sentence. Everything will be fine. My husband has died – I'm sure that will afford me some leniency and I have Jack to look after.

As I spray and wipe the kitchen cupboards, humming to the song on the radio, I know that the only way I will leave this house will be in a box. I love living here, and I'm going to fight tooth and nail to keep it.

Eventually, I sink into an armchair with a cup of tea. There's only five minutes to spare before the funeral celebrant is due to arrive. Even though I'm expecting him, I still jump when the doorbell sounds. I open the door to a darkly dressed, shiny-shoed man who holds his hand towards me. "Joseph Alexander. We have an appointment."

I accept his handshake, then invite him in. "Can I get you a drink?"

"No, not for me, thanks. I had one at the office before I left."

I don't ask him where the office is. It could be at the funeral home, or the crematorium. I don't know how people in the funeral service do the work they do, but it must be interesting. "Come through."

He takes the seat by the window and I swivel my armchair around to face him.

"I'll start by expressing my condolences for your loss, Mrs Matherson," he begins. "Your husband was so young."

"I know. Thank you."

"And to be taken so suddenly and tragically," he goes on. "I hope you're being well looked after."

"I was." My previous fury with Mum snakes back up my spine. I try to quell it. She wants me to feel shittier than I already do. I will not bow to her wishes. "My Dad *was* here but now he's had to go."

"OK, well, as Emma from the funeral home will have explained, I will conduct your husband's service, and I need to get some details to help me know your husband a little, and also to take some information in order that we can put the service together."

He looks at me and I nod.

"We haven't got a lot of time, with it only being on Friday, so we need to get through it all today."

"What sort of details?" Emma asked me to give this some thought and dig out some photographs. I haven't done either. I recall her saying I could have one photograph up on the screen throughout the service. My eyes fall on a recent one of Rob with Jack. They look like twins, though thirty years apart, both with exactly the same blue eyes, brown hair and even the shape of their eyebrows and the way they're smiling. They're both wearing navy, so look even more alike. "Can this photo be on display throughout the service?" I stand and pluck it from its corner in the bay window which looks over the garden. A cloud of dust would normally come with it, so I'm pleased I've given the house the once over today.

"Is that the only one? Most people have a carousel. It's not expensive."

"That one on its own is fine."

"Are you sure you don't want one with you in it as well?" He takes the photograph from me.

"No, just that one." I hope he will not challenge every one of my decisions.

"Right, as you wish. I'll get it scanned onto the system." He crosses one pin-striped leg across the other. "Before I go through the more formal questions, can you give me a flavour of Robert? His childhood, that sort of thing."

"Yes, sure." This is the easy bit. Talking about his past. "He was an only child, close to his parents. His dad died fairly recently, but his mother died before Rob and I met."

"What did they do for a living?"

"His dad used to be a miner, and his mum worked in a shop. They apparently spent their entire lives worrying about money and how they would get by. It sounds as though they worked themselves into early graves. His dad died of a lung condition and his mum died from breast cancer."

Joseph nods slowly. "Do you want your husband referred to as Rob throughout the service?"

"Yes, maybe give his full name, Robert Lee Matherson, right at the beginning."

"I take it you want me to deliver the eulogy; you've no desire to do it yourself?"

"None." I smile, despite the situation. "I can't imagine anything worse."

"How many people are you expecting? So I know which chapel to prepare."

"We're catering for seventy at the wake, so around that number."

"OK. Right, let's return to the background details. You were telling me about Rob's parents, and how they struggled financially."

"Yes. But there didn't seem to be a shortage of love." I think of my own mother and almost grit my teeth before continuing. "They had days out in Scarborough, on the bus, and he often talked about his mother's wonderful cooking and ability to make something out of nothing. He's said before, that he never heard a cross word between his parents." *Unlike us,* I resist adding. I glance around my lounge before absentmindedly continuing. I'm going to have to go through all these photographs. I can't stand Rob staring at me from every corner. Once Friday is over...

"What about his education?" Joseph asks, his pen poised over his clipboard. He has got one of the most groomed beards I've ever seen. Dad would be jealous of it. Rob tried growing a beard after we got engaged, but it was a different colour to the rest of his hair – he looked strange. I told him I wouldn't kiss him unless he shaved it off.

"He passed his eleven plus, so went to grammar school. Apparently, he was quite academic, great at sport too – he still is... was."

"It must be really hard for you, all this." Joseph glances up from his writing. "You're doing really well. Tell me about his sports."

"From what he's said over the years, he took part in everything," I reply. "He's always been modest, but he seemed to have been one of those popular boys at school, looked up to by others, and good at whatever he put his mind to." *Unlike me,* I want to chip in again. It's no wonder I ended up on the drink. I didn't stand a chance in life with the mother I've got.

"Did Rob have any other family?"

"He went on to marry, after his first engagement broke up."

"What was his first wife's name?"

"Denise. They have a ten-year-old daughter together. Simone." I really, really hope Simone doesn't come on Friday. She'll make it all about *her,* they both will. I glance at the photograph of her on the mantlepiece. That is coming down.

"Can you tell me about Rob's career?"

I can't tell him the truth – that he got sacked for embezzling money from his employers. It will have to be a partial truth. Rob's lucky I'm sat here, arranging all this for him. If the shoe had been on the other foot, with the betrayal, fraud, and deceit I'm having to endure, Rob would have had me burnt at the stake, never mind at a crematorium.

"He went from doing, I think, it was Maths, Physics and History at A-Level, to a Degree in Business and Finance. He spent most of his career with Bracken Furniture. I used to go on at him to be more ambitious. But he was happy there."

"And settling in a job makes some people happy, doesn't it?" Joseph loosens his tie. "Not everyone wants to move around."

"I'll open a window." In two movements, I'm out of my seat and letting some air in. "It's always too warm in here."

"What else can you tell me about Robert?"

"He adored his son, Jack, and got on well with my Dad, Roger. He had lots of good friends at his cycle club and his golf club. He loved both – he died whilst out on his bike."

"I heard. I can't imagine what you must be going through. No one expects to lose their spouse at your age."

I expect most wives would be in floods of tears in front of a funeral celebrant by now. Not me. I'm more curious about the word celebrant. It's a strange word to describe a person who officiates a funeral.

"Anything else? What about closer friends, or things he was passionate about? What made Rob, *Rob?*"

If Bryony were sat in my place, she'd probably be able to give a very detailed answer. She'd claim to have known him far better than I did. Rob and I never really had the sort of heart-to-hearts and intimacy that a lot of couples say they have. Either I was too drunk, or he was too tired. Our relationship became perfunctory.

I don't think he was far from leaving me. I'm unsure what to tell this man. But I must tell him something. "He loved the Hornby set, which he set up with our son. His own dad had apparently wanted one for him, but couldn't afford it back then. Rob loved *Only Fools and Horses,* and his favourite band was *Coldplay.*"

"Ah, that reminds me, what songs would you like, going in, and at the end?"

The end. I'm dreading that. When the final curtain draws around his coffin. I always thought they derived the term *the final curtain* from theatre performances, but I have a new perspective now. I've already thought about music. I didn't mean to, but it was going around and around my head in the middle of the night, like everything does. "It's got to be *Yellow* by Coldplay on the way in, and *Someone Like You*, by Adele, at the end. It was our song.

I'm devastated by what's come to light since Rob died, and that it's confirmed my suspicions about his friendship with Bryony. However, I am gutted he's dead. I miss him more than I could have ever thought possible. I've just got to get through Friday. Another thing I decided in the middle of the night is that I'm going to make an appointment to see him before his funeral. If I don't, I think I'll regret it.

* * *

Hopefully, no one will notice
that my eyes are bone dry
I'm just interested in getting beyond the day now.

Chapter 40

The shrieking, shouting and overhead thuds sound alien in a home in which a funeral service was being discussed just over an hour ago. It's true what they say about kids being robust. Jack is racing around with Sam like he hasn't got a care in the world. No one would guess that this is a boy whose dad died last week.

Once we return to some sort of normality, Jack will be the one who'll ensure I get through it all. Somehow. Looking after him will keep me going. Being his mum will provide the fire that will help me fight for this house, and to clear my name.

I get pizza delivered for the boys and call them to the dining room table. I've set up Jack's streamers and balloons. He gasps as he walks in. I listen to their conversation as I pour them a glass of pop. *Suspension bridges.* I pinch a slice of pizza and leave them to it. Settling down in the lounge, I smile at the rising noise. It sounds as though there are five of them in there.

"Mum!" Jack shakes my shoulder. I can't believe I've fallen asleep whilst looking after someone else's child. I don't think Sam's spotted me sleeping, thankfully. That would sound good being talked about in the school playground.

"Are you ready for your film?" I try to disguise my weariness.

The house falls silent as they become consumed by the latest Spiderman movie. I clear the pizza debris and begin tackling the ironing pile, needing to get moving. If I stop, I think too much.

I jump as the doorbell echoes through the house. It must be Lynne, though she's half an hour early. Smiling, I pull the door open and the cat shoots past me. There's nobody there. Puzzled, I look up and down the street. I wasn't hearing things. The doorbell really rang. "Jack, did you hear the doorbell?"

"Um, I dunno." He doesn't avert his gaze from the TV as I poke my head into the lounge.

I return to my ironing, burning myself when the doorbell cuts into my thoughts again.

"Hi Lynne, come in."

She steps into the hallway and looks around. "Have you tied them up somewhere? It's so quiet."

I laugh, the sound foreign to me. "I've hardly seen them since I brought them back. They're totally glued to Spiderman. Would you like a cup of tea?"

"Yes, if it's no trouble."

"None at all."

She follows me to the kitchen. "What a lovely home you've got." She sounds surprised. I should ask her what she was expecting.

"Thanks. Although Jack and I are going to be rattling around it now. Originally, we'd planned to have more children."

She rests her hand on my arm as I flick the kettle switch. "I honestly can't imagine what it must be like for you."

I'm getting sick of people saying this. It's one of the most trotted out after-death sayings. "Don't even try." I turn cups over from the draining board.

"Has Sam behaved himself?"

"I barely knew I had him. It's been wonderful for Jack. He can come anytime. How do you have your tea?"

"Have you got any fruit teas?"

Amazingly, I have a box of *five berries blend*. I don't tell Lynne that it's been in the cupboard for about four years. I bought it when I was trying to kick the drink back then. I thought if I had nice things in the house to drink, I'd stay away from alcohol. "There you go. Have a seat." I point to the breakfast bar.

"Thanks. How are you feeling about Friday?"

"I'm absolutely dreading it." I place the mug in front of her.

"Do you need any help with anything?"

Paying for it. I bite my tongue. "Thanks, but everything's under control."

"I'm planning to come along. Pay my respects. And look after you."

I should thank her, but I'm taken aback. "Oh." *Be nosy,* she means. We've looked after each other's sons a few times, and she's acting like we've known each other for years. I don't trust her. One wrong word about anything and it'll be all around the school. I'm sure of it.

If she notices my reticence, she says nothing. "I can collect Jack from school on Friday. If you want me to, that is. I'm sure you'll be needing to drown your sorrows at the wake."

"Didn't I mention I don't drink?" I'm becoming exasperated with her suggesting that I do.

"Well, yes. But, it's just, Jake's Mum, Meloney, saw you leaving the pub in the centre last week – what day was it?" She looks thoughtful, but I can tell she knows exactly what day it was. "Erm, Friday, I think."

She's fishing. Great. That one will be all around the school. "I fell off the wagon. Anyone would, in my circumstances."

"Gosh, I'm not judging you Fiona. Not one bit. I'd fall to bits in your shoes, never mind get drunk." She takes a sip from her cup and seems to pull a face. I can vouch for the fact that fruit berry blend tastes like floor cleaner. "Have they any idea who did it to him yet? You must be dying to get your hands on them."

"No. None whatsoever. It's not the greatest area for CCTV, is it? Around here?"

She gives me a strange look, and I wonder if she knows that I'm under investigation. I'm sure she does. Nothing stays secret in this little town. Instead she says, "Is Bryony planning to go to the funeral?"

At first, I think I'm hearing things. "What are you getting at Lynne? How much do you know?" My voice is shaky. I don't want to talk about it with her.

"You know what it's like around here? I knew she and your husband were friends. And that you went around to see her."

"Yes, on both counts. But, look Lynne. I'm sure you mean well, but this is an ongoing inquiry. I can't talk about it, to you, or anyone."

"But you can trust me, can't you?" She sips at her tea again. I'm glad I didn't quite boil the kettle. She might drink it faster. "You trust me with your son, don't you?"

"I trust very few people right now. In fact, I've never felt more alone."

"Oh, Fiona." She slides from her stool and lands at my side. "You're not alone." She throws her arm across my shoulder. It's a small comfort, having the warmth of another person's limb against me.

"Why did you mention Bryony?"

"My daughter Chloe, goes to Guides with her niece, Ella, and also your stepdaughter."

"Simone?"

"Yes. She's told them she was off school last Monday when it happened."

"When Rob died? What's that got to do with anything?"

"Rob and his ex apparently had a right go at each other. Simone was too upset to go to school after her dad had let her down."

"When did she tell them this?"

"On Thursday, at Guides. And Ella says that Bryony has been really upset. I thought you should know."

"Right." I say slowly, trying to think. So that might have been the reason for the delay in Rob getting to Denton Road. Though I can't imagine he'd have been rowing with Denise for one hour, twenty minutes. He's not usually in her presence for over five seconds. I bet he went to Bryony's as well. "I must pass this information onto the police." I want Lynne to go. It's all too much. I need to be on my own.

Luckily, Jack bursts into the kitchen. "Spiderman's finished."

Sam follows him, rubbing his eyes and heading straight to Lynne's side. "I'm tired Mum."

"We'd better be off," she says. "If I don't see you before, I'll see you on Friday. I'll be there for you."

Jack, for the first time since Rob died, is out like a light. Now I know he will not have any brothers or sisters, I must invite his friends around more. Both Rob and I grew up as only children, which was one of the reasons we'd vowed to have more children ourselves. But my drinking and our widening gulf put a stop to that. I can't imagine meeting someone else in the future – I mean, who'd want me, especially with all my baggage?

I glance out of the window. Although it's the middle of summer, the sky is dark. It looks like it will throw it down. There might even be a storm. That's probably what we need to clear the air. I flick the lamp on and pull the curtains across. It's strange to spend the evening alone – almost for the first time since Rob died. There was only the very first night, when he died, that I was on my own. Either Mum or Dad have been here since.

I flick the TV on. The local news is starting. There's nothing about Rob anymore. He's old news now. Until they charge someone, then it will be back up there again. No news is good news. I still haven't heard a thing about what's going on. Not even a court date for the aggravated assault. Although they might stall that, whilst they try to gather evidence for further crimes against me. I'll have to see. I'm trying not to worry, although these days I feel like the weather outside. The calm before the storm.

My thought's wander. It's half-past nine and this time eight years ago, Jack was on the verge of being born. Rob didn't leave my side the whole time and wept when Jack made his entrance at ten to ten. I couldn't have loved a man more than I loved Rob back then. He had been wonderful whilst I was pregnant. He more than made up for the indifference of my mother.

A fat tear plops from my chin onto the magazine I've been clutching since I sat down. I can't focus on reading, TV, or anything. There must be something severely wrong with me. Mum can't stand me, Dad follows her around like a puppy, Grandma's gone, and now Rob.

I haven't really got any friends to speak of. I'd hardly class Lynne as a friend, no matter how nosy she is, and Christina hasn't been near since I got arrested. I'll knock on her door tomorrow as I've got no phone. Normally I'd have replaced it by now, but it's slipped my mind with all that is going on. I don't like being ignored by Christina – I thought she cared about me. As for Jack, I feel sure he'll turn on me one day. Everybody does. The TV drones on. More self-pitying tears slide down my face. I feel so alone.

I freeze as I hear a bang from outside. Like something has been knocked over. Then the shattering of glass. Unless it's an animal of some description, someone's in the back garden. The front door is locked, but I don't think I locked either of the back doors.

Throwing my magazine to the floor, I bolt from the lounge, through the dining room and into the conservatory. The door isn't just unlocked, it's swinging in the breeze. Sweat runs down the side of my head. It's so warm. Fear grips me. Where's the key? I grapple around the conservatory, desperate to get the door locked, so I can check the utility room.

Movement in the corner of my vision diverts my attention from my search. Someone is at the bottom of the garden. And I can't find the bloody key.

"Who's there?" I call into the dusk. I should call the police. But the landline is in the lounge and I daren't risk walking away from this door, leaving it unlocked. I think of Jack sleeping upstairs. What happens to him if someone hurts me?

Mum's smug face swims into my mind. If she hadn't taken Dad away, then I wouldn't even be here on my own. Self-centred cow. If someone is out there, they're not making themselves known to me. I need to either get this house locked up *or* ring the police. Sharpish. In the absence of a key, I decide on option two and dash back through the house.

Who would prowl around my house at this time of night? Then I remember. I'm not exactly short of enemies at the moment, that's for sure. Perhaps Turner has come to finish what he started. I can't imagine it being Phillip Bracken – skulking around someone's garden in the shadows wouldn't be his style. It could be Bryony, having sent someone round after what I did to her, or Denise – I'm not exactly her favourite person either, especially now I've given the details of her car to the police. And I've yet to let them know she was with Rob before he died.

The call connects straight away. I hear a bang. It sounds like the conservatory door. I grab a heavy vase from the windowsill. "I think someone's in the house," I hiss at the operator as my breath catches. "And I'm here on my own with my eight-year-old son."

"There's a police unit on its way," she assures me after getting my address. "I'm going to ask you to stay on the line until they get there. Just to make sure you're both alright."

"Thank you." I'm clutching the phone like it will save me.

"Can you hear anything now?"

I sit, as still as Jack would when he's trying to extend his bedtime and not be noticed. "Nothing," I reply. "There was someone in the garden though, and they could have got into the house. I heard a door bang when I first got on the phone to you. But, I daren't look."

"Can you get to the room where your son's sleeping? Make sure he's OK? It's probably best if you stay together until the police get there."

I swing the lounge door open, look both ways along the hallway, and shoot towards the foot of the stairs. There doesn't seem to be anyone here. Thank God I've got a landline after my phone was smashed. "I'm on my way upstairs," I say to the operator. "How long will they be?" If there is anyone in the house, hopefully they can hear me on the phone to the police and will make a run for it.

"Just a couple more minutes," she says. "They're coming through the town centre. Stay on the phone. Are you with your son yet?"

"I'm outside his room." I peer around the door, noticing his shape in the semi darkness, his arms around the bear he's started to need at bedtime again. "He's fine. I'm going to stay out here, right outside his room. I don't want to wake him whilst talking to you."

I jump as there's a noise from the dining room. "There's someone in the house," I whisper to the operator. The phone against my ear shakes in my grip. *Who is it? What do they want?* Mercifully, I can hear sirens in the distance. "I think they're coming," I say, heading to the top of the stairs, whilst willing Jack to stay asleep. This is the last thing I should put him through on top of everything else.

The utility room door bangs, and I hear the sound of footsteps dying away from the house. I rush to the side window where I can see the blue flash of an approaching police van. Then the back landing window, where only the dark shapes of conifer trees are visible. Whoever it is, or was, could have got over the back fence and away down the snicket. I don't think they would have risked escaping via the front of the house, especially with the sirens.

I swing the front door open as four police officers jump from the van. The cat runs back in with them. *Thank goodness she's OK.* Two comb the garden, whilst the other two, both women, do a check of the house to ensure whoever was there has gone. They introduce themselves as PC Richmond and PC Ellison. I follow them around.

"Who lives here with you?"

Something inside me plummets as I explain my husband has just died.

"They seem to have been scared off by our arrival," PC Ellison says, looking around.

"There's several people with an axe to grind with me." I reel off my enemies and their possible 'axes.' But if someone wanted to attack me, they had plenty of chance before the police arrived, especially with both back doors being open.

"You must keep everything locked now." PC Richmond shines a torch into the utility room. I can see the two male officers through the window, shining torches under bushes in the back garden.

"Whoever was here seems to be long gone," she says. "But we'll have a drive around and double check no one is hanging about." She glances at Milly, sat, obliviously licking her paws. "Never mind this cat – perhaps you should get yourself a dog!"

I'm in no mood for jokey comments. "Can't you take fingerprints to find out who was here?"

"Has any property been taken?"

I glance around the kitchen, then go through to the dining room. "Not that I can see."

"I'll put a request in for the forensics team, they'll get in touch with you. Looking at the door handles though, it's unlikely we'd be able to get prints from them. But we should at least try."

"I can't take any more." I sink to a chair. "I don't feel safe and I've got my son to think about."

"Is there anywhere you could stay tonight?" PC Richmond looks at me, her voice soft and her eyes full of concern. "You shouldn't be on your own."

"My eight-year-old is asleep upstairs. I can't go anywhere now."

"What about someone staying here with you?

I shake my head. "My parents are away on holiday."

"OK. We'll have a patrol car come past every half hour. We'll keep an eye on everything."

"Thank you."

I must look more shaken than I feel as she asks again, "are you sure no one could come and be with you?"

I shake my head again. How can I tell them I've got literally no one to ask? I know it's my fault. I'm my own worst enemy.

* * *

Midsummer.
A turning point.
Tonight, I feel as heavy as the sky
with a sense of foreboding.
Hopefully, it's the storm before the calm,
not the other way around.

Chapter 41

Thankfully, Jack is blissfully unaware of our late night intruder, and the police having been here. "When can Sam come again Mum?"

He'd never go to bed again if he had an inkling that someone had been prowling around the house. He's a child who hears and fears noises as it is.

"Fiona. Hi." Lynne is hurrying towards me as I make my way over to the playground gate. She's impeccably groomed as always, more like she's going out for dinner than dropping her son off at school. Her friends look on. None of them ever talk to me. I wonder why she does. "I had a right job getting Sam out of bed this morning. He says he had a great evening, so thanks again."

"Good." I try to smile and pretend we're not twenty-four hours away from my husband's funeral. "He's welcome anytime."

"Do you fancy a coffee?" She glances at her watch. "I've got a spare hour."

"I'm sorry. I'm due at the doctor's shortly." It's the first time I've ever been invited for a coffee by one of the other mums. It feels quite nice, although I know she will most likely be fishing for information again.

"Oh? Is everything alright?"

"Fine. Just routine." God, she's so nosy. *I'm off to get some Antabuse tablets, so if I go anywhere near a drop of alcohol, I'll be violently sick.* That information would shut her up. Personally, I think she's in league with Bryony somehow, after her mention of her last night. Or has such a boring life herself, she wants to be part of my chaos. I'd swap lives with her right at this moment if she wants drama.

Even when I tell him what's going on with me, the GP refuses my request for Antabuse at first and suggests *Alcoholics Anonymous.*

I tell him what I did last Friday after being sober for twelve months, and having attended AA meetings for two years.

"OK Fiona, I'm going to let you give it a go. I'll put you onto a five hundred milligrams a day dose. We can alter that after a couple of weeks if we need to."

"Will it definitely stop me drinking?"

"It can't stop you, but if you try, you'll wish you hadn't. The medication is so responsive, that you shouldn't be anywhere *near* alcohol – that goes for mouthwashes, perfumes, hand gels, or anything like that. Are you having any trouble sleeping?"

"It varies. My sleep is either terrible or really heavy."

"Well, if you take the medication at night, rather than in the morning, it can have a sedative effect." I watch as he types onto his keyboard. "I'm also referring you for counselling. Can I have your arm for your blood pressure?"

"Counselling? But I'm already going to AA."

"And that's good," he says as he wraps the blood pressure sleeve around my arm. The human contact is soothing. "But we need to explore every aspect of your life, not just the alcohol addiction. It sounds as though you're really struggling."

The tears let themselves loose again. They're never far away. The gentle voice and the concern in the doctor's eyes are too much for me.

"Is anyone looking after you, Fiona?"

There it is, the question guaranteed to make me feel like crap. "No,"

I admit, my voice wobbling uncontrollably. "I've all sorts going on." Then it all comes tumbling out. My money worries, the allegations and charges against me. "If it wasn't for my little boy, I would..."

Clutching a prescription and the number for the Crisis Counselling Service, I scuttle through the packed waiting room and out of the automatic doors, ignoring the impatient glares, probably peeved at being kept waiting. At least I've got the Antabuse. There's no going back now. Hopefully, I can stop craving a bloody drink.

I've got a couple of hours to kill before I'm due at the funeral home for my viewing appointment. I decide to return home and give Christina a knock whilst I'm at it. I wonder if she's planning to come tomorrow. I need all the support I can get.

I start up the Jeep and head towards the chemist first. I might as well get started on these tablets tonight. But they haven't got the tablets in stock at either of the Otley chemists. I'm told they will be in tomorrow. I can't wait. "I'm at my husband's funeral tomorrow," I say. If I don't have them, I know I'll drink. At that, the pharmacist must take pity on me, and a phone call reveals they have them in stock at the Ilkley branch.

I glance in my rear-view mirror. Someone's trying to get past me. These country roads are notoriously narrow, especially for overtaking. Perhaps I've been dawdling. With so much on my mind, I'm often driving on autopilot. And I'm so tired that I probably shouldn't be driving anyway. I speed up. So does he, or she. I can't tell as their windows are darkened. I think it's a Range Rover. Whatever it is speeds up. I try to focus on what's in front, not behind, but I can literally feel how close the car is. The irony of the stretch of road I'm on isn't lost on me. "Oh my God." I scream as the pursuing car nudges the back of mine. I grip the steering wheel, tempted to hit the brakes, but if I do, the car will slam into the back of me. So I accelerate but it bumps me again.

"Shiiiit," I yell. I will not die. Not on this stretch of road. Not when I have a son who needs me. My steely resolve returns. At one point I feared it had abandoned me. I grip the steering wheel tighter as they bump twice more into the back of me, harder this time. As the road widens, I see the car speed up in my side mirror, pulling around the right-hand side of me. Ready for this, I brake hard and it flies past me, swerving to the left as it does. No doubt trying to hit me from the side, not having expected me to brake so hard. I still can't see who's driving, only that the car is black. I scream as it stops and starts reversing back. Whoever it is, is definitely trying to run me off the road.

Then, as another vehicle comes up behind me, the black 4x4 stops reversing before speeding away. There's no rear plate for me to take a number. I also know from Rob's death that there's no CCTV on this road. I pull my car over to compose myself. Another car behind sounds its horn. Its furious occupant shouts obscenities as they're passing and also speeds off.

Pulling further into the side, I flick my hazards on. Someone's trying to frighten me. They've targeted me. They will be back; it is probably the same person who was in my house last night.

Wrapping my arms around the steering wheel, I lay my head on them, exhausted sobs wracking my body. I didn't want to, but I must move to a new house – a new start. No one can live in fear like this. I'm not even safe at home. My thoughts race for several minutes, until they're broken into by someone pulling up alongside me. A woman calls out. I open the window.

"Are you OK? Do you need any help?"

"I'm fine. Thanks for stopping. I had a near miss, that's all. I'll be on my way in a minute."

"So long as you're alright."

She drives away. Her small kindness has lifted my spirits though. When I was really poorly with depression in between Grandma dying and meeting Rob, my counsellor suggested keeping a gratitude diary. I had to note three things each day that I was grateful for. This training has stayed with me and I still try to look for the good in each day. Usually. Within a few minutes, I've calmed myself enough to progress onto the chemist. I need to get off this road. I don't feel at all safe anymore.

I collect my prescription and head for the police station again. DI Green is on her way out as I arrive. "Can I have a quick word?" I call across the car park.

"You certainly can. I was on my way to see you, so you've saved me a trip." PC Robinson gets out of the car with her and we walk together into the station. "How are you doing?"

"Did you hear what happened last night?"

"Yes, I was told about it at handover this morning." DI Green holds the door for me. "They didn't find anyone around your house, did they? Are you OK?"

"Not really. I feel as though someone's out to get me."

"And did you find anything missing?"

"No."

She and PC Robinson appear to exchange glances as she gestures for me to sit in the all-too-familiar spot inside the green interview room. It smells of stale sweat. "Was everything alright after my colleagues left you? They had a look around and we've had our patrols doing drive-bys through the night."

"Yes. I locked everything up. I got little sleep though. I was hearing noises all night. But, as if things aren't bad enough, a car has just tried running me off the road. In the same spot where Rob was killed."

DI Diana Green's face visibly changes from complacency to concern.

"Get this down John?" She nods towards her colleague who pulls his notebook from his shirt pocket. "What do you mean, someone tried to run you off the road?"

"A car came up behind me. I thought it was going to overtake, but it bumped me four times instead. I couldn't see the driver. The windows were blackened. Could I have a drink of water, please?" My usual anxiety and nausea is rising. After the funeral, I'm going to have to sort myself out. Take up yoga or meditation or something. Maybe I could join Bryony's classes. The thought almost makes me laugh, despite all I'm facing right now.

PC Robinson presses a button and requests the water. "Did you get any details from the car? Even a partial number plate?"

I shake my head. "It all happened so quickly. I only got a look at the back of it, and the number plate had been taken off. It looked like a Land Rover, or maybe a Range Rover. It was big, and black. I think it only stopped bumping me because another car came up behind us."

"How many times did it hit you?"

I'm shaking again at the thought of it. "Four from behind. Then if I hadn't have slammed on when it overtook me, I'm sure it would have slammed into the side of me."

"Is there any damage to your car?"

"I'm not sure. It's pretty robust, my Jeep, so it's still drivable."

"It sounds as though they were trying to intimidate you, rather than anything more serious."

Oh well, that's alright then, I feel like saying. *So long as they were only trying to intimidate me.* "Look, maybe you're trying to make me feel better, but is that not serious enough?"

DI Green straightens up. "John will come out and have a look at your car before you leave. See if there's any paint scrapes. Have you any idea who it could have been?"

Misery drags at my stomach. "Well, as you know, there are a few possibilities. Rob's boss. Rob's ex-wife. Turner, Rob's financial associate. Or it could be repercussions for what I did last week." I count my enemies on my fingers as I speak.

"To Bryony Rose, you mean?" DI Green clasps her hands on the table and looks at me.

"Maybe. Have you questioned Denise Matherson yet, about her car? It's different from the one that came after me this morning, but who knows, she could have borrowed one. She certainly hates me enough."

"Yes, we've spoken to her."

"And?"

"It's an ongoing Inquiry Fiona. There's only so much we can share with you."

"Do you still think I did it?" There it's out. The million dollar question. I've been read my rights and interviewed, but never charged. Surely they'd have charged me by now if they were going to.

She gives me a half smile. "Personally, I'd like to think you didn't, but obviously whilst things are ongoing, I have to keep an open mind."

"What about Turner?"

"We went over to Manchester yesterday, hoping to catch him at home, but he wasn't there. His wife claims not to have seen him for two days and has said she doesn't know of his financial transactions with Rob."

"What about the phone recording?"

She shakes her head. "Nothing, I'm afraid. We really need to speak to James Turner. You can be assured we'll keep trying."

"So, he's gone missing. Surely that must make you more suspicious of him. I'm telling you, I really think it's him, who killed Rob. He half admitted to me."

"It's such a shame you didn't save the recording." Her face bears a hint of regret. "Without that, it's your word against his."

"I reckon it's probably him who was driving like a maniac this morning – right on the same stretch of road that Rob died. If he's gone AWOL from Manchester, that would tie in, if he's over here, I mean."

"We'll certainly have a look at nearby CCTV, see if anything has been picked up in Ilkley or Otley."

"The car also looked like the same one Rob's boss, Phillip Bracken has."

"A black Range Rover or Land Rover?"

"Yes."

"And does his car have blackened windows?"

"I've no idea. Running me off the road doesn't seem his style though, nor can I imagine him stalking my house late at night, but there again, he could've got someone to do it for him."

"OK Fiona." DI Green stretches her arms out in front of her. "Leave this with us. Get through your husband's funeral, then we'll talk again at the weekend. John will come out with you to give your car a look over."

It's alright for you, I want to tell her. The reality is I've got to drive around with Jack in the car, worrying if we're being followed, or if someone is going to break into the house at night and it's making me feel ill. I'll have to make the house like Fort Knox. And go on foot to collect Jack from school.

But first, I've got to go and see Rob. It's my last chance. To make matters worse, PC John Robinson only finds a couple of scuff marks on the bumper of the jeep.

I can still remember Grandma when I viewed her body the day before her funeral. She looked tiny in her white coffin. I'd sat with her for about half an hour, making her endless promises about how the rest of my life would look. She'd be so disappointed if she could see how I'm doing, despite all she did for me.

I exchange the street bustle for the silence of the funeral home.

"We've dressed him in the clothes you brought in. He's all ready for you," Emma says. She smiles at me. I guess this is business as usual for her. "I gather you got all the service arrangements sorted yesterday."

"Yes. Thank you. Your colleague, Joseph, was very kind. Oh, and I got your bill. I'll have to sort it out early next week."

"That's fine." She rises from her seat. "It's not as if you haven't got enough to be thinking about over the next few days."

"He's in here," Emma says, as we approach a door with a number one on it. I'm shocked when she knocks before going in, as though he's going to call out *come in.*

Nothing could have prepared me for the sight of my husband, laid in a coffin, his hands resting on his ribs. He's still wearing his wedding ring and they've combed his hair. I'm amazed there's barely a scratch on him after what happened. Apparently, it was the top of his spine that took most of the impact.

Emma must notice me staring at his ring. "That can't go with him tomorrow, for cremation, I mean. So we'll let you have it either when you leave today, or after the service."

"I'll get it tomorrow." God knows what I'm going to do with his wedding ring. Sell it, I reckon. It cost enough and I need every penny I can get hold of. Bloody hell, as if I'm even considering this.

"Would you like me to stay with you, or do you want some time on your own with him?"

"I'd like some time on my own, if you don't mind." I point at the rose stem laid across Rob's chest. "Where has the flower come from?" I immediately suspect Bryony. Surely not.

"Oh, we do that for everyone. It's a symbol of respect from us. Right. I'll give you some time." She touches my arm as she steps away. "I'll be outside if you need anything."

The door closes softly behind her. I notice the coffin lid resting against the wall at the side of Rob. Then I stare at my husband's ashen face.

"It's me." My voice sounds strange in the silence. "I thought I'd better come and see you, whilst I've got the chance." I step closer. "I can't believe what's happened." Talk about an understatement.

A rush of misery sweeps over me. "I loved you so much Rob. I just didn't really know you, did I? Not like Bryony did." Then I decide I won't talk about her. I won't sully the final moments I have with him. But they're not with him. Not really. He's gone. Lying here, is his shell. Which will soon be incinerated. All that will be left of him is his wedding ring, the memories, and Jack of course.

"Why, Rob? Why did you tell me so many lies? Why did it have to end like this?" Tears are burning my eyes. I need a drink. *No*, a voice suddenly says inside me. Then I remember the Antabuse in my handbag. I must take it later. At least I might get some decent sleep. I'll need it with the day I've got in front of me tomorrow.

"I'll take good care of Jack, I promise. Please watch over him – and me. I know things had gone wrong, but I was still your wife." My voice is rising, so I lower it to a whisper. I reach for his hand. It's cold and waxy, which is to be expected, but it still comes as a surprise.

"Rob." I feel stupid now, but the words tumble from me. "I've looked everywhere for your life insurance, and your will. Turner has disappeared and it feels as though someone is out to get me. There was someone in our house last night Rob, and someone has just tried to run me off the road. If there is such a thing as an afterlife – if you can somehow hear me, please help us. Rob, I've got our son to look after." Tears are streaming down my face. "I've got our son." I really hope Emma isn't listening.

This is how desperate I am. I'm standing in a chapel of rest, asking my dead husband to pull some strings from beyond the grave. Rob was savvier than to not leave a will or any life insurance.

256

It's impossible to think that Rob would be so taken in by some charlatan, who had claimed to be able to multiply his investment ten fold. I thought he was more astute than to trust someone with nearly half a million pounds. Even if they went back a long way. But now, even more than the money, I'm worried about my own safety.

I stare at him as though trying to drink in every detail. "I'm going to leave you now Rob. I loved you so, so much, you know." I touch his hand again. "Perhaps I'll see you again one day."

* * *

Nobody goes to a funeral unless they absolutely must.
And tomorrow I must.

Chapter 42

Christina moves the curtain aside. "The car's here. Are you ready for this Fiona?"

"I haven't got a lot of choice, have I?" I smooth down my ill-fitting dress. I've lost so much weight since I bought this last year, that it's hanging from me. It's a beautiful midsummer day, probably too warm for the black tights I'm wearing, but I can't wear my black court shoes without tights. For the first time since Rob died, I've blow-dried and straightened my hair, and I've even got makeup on. I feel better for it.

Christina jangles her car keys. "I'll drive us. Try to relax."

I grab my bag and follow her from the house.

"Don't forget to lock up," she says, as I walk away from the front door without doing so. God, there's some maniac on the prowl, and I'm forgetting to lock up my house.

The driver of the hearse doffs his hat as I walk towards it. I stare at the D-A-D flower arrangement. Jack asked about coming, but thankfully agreed that it would probably be too much. When I dropped him at school, his teacher promised to keep a close eye on him. A funeral is no place for an eight-year-old. Today will be hard enough for me to get through, without having to focus on Jack as well. Plus, I don't know who's going to turn up.

"We're going to follow you there," I say to the driver as we turn towards Christina's car.

"Right you are."

"How come you didn't get a family car to follow?" Christina glances at me as we set off, following at a snail's pace. The other undertaker is walking in front of the hearse. At the end of the street, he stops, turns to face it, and bows his head. Several neighbours are out, watching our small procession. I hope some of them will come along. If only so I can say thank you for the bits and pieces that have been left on the doorstep over the last couple of weeks.

"What would have been the point in getting a family car?" I reply. "Rob was an only child. Jack's at school, and I wouldn't have wanted to share a car with Denise and Simone." We scheduled the journey to pass their house so they can follow in their own car from there. I got a text message from Denise to say they were both coming, and she expected to speak to me at the wake about the financial situation. Like hell.

"I'd have travelled with you."

"Would you really? To be honest Christina, I thought you weren't speaking to me. I've not seen you since they arrested me."

"I thought you had enough on your plate without me turning up every five minutes. I decided I should leave you be."

"Turning up once would have been good. To start with, you were great."

"I'm sorry." She's quiet for a moment. "Have they let everything drop against you? I've not heard anything else in the news."

"I don't know what's happening." We pass the local bike shop. The staff are out and bow their heads as our cortege passes them. Rob was probably one of their best customers. He was always in there, buying accessories or having his bike serviced or realigned. "I don't want to think about all that today."

"Where are your parents?" She flicks her hair behind her shoulder. "Are they meeting you there?"

"I don't know. I haven't heard from them. And my phone's broken."

"I wondered why you weren't replying to my texts. See, I tried to keep in touch with you."

"I'll get a new one sorted this weekend."

"What's up with your old one? Can't it be fixed?"

I don't answer her. Hopefully, she'll get the message that I absolutely don't want to be having a trivial conversation about a mobile phone whilst following my husband's coffin to the crematorium.

I feel even more disorientated than normal this morning, probably in part with what I'm about to face, and it might also be the effects of my new medication. At least I hope the tablets have removed all temptation to have a drink at the wake. I fiddle with the bracelet Rob bought me whilst I was expecting Jack.

People pause and even cross themselves in the street as we turn and embark on the final stretch of our journey. It's a similar day, weather-wise, to the one on which he died. I feel the weather is taunting me somehow. It should be stormy and grey, with driving rain.

The hearse turns into the crematorium driveway towards the throng of darkly dressed people awaiting its arrival. At the other side of the building, there's a group of mourners emerging into the back courtyard. It's one in, one out here – a conveyer belt of dead bodies and their mourners.

I scan faces for Dad as we pull up beside the crowd. No sign of him, or Mum. Anxiety rises in me like bile. Surely, he wouldn't leave me to face this without him. Simone's face crumples as she sees the coffin. I don't particularly like her, but the sight of her dad in a hearse is something no ten-year-old should have to witness. Denise draws her towards her.

Bloody Bryony's here. I must stay away from her. It's part of my bail conditions. If anyone should have to leave the funeral, it'll have to be her. DI Green and PC Robinson are standing close to her. What the hell are they doing here? It's not as though they knew Rob.

I think back to the crime dramas I've watched, where police attend funerals to watch how people interact with one another. This sometimes leads them to *whodunnit*. Who'd have ever thought that I would end up in the middle of my own crime drama? I wonder if Turner is here somewhere, perhaps they'll collar him. I can't see him turning up, somehow.

Christina's voice slices into my thoughts. "I'll drop you off here Fiona and find somewhere to park."

I don't want to be dropped off. I frantically look around for someone I can stand with. Where's bloody Dad? As I open the door, Lynne steps out of the crowd and wraps an arm around my shoulders. I'm grateful for it. Some of my neighbours are here too – I'll get through this. People are rooting for me.

They slide the coffin from the hearse onto a trolley. I stare at the lid, recalling it standing against the wall in the chapel of rest yesterday. I can visualise Rob's face, now encased within the coffin. I wish I could have one more look. I bet everyone else here is curious too. What a macabre thought.

"Do we have any pallbearers? Mrs Matherson?"

My head jerks up in response to the undertaker's voice. "Erm, I'd not even thought about that." I don't think Joseph mentioned it in our meeting. Wednesday seems such a long time ago. Life is so strange. The days seem long, yet in retrospect, everything seems to be happening so fast.

People are staring at me. I can't breathe. I need to get in and out of there. If only I could hit that golf club and get wasted. I shouldn't have started those Antabuse.

"I'll be one of the pallbearers. I'm Rob's friend." A man, who I don't recognise, steps towards the coffin.

Another man comes forward too. "Rob and I played a few rounds." He beckons towards someone else. "Tom, we're about the same height."

Three more men come forward and arrange themselves according to height as best they can to carry Rob in. I'm thankful to them. There's no sign of anyone from Rob's work, which is disgraceful, to say he worked there since his university days. No matter what he's been investigated for, surely he had friends? Maybe Phillip Bracken has forbidden them to attend.

As the pallbearers move along to the strains of the Coldplay song, we follow, me first, with Lynne linking my arm, through the foyer of the crematorium. The song has nearly finished by the time everyone is in.

The D-A-D display has been placed at the foot of the coffin and the beautiful spray of roses, lilies and carnations is sat on the top. I absently wonder what happens to the flowers afterwards. Am I expected to take them home, or do they get binned? There's nearly three hundred quid's worth there.

"I'm sorry we're late love. Traffic." I want to cry at the sound of my dad's voice as he slides into the pew beside me. Lynne, on my inside, shuffles up.

"Where's Mum?"

"She's here. Just gone to find a loo. How are you doing?" He pulls me towards him, and I feel myself let go. I'm comforted by the scratch of his beard and the scent of his aftershave. He'll catch me if need be.

"I'm OK. Numb. Sad. But I'm glad you've come."

"Of course we have. We wouldn't let you go through this on your own."

I notice an emphasis on the word *we*. I hate this sudden feeling of unity he's found with my mother. Especially as I know if she'd had her way, neither of them would be here.

Lynne squeezes my arm as Joseph Alexander steps up to the lectern. After addressing us all, he delivers a wonderfully put together eulogy, which he's written in record time. It's got the lot, Rob's childhood, his relationship with Jack, his friends, the ability he had both academically and in sport. Our marriage has been made to sound more robust than it turns out it was, but I didn't want to contradict it. Joseph sent the eulogy to me yesterday for approval, and it made me cry, despite everything.

I look over my shoulder in time to see Mum creep in and take a seat at the back. I wonder why she's staying there. As I bring my gaze forwards again, I notice Bryony crying her eyes out, being comforted by the person sat next to her. Bitch. How dare she come to my husband's funeral and act like the grieving widow. She can get lost if she thinks she's coming to the wake.

Simone's sobs can be heard echoing through the room as well. She's sat with her mother in the front row on the other side from me. Denise is consoling her. She must sense me watching them, for she looks straight at me with an expression that's a cross between fury and pity. I'm close enough to notice that Denise's eyes are dry. I stare at the photo on the screen of Rob and Jack. It was one of my favourites, though I don't think I'll be able to display it at home again after this.

We say the Lord's Prayer, or at least everyone else does, then it's the committal. Crematorium services are always over in record time. They allocate only twenty minutes. This is the part I've been dreading. The piano introduction of *Someone Like You* reverberates around the chapel. Everyone's eyes are on me again. I guess that, as his wife, I'm expected to leave the room first. Dad links arms with me as I get to my feet. He steers me towards the coffin. If it were up to me, I would just run out of here.

"Bye Rob," I whisper at the coffin. I will not wait until the curtain draws around. I will not look on as Simone sobs over it. I will not watch as Bryony does whatever she will do. Hopefully, she'll keep a grip on herself. He was married to me, not her. "I need some air." I turn to Dad.

"Come on then love."

Lynne follows us out. I look for Mum, but there's no sign. The ground outside is partitioned into squares for the flowers to be brought out. The previous funeral, only twenty minutes before, has dispersed, leaving their flowers behind. I stare sadly at the letters spelling out G-R-A-N and M-U-M. The woman probably lived to a ripe old age. I try to imagine how I will feel when my Mum dies. Right now, I wouldn't feel like shelling out three hundred and fifty pounds on flowered letters for her – in fact, I would not want to spend three pounds fifty. Still, she's here, which I'm surprised about. Even if Dad forced her to get in the car.

"Did Mum take much persuasion to come?" I can't help myself. I have to know.

His reply is drowned out by the sudden swarm emerging from the crematorium. One by one, people who I've never met hug me and shake my hand. They tell me *how sorry they are for my loss* and say, *if there's anything I can do...* I nod repeatedly and thank them, noticing how Bryony, Simone and Denise keep their distance. But Bryony barely takes her eyes off me.

"Can I come in the car with you Dad? We're only going to the golf club."

"There's no room in the back." Mum sidles up to Dad's side. The back seat is full of our cases and other stuff."

"So you're staying then?" Despite my mixed feelings towards Mum, I want them to come back after the wake. I don't want to be on my own tonight. Especially with the intruder from two nights ago. Thankfully, there was no sign of anyone last night.

264

"I can move your cases into my car if you like," Lynne offers. "Then you can all go together."

"No. Don't worry. It's too much hassle." Mum waves her hand. "We'll see you at the club Fiona."

I start to respond, but DI Green and PC Robinson look as though they're waiting to speak to me.

"How are you doing Fiona?" DI Green asks.

"You know."

"We'll be in touch tomorrow. We need to talk."

"What about? Have you located Turner yet?"

"I'm afraid not."

"Can't you give me some idea of what you want to talk about? I'll be worrying if you don't tell me."

"It's all positive, depending on which way you look at it. Now that we've spoken to Turner's wife, and got some information on his car, we've had some CCTV sightings of one like it in Ilkley. Two of them were on the day Robert was killed."

"*Really?* I told you it was him."

"The same car has been checked in the vicinity on the night you had an intruder and the next morning when someone was trying to run into you as well."

"Well at least I know who it probably was."

"We'll talk more tomorrow," PC Robinson says. Even though he's dressed head to foot in black, he stands out from everyone else here. It's obvious he's with the police. "It was a good turnout, wasn't it?"

"A nice service too," DI Green adds. Her too. They've got an air about them that shows they're watching, rather than taking part.

Good turnout. Nice Service. Stock funeral talk. James bloody Turner. He's ruined my life. And now it seems he is out to finish me off, or at the very least, to do everything in his power to frighten me as much as possible.

265

I want to know who Mum's on the phone to. She's walked to the edge of the car park and seems to be having a heated conversation. Dad's watching too. He and I look at each other. We're probably thinking the same thing. *Is it him?*

The funeral guests, mourners, or whatever you call them, are disbanding into the car park. All probably ready for a stiff drink. I don't know whether to envy or pity them. Joseph comes out and presses an envelope into my hand. "The collection," he says. "You held up really well. Robert's wedding ring is in there too."

"Thank you." I clutch the envelope towards my chest. "The eulogy was perfect. You got everything in that we talked about."

"You're welcome. We'll be in touch when your husband's ashes are ready for collection." He makes it sound like the dry cleaning.

* * *

I had no respect for Robert Matherson,
so what will I pay instead?

Chapter 43

Lynne chatters away on the short journey, like we're going on a shopping trip. "Your mum's not what I expected," she says. "Doesn't she look good for her age?"

Mum looks great, far younger than she is. I probably look older than her at the moment. I'd hate to be the person she is inside though. There's absolutely no love in her. As far as looks are concerned, I'd hate to have eyes as cold as hers or the mouth that's permanently set in a firm, hard line. If it wasn't for Dad, I don't think I would have anything to do with her.

Before Lynne had started talking about Mum, I'd asked her to take her time getting to the wake. This was to avoid having to greet everyone, so we have gone the long way around.

When we arrive, there's already a huddle of smokers at the entrance of the golf club. "Thanks for the lift Lynne." As we pull up I see Christina's car parked at the back too. I noticed she integrated herself amongst our other neighbours as soon as we'd arrived at the crematorium.

"Can I get you a drink?" A man's voice is close behind me as I'm waiting at the bar. "You look like you could do with one."

It's on the tip of my tongue to request a gin and tonic, but then I remember I can't. "Just a soda water, please." I'm well out of my comfort zone here, amongst all these people. I long for the sanctuary of home. Then I remember that home is no longer a sanctuary. Not after the other night. Normally, a drink in hand would allow me to be less reserved within this sea of strange faces. As is always the case at funerals, the atmosphere is calmer now we're at the wake. The snippets of conversation I catch are more normal than they were at the crematorium. Most people have their drink now and are tucking into the buffet. I massage my temples, which are throbbing after swapping the sunshine for this gloomy but well air-conditioned room.

"I'm Kev," the athletic-looking man says as we wait for the barman. "I was in the cycle club with Rob. I'd got to know him well over the last year or so."

"Nice to meet you." I hold my hand out. "Though I wish it could have been in different circumstances."

"Me too." He shakes my hand. "He did really love you you know. All that trouble he got into with his work. He only wanted to make you happy. Somehow, he thought he was doing the right thing."

"You know all about that? Have you spoken to the police? They've been trying to implicate me."

"I only got a rough gist of things from Rob, and I didn't know about the police involvement until today. I've been away on business. But I'll certainly speak to them if you think it'll help."

Dad doesn't know I'm on the medication and swoops to my side. "I'll get this," he says to Kev. He's probably worried that I'll get blitzed. Especially after last Friday. "Have you seen your mother love? I think she's disappeared with her bloody phone again."

I glance out of the window. It's hard to see clearly, as they haven't fully opened the shutters. But Mum's there on her phone, looking like before, as though she's arguing with someone.

"I thought things were getting better between you two. You've just been away, for God's sake."

Dad looks utterly miserable, and I see shadows of how he was when in the throes of his previous depression. I'm going to have to keep an eye on him if he and Mum split up. There's only me who will. My grandmother flashes into my mind. I've missed her today. Rob's death and funeral have brought to the surface some of what I went through when *she* died. I make a mental note to drive over and lay some flowers on her grave this weekend.

"I thought we might be getting somewhere, your mother and I, only she's been talking about moving away, really moving away. If I'm honest, I don't want to." Dad avoids my eye. "I think she'd regret it if we uprooted ourselves. She seems desperate though - it's almost like she's trying to run away from something."

"From herself." I watch her, waving her arm around as she speaks into her phone. She looks like she's crying. "Though she'd have to run a long way."

Mum drops her phone into her bag, and sinks to the wall behind her, shoulders hunched. "Are you going to see what's up with her Dad?"

"Soon." He puts an arm around my shoulders. "Today, however, is about you, helping you through it. Starting with getting some food down your neck. I'll fill a plate before it all goes."

As he walks away, Lynne returns to my side. "I'm going to make a move Fiona. Are you alright for getting home later? I need to do some shopping before I pick the boys up."

"I'll be fine. And thanks, for picking Jack up, I mean. I really appreciate it."

"What are friends for?" She gives me a smile so genuine that I decide to put aside my suspicions about her having an agenda. Maybe, just maybe, she's sincere and wants to be my friend. I must start letting people in apart from Jack and Dad.

"Do you want me to check if your mum's OK on my way out?" I

follow her gaze to the window. "She looks like she's struggling."

"No. Leave her. Dad's going to nip out after he's got me some food. I'd stay well away, looking at the mood she's in."

"OK, I'll slip past her. I'll see you later. Be as long as you need."

"Get that eaten." Dad thrusts a plate laden with sandwiches and vol-au-vents at me. "They're vultures, that lot."

I'm glad he's come back before anyone else has come over to express condolences. Hopefully, they'll see I'm having something to eat now and give me a few more minutes' peace. I'm happier standing out of the way with Dad.

"How are you doing?" He sprays sausage roll crumbs into his beard as he speaks. "Now that the service is over?"

"Just putting one foot in front of the other, to be honest. I can't do a right lot else, can I?" I nibble at a sandwich. "The police want to talk to me again tomorrow. It sounds as though they have a new lead with the man who's taken our money." I'm about to fill him in on what I know, when Mum bursts in, pursued by some man. He stands in the doorway, scanning the room. There's something familiar about him.

"Shane, no. Not now. Not here!"

Shane. No wonder he looks familiar. I stalked him on Facebook when Mum first started using me as a decoy.

"Which one of you is Fiona?"

I raise my hand, as though I'm in class or something. The clattering of plates from the back of the room has paused. Conversations have stilled. All eyes are on Shane. He walks towards me.

"Shane, you say anything and I'll…"

"Shut up, Maggie." He raises his palm in her direction. "I know I should really have gone to the police first. But I wanted you to hear this from me."

"It's *you* that's been carrying on with my wife?" Dad is trembling at my side. "You've some nerve, turning up here."

"Let him speak Dad." I put my hand on his arm, feeling strangely stronger than I have in a long time. After losing Rob and coping with everything else over the last fortnight, things can't get any worse.

Mum's heels clip-clop across the parquet floor as she rushes to Shane's side and tugs at his arm. I've never seen such desperation in her face. "Shane! I wasn't telling you the truth! I made it all up!"

Someone's brought the flowers from the crematorium. The stench of lilies is overpowering, making my head feel woozy. What is this truth, or not-truth, that Mum's wittering on about? The crowd has moved closer.

"You might have been wondering why Maggie came back so suddenly the other week." Shane looks from me to Dad. He's a nice-looking man and reminds me of Richard Gere. He's easily half a foot taller than Dad, but perhaps ten years younger.

"I thought she was staying with our daughter and grandson," Dad replies. "But whatever has happened, you shouldn't be turning up at my son-in-law's funeral like this."

"Just leave," Mum hisses, tugging at his arm again.

"Get off." He shakes his arm away. "Don't touch me." He turns his attention back to me. "I'm here to tell you what happened to your husband."

Mum, with the wide-eyed expression of an animal caught in headlights looks from Dad to me, then bolts towards the doorway.

* * *

I've got to get away.
And if they catch me,
I'm taking her down as well.

Chapter 44

I wasn't going to come to Mum's hearing.

Whether she gets bail has been left for the court to decide. She's been in custody for the entire weekend, so I haven't had the chance to hear her side of things. Not that there's much she could say after what she's done. Soon, she'll be brought up from the underground cells and I'll face her across the courtroom.

"Fiona. Can we have a word before we go in?" DI Green and PC Robinson hurry towards me. I expect they're knackered after hours of interviewing Shane and my mother over the last couple of days. No one could accuse them of not putting the hours in.

"Sure." I follow them into a room off the corridor, glad to leave the marble walls and floor with sunshine glaring through the glass roof. I'd have a migraine if I sat there for much longer.

The green of the room I step into reminds me of the interview rooms I've recently been in. I'm thankful they're a thing of the past.

"Is your Dad not here with you?"

I take a deep breath. "He's really struggling with all this. He's taken Jack to school and then he's driving home to see his GP."

"He's had a lot to cope with." There's genuine concern in PC Robinson's tone and face as he gestures for me to sit down. "As have you. Is he coming back afterwards?"

"Yes. He needs to. He's got a history of depression, so I need to monitor him." I sit facing them, as I have in interviews.

"You're doing really well." DI Green speaks now. "It's admirable, how well you're holding up."

"I've got little choice. I must stay strong for my dad, and I've also got a young son to look after." I glance at the clock. It's approaching ten o'clock and I'm aware that this time a fortnight ago, my world was still *normal.* Or so I thought.

The events leading up to Rob's death were made known to me and Dad when DI Green and PC Robinson visited us yesterday.

Rob's work fraud, the loan and the re-mortgage had been Mum's idea. How Mum had convinced him with her and Rob not seeing eye to eye over the years, I'll never know. Apparently, they'd both been eager to make some serious money. She'd taken on the administrative side of things, and Rob had handled the money. Some of Dad's savings, unbeknown to Dad, were Mum's stake.

She believed, DI Green said, that any monies coming were rightfully hers, after losing out with Grandma's will all those years ago. She'd become greedy though and was threatening Rob with exposure if he didn't give her a bigger cut than what they'd agreed.

When the police had interviewed her, she had apparently tried to implicate me. Eventually, it had been a handwriting analyst, as well as internet provider address checks that had exonerated my involvement in the fraud.

With Turner not responding to any contact attempts from Rob, Mum had become angrier and was suspecting Rob of having duped her. He had told her, like he had told me, that it was a done deal – a deal which should have been done a week before.

"I've been wracking my brains all night, and I never got a hint of what was going on." I tell DI Green. "But I have remembered one thing."

"Go on."

"My mum arrived the night before Rob died, and they were having words in the garden. I was in the house and couldn't hear what they were saying. But something was *off*. She seemed quite normal the next morning, though me and her had disagreed strongly over how she was treating my dad. But she took Jack to school." I feel sick to the stomach for ever trusting her with my son.

"Rob, as we know," continues DI Green, "called in at his ex-wife's house. According to Denise's neighbour, who was around there, he gave her some maintenance money and was apologising for getting mixed up with the arrangements at the weekend."

That's not what Denise told me. "At least she can't blacken his name anymore."

"Rob then met your mother at the farmhouse shop café. We eventually got footage of their meeting off their antiquated security camera system." PC Robinson leans back in his chair and yawns. "I'm sorry. It was a late one yesterday."

"The café is about a mile before the site of his accident," I say.

"Which explains the time of it." DI Green adds. "Your mum didn't believe Turner had simply disappeared. She wanted what she believed she was owed, before setting off to Devon. On the day she left, she apparently had no intention of returning."

"Poor Dad," I stare down at the table.

DI Green takes a sip from her paper cup. "She was angry. Not only was she not getting her cut of the money from Rob, but she said Rob had threatened her at the café with telling your Dad about her affair."

"She was desperate for my dad not to find out. I thought it was mostly because of his depression."

I've realised that Dad married someone who replicated what he'd known in childhood. His own father had led a double life with a secret family, eventually walking out when Dad was in his teens, never to be heard from again. I was shocked to discover that Grandma had known about the other woman and her two kids and had chosen to accept being treated in that way. All this acceptance of poor treatment must be hereditary. First Grandma, then Dad, now me. I'll do everything in my power to make sure Jack doesn't follow in our footsteps.

PC Robinson rubs his eye. "It seems to have more to do with what she stood to lose. She's very bitter."

DI Green looks at her watch. "Your mum wanted everything on her terms, and to let your Dad find out, or not find out, whenever and however it was best for *her.*"

"It's very noble of Rob to have wanted to put a stop to my mum's affair, but I don't see how he could come over all high and mighty with *anyone,* not after his relationship with Bryony."

"Bryony has told us it was strictly a platonic friendship, albeit a deep one," says DI Green, with an expression like she's trying to make me feel better. "From what I've heard from you all, your husband's anger towards your mother was mainly due to how she was treating you." She flicks her fringe from her eyes. "Making you lie, whilst pretending she was spending time with you and your son."

"It was this threat of the money being scuppered, and your Dad finding out before she was ready for him to know – that's what seems to have tipped her over the edge."

"What do you mean? Tipped her over the edge."

"Fiona." She pauses for a couple of seconds. I know what she's going to tell me, and I do not want her to say the words. But she does anyway. "It's your mother who killed your husband. Though she claims to have set out to only injure him. To give him a warning. Obviously, she didn't bank on him landing on his neck and severing his spine."

I rub at my head again. The room feels like it is tilting. "And then she brazenly drove on to Devon?"

She nods. "After, it would seem, she pretended to be *you*, having her blown out tyre fixed."

It's all falling into place. She's looked nothing like her age. "But – they had my registration number."

"She gave it to them. We've been back again first thing this morning and checked. They did the tyre replacement outside and then went into the office to fill in the paperwork. The young mechanic couldn't be bothered checking on the exact registration of the car he'd fixed. He said he had no reason to suspect your mother was giving him a different registration. I think she'd been very flattering towards him and had promised to come to him for more repairs"

I can't help feeling aghast at my mother being so brazen. "The young lad was only about twenty-two."

"Don't worry. He's in plenty of trouble with his boss," PC Robinson adds.

"I was thinking it was Denise who'd killed Rob. She's got damage to her car too."

"Coincidence, it would seem. She made no secret of her disdain for Rob when we spoke to her, but you were our main suspect."

"It was the information from the garage that went against you." A dark look crosses PC Robinson's face. "We got it wrong. Sometimes we do."

"And what did Shane have to do with it all? Other than having an affair?"

"We've charged him with perverting the course of justice. If he'd come forward earlier, he could have saved a lot of heartache."

"How?"

PC Robinson looks at DI Green as if to check how much he's allowed to tell me.

She nods at him.

"When your mother arrived in Devon that Monday, Shane had already decided he was going to return to his wife and two sons."

"I already knew that. She showed up at mine in a right state. Got drunk out of her brains. That was two days later though."

DI Green carries on with the explanation. "Your mother told Shane on the Tuesday what she'd done to Rob. It was given as a warning what she would be capable of doing to him, his wife or his sons, if he proceeded with his decision of ending things with your mother."

"According to Shane, your mum can't have actually planned to tell him what she'd done," says PC Robinson. "When she saw Shane's reaction, she backtracked - told him she'd made it all up to scare him."

I massage my forehead. She's utterly evil.

"But he couldn't get it out of his mind." DI Green raises the paper cup to her lips again. "Obviously. And when your mum kept begging and pleading, even after she'd returned to Yorkshire, Shane knew he had to tell us what she'd confessed to, even if she had tried to retract it. Plus, deep down, he feared she would carry out her initial threat to hurt him and his family. She'd already proven herself to be more than a little unhinged. He's come up here as he says he wants to see her put away, with his own eyes."

I'm as numb as I was when I first discovered Rob had died. My mother has killed my husband. *And for what?* Because, as always, she couldn't control her impatience, or her anger? Had Shane not come forward, she would probably have let me be tried for it. Not only was she prepared to do that to me, but to Jack as well.

"And what about Turner?"

"We believe he got on a plane to South America yesterday. Interpol have been informed, but I wouldn't hold your breath." PC Robinson tilts his phone screen towards him, either checking the time or an autopilot check of any messages. "We're keeping in touch with his wife. She's not happy with his dealings and disappearance and will contact us with anything she hears."

"So she didn't know anything about it? I thought so. I threatened that I was going to tell her."

"You should have left things to us." DI Green frowns. "We can't say for certain, but the footage of his car that we've seen on several occasions says to me that he's behind the personal threats you have suffered. Things could clearly have been much worse - we feel he was trying to frighten you more than anything."

"My head's spinning with all it all. To be honest, I really thought it was Turner who had killed Rob. I can't believe it was my own *mother*," I spit the word out, "that has killed my husband."

"It's a lot for you to take in, I know."

Can all parties in the case of Margaret Ann Mortimer please attend at court number three?

"Are you sure you're up to facing her?"

"I'd like to speak to her. Will that be possible?"

"It depends whether she gets bail. I'll have a word for you in court."

* * *

They've ruined my life.
There's no coming back from this.

Chapter 45

"You can have a few minutes."

I stand in response to the police officer's words. "That's all I need. Thank you."

I follow her as she jangles from the sunny court corridor to the bowels of the building. I feel as though I should make conversation with her but wouldn't know what to say. As we leave the lift, I shiver. The officer taps a code into a keypad and a door swings away from us.

"The prison van is due soon." She turns to me as we walk along the gloomy passageway. "And I must stay in the cell with you, for obvious reasons."

"I understand." I'm amazingly calm. I wonder if at some point, I'm going to fall apart. Or maybe my blow out occurred when I got drunk the other week. Perhaps I've got a strength within me I've never acknowledged before.

The officer unlocks a metal door and beckons me in after her. My mother slumps on the bench at the far side of the cell, her usual larger than life presence shrunken in the gloom of her surroundings. She's wearing the skirt and blouse Dad dropped at the station yesterday. She doesn't look up as I walk in after the officer.

"Mum." My voice reverberates around the cell. "Or should I say *Maggie?* You're no mother of mine anymore."

"What do you want?"

"I want to know why you did it?" My voice wobbles.

"They've remanded me." She looks at me now, desperation in her eyes. "What's going to happen to me? I can't go to prison!"

"That's right. You think of yourself. Poor Maggie Mortimer. Never mind that you've murdered my husband and Jack's father. Because of your mastermind plan, we've been left with nothing." I glance around the cell, the sight of it reminding me of my own recent incarcerations. It smells nasty in here too – urine mixed with bleach.

"It's nothing less than you deserve, *Fiona*." She says my name like it's a swear word. "You owe me. That money you got when Roger's mother died – it should have been ours. The life you secured for yourself when you married Rob – with your posh house and holidays - you weren't worthy of any of it."

"You were jealous. Of me? That's madness." I stare at her. "You need help, you do."

"Do you know Rob and I had a fling? Whilst you were pregnant with Jack."

I stare at her. "I don't believe you." As I say it, the absurdity of her claim hits me and something deep inside shifts. I should feel winded at this so-called revelation, but I feel nothing for her. I see who she truly is.

"I don't care if you do or you don't. Food for thought though, isn't it?"

A calmness I've never known whilst in her presence floods through me. "What did I ever do to make you hate me so much?" I search the coldness of her eyes for a flicker of remorse. "You're a psychopath."

Her expression suggests that she doesn't enjoy being called that. "I didn't mean to kill Rob. Just to warn him."

"That didn't stop you trying to frame me for it all, did it?" I cannot believe how calm I feel. With it, a sense of freedom from her comes over me, and the revelation hits me. "It's no wonder I've spent most of my adult life so messed up. How can a mother do that to her own daughter?"

"You're no daughter of mine." There's froth at the corner of her mouth as she speaks. "I want nothing more to do with you."

"I know you didn't sleep with Rob."

She smiles slyly, obviously trying to re-exert the power she's always had over me.

"I want you to stay away from my son. From both of us."

I can tell she doesn't understand what's happened within me. Sitting up, she hisses her next words. "Once I get out. You can't stop me seeing him."

I look straight into her eyes and with more conviction than I've ever felt say, "watch me." I turn to leave before looking over my shoulder and add. "Besides, I don't think you'll be seeing daylight for a long time. Have a nice life *Maggie.*"

"It should be you in here," she mutters without looking at me. I feel a slight pang of sympathy for her as she slumps back on her bench. But by the time the door has slammed behind me, it's gone.

Before you go...

Join my 'keep in touch' list to receive a free book, and to be kept posted of other freebies, special offers and new releases. Being in touch with you, my reader, is one of the best things about being an author.

If you want to read another of my psychological thrillers, find out more about *The Hen Party* on Amazon.

Book Discussion Group Questions

1. What did you think of Fiona's initial reaction to the news of her husband's death?
2. What can a person do to educate themselves financially? How could this make any difference to their life?
3. Talk about the supposed non-physical relationship Rob was having with Bryony. Why might they have felt compelled to continue it? How might it have developed if he had lived?
4. Which character did you feel the most sympathy towards in the story?
5. Which character did you feel the least sympathy towards?
6. To what extent did Fiona affect her future by giving her husband financial control?
7. Did Fiona's relationship with her mother have a bearing on her own relationship with Jack?
8. Discuss how money polarises the characters in this book.
9. Do you believe there was any truth in Maggie's revelation that she and Rob had a fling?
10. Examine the dynamic between Fiona, her parents, and her grandmother.
11. To what degree did Fiona's addiction to alcohol limit her quality of life?
12. Mental health is a factor in this novel. Talk about how this plays out amongst the characters.

13. Put yourself in the shoes of Rob's daughter, Simone. How would the situation appear from her point of view?

14. Talk about Fiona's friendships, or lack of them.

15. Shane appears in a scene at the end. Talk about his conduct throughout the story and the reasons behind his eventual appearance. Did he deserve to be punished?

16. What could cause a mother to behave in a way to their daughter like Maggie did towards Fiona?

17. How has each character's life and perspective changed as a result of what they have been through in the story?

By the Same Author

Psychological Thrillers
Left Hanging
The Man Behind Closed Doors
The Last Cuckoo
The Yorkshire Dipper
The Hen Party
Last Christmas
Drowned Voices

Memoir
Don't Call me Mum

Poetry
Poetry for the Newly Married 40 Something

How-to Books for Writers
Write your Life Story in a Year
Write a Novel in a Year
Write a Collection of Poetry in a Year
Write a Collection of Short Stories in a Year

All available on Amazon

The Hen Party - Prologue

(The next psychological thriller - find out more on Amazon)

It takes a moment for my eyes to grow accustomed to the darkness. My heart rate quickens and I hear the whoosh of my breath in my ears. As I tiptoe to her side, she doesn't stir.

I hold the pillow, my hands gripping either edge as I prepare to lower it.

She barely flinches to start with. I wonder if she will just drift into an eternal sleep without waking first.

Her body becomes rigid, but then, some fight must kick in, her arms and legs flail in all directions. Taken aback, I press down. Hard. I hear her gasps beneath the pillow. She doesn't thrash for long before going limp. Then. Silence.

I hardly dare move the pillow for a moment. When I do, I know there's no going back.

She's gone.

Available at Amazon

Acknowledgements

I'd like to firstly thank my husband, Michael, who acts as my first reader and is additionally an eagle-eyed proof reader. But more importantly, his support and belief in my author career keeps me going on the tough days when the words will not flow!

Next, a thank you to my talented book cover designer Darran Holmes, who has once again worked his magic with the cover design. He somehow always manages to turn my vision into something even better. Thanks also to Sue Coates, the photographer who took my 'author photo.'

A huge thank you also to my wonderful Advance Reader Team for your later stage feedback. Your support means the world to me and I don't know what I'd do without you!

I am forever grateful to Leeds Trinity University and my MA in Creative Writing Tutors there, Martyn, Amina and Oz. Without graduating from the Masters degree in 2015, I'm not sure I would have ever made the transition from an aspiring to a professional writer.

And finally, to you, the reader. Without readers an author is nothing. I am truly thankful for your interest in my work. I really hope you enjoyed Hit and Run.

About the Author

The domestic thrillers I write shine a light into the darkness that can exist within marital and family relationships. I have been no stranger to turbulent times myself, and this has provided some of the raw material for my novels.

I am a born 'n' bred Yorkshirewoman, and a mum of two grown up sons. In my forties, I have been able to pursue a long-held ambition of gaining an MA in Creative Writing and make writing my full time occupation. Recently I have married for the second time and have found my 'happy ever after.'

This is not something you will find in my novels though! I think that we thriller writers are amongst the nicest people you could meet because we pour all our darkness into our books – it's the romance writers you've got to watch…

I plan to release four novels per year and if you'd like to be kept in the loop about new books and special offers, join my 'keep in touch list' or visit www.autonomypress.co.uk. You will receive a free book as a thank you for joining!